REVENGE PUCK

A FAKE DATING, GRUMPY SUNSHINE HOCKEY ROMANCE

SHOT AT LOVE
BOOK ONE

L.A. HART

COPYRIGHT

This book is a work of fiction. The characters, incidents, and dialogue were created from the authors' imagination and are not to be construed as real. Any resemblance to actual people or events is coincidental.

The authors acknowledge the copyrighted and trademarked status of various products within this work of fiction.

Editor's Choice Publishing

P.O. Box 10024

Greensboro, NC 27404

Illustrated Cover Design by Gowtham Thangaraj
Discreet Cover Design by Jessica Mohring | Raven Ink Covers, www.
raveninkcovers.com

After Elle Townsend is dumped by her hockey star boyfriend Christian Riley on the eve of the championship playoffs, she devises a plan for sweet revenge—a fake romance with Christian's arch-rival.

Preston Lawrence takes his hockey career very seriously because brawling on the ice is the only thing he's good at. With the championship trophy and his contract extension on the line, he needs to figure out a way to control his temper that always flares and gets him ejected whenever he faces his rival.

So, when a heartbroken blonde asks Preston for a photo with him to try to make Christian jealous, he raises the stakes. Known for avoiding the spotlight, Preston kisses Elle in front of a crowd of sports reporters, certain the video will go viral.

Their "fake" kiss felt a little too real for Elle and Preston. It looks real to Christian too, who goes ballistic when he sees Elle in the stands wearing Preston's jersey, and holding up a sign that insults the size of Christian's "stick."

Infuriating Christian helps Preston keep his head in the game so his team could win game one of four. That's why he suggests to Elle that they keep up their charade through the championships.

Christian and Preston have a complicated history. Their rivalry intensifies further when they begin to fight over Elle.

As Elle and Preston grow closer, secrets unravel, causing

Elle to question if Preston's feelings are genuine or just a part of his revenge plot against Christian.

Will Preston be able to convince Elle that his feelings for her are real, or will Christian find a way to win her back?

For David.

Thanks for being the sunshine to my grumpy for twenty-one years.

1

Elle Townsend

"That…was great," Christian Riley, my professional hockey star boyfriend, says just before he rolls out of my bed to get dressed. Clutching the sheet to my chest, I roll to my side and prop my head up on my elbow, watching in awe as he struts naked around my tiny apartment in all his six-foot, muscular perfection picking up his discarded clothes. "Too bad it was the last time."

It takes me longer than it should for his words to break through my blissful haze.

"The last time?" I repeat in confusion.

He hops around the floor, pulling on his jeans, both legs as once. "It's the playoffs, baby! If I win the trophy, shit is going to get crazy."

I sit up in the middle of the bed, gripping the sheet tighter as understanding unfortunately dawns on me. "You're breaking up with me?"

"I can't be tied down now, not when everyone is gonna want a piece of Christian Riley. Besides, it's not like we were really together," he has the audacity to say while zipping up his pants.

Oh my god. Did he ask me for a lunchtime quickie today, knowing it would be the last time?

Wow.

And I don't think I've ever hated how he refers to himself in the third person as much as I do now.

Not really together? He doesn't think we were together?

"We've been seeing each other three or four times a week for five months!" I remind the pretty blond bastard.

His Greensboro Bobcats tee slips over his head as he says, "Not exclusively."

"You-you've been with other people?"

The man shrugs at me. "Why wouldn't I be with other people?" he asks, as if it's a stupid question. "I'm always on the road with puck bunnies crawling all over me. You know how it is, right, Ellie?"

I keep telling myself that "Ellie" is a cute nickname, that he hasn't simply forgotten my name is Elle after all this time.

"So, I was what? Just a casual booty call on standby for when you're in town and wanted to get laid?"

"Exactly!" He flashes me his perfect smile, a rarity for hockey players, as if happy that I'm finally catching on. "And I was just a brag for you to tell your friends about, right? I get it. I am the best forward in the league. I just don't think I'll have time to keep this up with you over the summer once I win my first championship. At least I told you to your face and not by text, right?"

"So decent of you," I mutter through my teeth sarcastically as I fall back onto my pillow.

"I know. Most of the time, I just block numbers and move on."

How did I not realize what a callous prick he was?

Oh, because he's pretty, and he liked kissing me and doing lots of other yummy things.

"Why did I merit this talk instead of you just ghosting me?" I ask curiously while staring up at the ceiling rather than his too pretty face.

"Because you're the only one who can do my fade the way I like," he responds, as if it's obvious. "Just because we're not fucking doesn't mean I want you to stop cutting my hair and shit."

Oh, wow.

"By the way, you're welcome for me sending my teammates to you," he says, as if the new clients make up for him being an asshole. "Hey, you could probably sleep with one of them from now on!"

Is that what he thinks of me? That I only wanted him because he was a professional hockey player, so it's no big deal for me to replace him with a teammate?

Cutting my eyes to him, I ask, "You wouldn't be jealous if I hooked up with one of your teammates?"

"Why would I be? Those guys are all my friends. They won't mind my sloppy seconds."

I slap my palms over my burning face, so embarrassed and ready for this conversation to be over. "Oh my god. Did you just refer to me as your 'sloppy seconds'?"

"You could sleep with every player in the league, and I wouldn't care," he says confidently. "Well, except for Preston Lawrence."

Good to know there's at least one exception. "Why not him?" I can't help but ask through my palms.

"Because he's the guy who is gonna try to take me out of every game in the finals. He'll slam me into the boards and beat the shit out of me just to keep me from scoring."

"No kidding?" I'm suddenly a great admirer of this man I've never met. I have heard of him, though. Over the past five months, when Christian and I would come up for air, he would bitch about a rivalry with Preston Lawrence. He talked about him like he's terrified of the other man.

"But it's not like Preston would ever speak to a nobody like you, much less sleep with you," Christian continues to kick me while I'm down.

"Wow," I whisper indignantly at his insult. *I'm a nobody.*

"I didn't mean he wouldn't want you personally, Ellie. He just doesn't date anyone. Ever. Hockey is his whole little world. He doesn't allow any distractions from being the most violent prick in the whole damn league."

Sitting up again, I study the handsome man's scowl and furrowed brow. "It sounds like you're scared of him. Christian Riley isn't nervous about facing some big, bad bruiser in the playoffs, is he?" I can't help but taunt him, referring to him in third person since that's how he usually talks about himself.

"What? Hell no, I'm not scared." He pinches the front of his shirt and says, "The Bobcats are gonna win, and I'm gonna be MVP. Nobody can stop me, babe, especially not Preston fucking Lawrence."

We'll just see about that.

~

The day doesn't get better when I drag my ass back to the salon, now sad and hungry because I skipped lunch for Christian's final quickie. Not that skipping a meal is necessarily a bad thing for me…

"You look like crap," Audrey says when she sees me.

Unlike my beautiful best friend and salon co-owner, who never has a brunette hair out of place, I do look like crap. If I were thinner, prettier, maybe Christian wouldn't have wanted anyone else.

"No kidding. I just got dumped."

"What? No!" she exclaims.

"Not that *he* thinks we even qualified as being together. I was just a hookup for Christian. Nothing else."

"That's awful. I'm so sorry, Elle."

"It's fine. Really. I never actually thought the notorious playboy would give up all women for me or anything. It was nice to pretend for a while," I tell her as I slump into my salon chair and use the toe of my slip-ons to spin it around to face her. "Is it wrong that I want to shave his eyebrows off or slash his tires to get back at him?"

"Those are perfectly reasonable desires after a breakup."

"I can't mess up his looks or the puck bunnies would full on attack me whenever I go out in public."

"True enough. They are rabid."

"And I don't want to get arrested for assaulting his tires."

"I think the police would charge you with vandalism, not assault, but it could get you a court date which would require an expensive attorney."

"He's not worth those kinds of headaches. It just sucks that he tossed me aside so easily, like I was nothing. Can you believe he told me that I could sleep with one or all of his teammates and he wouldn't care?"

"Huh. That could help you feel a little better."

"No, it wouldn't! Not if he doesn't care!" I throw my head back on the chair and stare up at the ceiling tiles. "The only stupid exception he made to that offer was some rival on the Warhawks he's facing in the finals. Preston something."

"There you go!" Audrey exclaims. Coming over, she spins my chair around one full, quick time, causing my head to snap up. "Go sleep with him."

"Ha! Funny. Christian said this Preston guy wouldn't ever want me."

"Well, you wouldn't have to actually go through with it, right? Just make Christian think you were hooking up with his rival."

"I don't even remember his last name now…" I tell her when I notice her phone is already in her hand, thumbs typing away.

"Found him! His name is Preston Lawrence. He's a defenseman for the Warhawks. He could really use a cut and a shave, but he's not bad looking from what little I can see of his face." Turning her phone's screen around, she shows me his photo.

"Eh. Christian said he doesn't date, even if I could figure out a way to meet him."

"Again, you're not actually going to date the man, just pretend. And if Christian doesn't like him, then Preston probably feels the same, right? Maybe he would be willing to play along. You know what they say: the enemy of my enemy is my friend."

"That guy looks scary, Audrey. Even Christian is terrified of him."

"Scary? Really? That's hot," she whispers. "Let's look at some videos of this guy in action."

Once she finds a few videos, Audrey comes around so we can both watch on her phone.

Hit after hit, I can't help but wince at the force with which the big, hairy man runs people into the boards.

"Jeez," Audrey says. "This guy is a violent beast."

"No wonder Christian is worried about surviving the finals. He may have to face that dude in seven games! Do you know how many times he'll probably hit him?"

"A lot I'm guessing."

"Yes. And you think I can just walk up to this guy and say, *'Hey, you don't know me, but could you pretend we slept together?'* I'm sure he'll get right on board with that."

"I mean, you don't have to pretend if he's willing..." Audrey teases with a grin.

"I'm not going to sleep with some random guy just because Christian broke my heart!"

Shaking her head, Audrey clicks her tongue. "I knew that pretty man was too good to be true."

"He was. And I was stupid to think I could be enough for him. Have you seen me?"

"Yes, Elle, and you're beautiful."

"I'm twenty pounds overweight and have only been called cute by the guys I've gone out with before Christian. He told me he thought I was hot, and I stupidly believed him. He probably tells every woman that to sleep with her."

"Ah, Elle, the man is gorgeous and rich. I don't think he has to spew any lies to get women into his bed."

"You know what I mean."

"What I'm trying to say is that while Christian may be a manwhore, I don't think he would've given you compliments that he didn't mean. There was no reason to when women throw themselves at him."

"I guess so," I mutter. "I just—I thought I was special because Christian Riley wanted me. I know I shouldn't put my worth on what one man thinks, but I did. He made me feel more confident because I thought that out of all the women who wanted him, he chose me."

"And he did. You just weren't the only chosen one."

"Yeah. Bastard."

"If you want to get back at him, show him that you're not wasting a second crying over him and that you're already moving on."

"With his enemy? Right. That will be very believable."

"Hey, all you need to say is that you and the caveman ran into each other and bonded over your shared hatred. Then, the next thing you knew, he was offering to make your toes curl to help you forget the jerk."

"I wish forgetting Christian was that easy. Do you know how many incredible nights we had over five months? It's not fair that he's also good at sex as well as being pretty and one of the fastest guys on the ice."

Audrey flops down into her chair with a sigh. "No, it's not fair. He should share his knowledge with the rest of the male population."

"He should. But no, he's a selfish bastard who keeps all the good stuff to himself so that no other man can ever live up to him!"

"Oh, Elle. You will find someone better than that jerk. Right now, it may not feel like your broken heart will heal, but it will. And you know the best way to start the healing process?"

"Pretend like I'm moving on?"

"Yes! Pretending to move on is almost as good as the real thing."

"Right. Sure."

Getting to her feet, Audrey claps her hands together. "Now, how can we get to that woolly mammoth of a man to make this happen?"

"How do I get face time with a professional hockey player on the rival team for the finals? No freaking clue."

Biting her lip, Audrey paces in front of the salon windows. "Tomorrow is the first game of the series, right?"

"Yes."

"And it's here in town?"

"Uh-huh."

"And you've been to the arena a few times with Christian, right?"

"Yes, I've met him in the arena's player parking lot after the games. He got me tickets like twice."

"Then you have the perfect in. Nobody who works there needs to know you two broke up."

"I don't know if any employees at the security gate will remember me. But if I could get a ticket, I could pretend like I'm lost…"

"Then you could get into the lot and possibly run into the woolly mammoth?"

"That's a long shot," I say, dubiously.

"One you're willing to take, though, right?"

"How will I get a ticket the day before the first game of the freaking championship series?"

"We must know a client who has tickets. It's the only decent professional sport in this town."

"True. But who would be willing to give up a ticket to the first game of the finals? One ticket is probably going for a thousand dollars online." I spin the chair around slowly.

"Then we call in every favor and see what we can do."

"Okay," I agree. "But first, I have to go get tested for every disease under the sun."

"You always used protection, right?"

"Yes, of course we did. Except…you know, for oral?"

"Ah, right. Hard for me to forget, since I've been in the back more than once while you were out here on your knees."

"Sorry," I tell her with a wince. "The chair was always turned around so nobody could see in the window."

Audrey waves her hand through the air. "Eh, it's fine. I enjoy living vicariously through you. Too bad Christian was a player on and off the ice."

"Yeah, it's too bad," I agree.

"Well, forget that jerk. You go get your tests, and I'll start making some calls."

"Great, thank you." I hop out of the chair to give my best friend and partner a hug, grateful I have her for support.

2

____

Preston Lawrence

"I t's not a great time, Tommy. The bus just pulled up at the arena in Greensboro," I tell my agent as my teammates all stand up from their seats to gather their things before heading into the Bobcats' visiting team locker rooms.

"My sources tell me that management in D.C. is nervous." One of the few things I like about my agent is that he gets right to the point without wasting my time. He's also made me a ton of money.

"They're nervous about winning the trophy? I wouldn't be surprised. It has been nineteen years since the last time."

"No, Preston, they're not nervous about the championships. They're nervous about *you*."

"Me? Why? I've been playing longer than most guys on the team and won the trophy four years ago with the Wolverines."

"Are you really asking why?" he huffs. "Every time you've faced Christian Riley, you've been ejected!"

I can't help but wince since it's true. Not my proudest moments. "I've only been ejected twice in five years."

"Yes, and both times were when you played Riley and went after him! Tell me that's not some kind of coincidence."

"It's not a coincidence. You know I hate that son of a bitch."

"So, I've heard. Not to mention the shitstorm you caused last year when you punched a fan…"

"I was enjoying a day off with my family, and the jerk wouldn't stop videoing us on his goddamn phone."

"You're a famous hockey player who never speaks a word to the press or on social media. Of course, fans are curious about your life…"

"My life is none of their business," I grumble.

"It doesn't work that way when you live in the spotlight, and you know it," Tommy points out. "Why do you let shit like that bother you or let Riley get in your head when you know he's doing it on purpose?"

I sit there silently on the now empty bus until he gives up on waiting for me to respond. He knows why.

Sighing, Tommy finally says, "Fine. Whatever. Just don't get thrown out of today's game, or any other game during the playoffs. If you do…"

"If I do, then what?"

"If you're thrown out of a game, your bonus under the extended season clause of your contract goes down the drain."

"What? All of it?"

"All of it. Not to mention D.C. probably won't offer you an extension if you have to bow out early."

"Are you kidding me? I'm part of the team that's taking them to the playoffs for the first time in nearly two decades!"

"I know that, Pres. And they know your temper and brutality on the ice helped get them to this point. But management said they're getting tired of waiting for you to become a team player."

"What are you talking about? Hockey is always a team sport."

"Pres, being a grumpy loner doesn't win you any Mr. Congeniality awards in the locker room."

"The guys respect me."

"Sure, they respect you. You're a vet with a record for bloodying and breaking the bones of opponents. That doesn't mean they like you or want you to stick around another year chewing them out whenever they mess up."

"We play hockey together. There's no need for us to have sleepovers and braid each other's beards," I huff. "And if coach won't tell them when they make mistakes, then how can they fix their shit if I don't educate them?"

"I just wanted to warn you that if you do something stupid to get ejected, I think you'll have to wait and hope another team will want to put up with your cranky ass."

"I don't want to leave D.C. You know I can't."

"I know that moving is a last resort. So, keep your head on straight during the finals and help the Warhawks win the championship trophy. Don't waste a single minute in the penalty box for that prick Christian Riley. He's not worth it."

I wish keeping my fists out of Christian's smug face was as easy as it sounds. It's not.

Riley is the league's golden boy. He scored more points than any other player during the regular season and is looking at a potential MVP award. That is, if the Bobcats weren't going to lose the finals to us.

I don't despise Riley just because he's a good player. I hate him for a whole other list of reasons. Ones that date back to the days when we played together in the minor leagues.

There's so much on the line now, though. Deep down I know I can't screw this up, that Riley's not worth losing a contract or my bonus money.

At the same time, whenever I see the asshole's smug face, my anger just takes over and I lose my shit. All I want to do is hurt him. Winning the game isn't nearly as important as that when we meet on the ice.

"Listen," Tommy says. "I'll put out some feelers, try to get another team to make an offer before the playoffs are over. Best case, it'll light a fire under D.C.'s ass, make them wake up and want to keep you around instead of losing you to a team they may have to face. Worst, at least you'll have backup options in case they pull the plug."

"Do what you need to do, but I'm not leaving D.C.," I tell my agent before ending the call.

3

Elle

Audrey was able to snag us two seats thanks to clients of ours having zero interest in accompanying their husbands to the game. It only cost us a year's worth of free cuts for the whole entire family. I feel bad for the husbands' friends that got booted, but my needs are greater than theirs. Audrey wanted to come with me to the parking lot, but I told her that there was no reason for both of us to get arrested and/or permanently banned from the Bobcats' arena.

Tickets were the easy part. Sneaking into the Bobcats' back parking lot will not be. Sure, I've gotten through the gate a few times before, but that was only because Christian vouched for me.

Today, the first game of the series for the finals, I don't even recognize the short but stocky man in black standing closest to the players' back gate entrance. I stroll up to the chain-link fence, shouldering my way between dedicated sports reporters with their phones out, hoping to catch glimpses of players.

The man standing guard at the charter bus has a small hawkish bird logo on his polo. I'm guessing he's part of the visiting Warhawk's security team.

"Players and staff only," the one and only burly security guard in the lot says when he glances at me.

"Hi. I know it's player's only, but I was hoping you would make an exception."

"No exceptions. You'll need to go to the fan entrance on the other side of the street."

"But I'm a friend of the team." I don't tell him I have connections because I used to sleep with the star player of the Bobcats. "I just need to talk to Preston. Preston Lawrence. He plays for the Warhawks. It won't take but a moment of his time."

"I know who Preston Lawrence is, woman. Are you press or something?"

"Sure," I say, hoping it'll get me in.

"Yeah, right. Even if you are, Preston doesn't do interviews before, during, or after games."

"Ah, right. He's not a people person, doesn't date, doesn't take questions about his personal life, punches people who try to take photos of him without his permission. Trust me, I'm aware of all that," I tell the guard because I've done my home-work on the defenseman. "But this is super important."

The man lifts his eyebrows as if to challenge that statement.

"Okay, so maybe it's not super important to Preston Lawrence. It's important to me and I…"

"The answer is no, blondie. Preston Lawrence doesn't do puck bunnies. Now don't make me arrest you for trespassing."

I start to tell him he's not an actual cop so he can't arrest me when, by some miracle, the big, and I mean BIG man himself walks off the bus. At least I think it's him based on the image search Audrey and I did on the web. It's hard to tell since he's wearing a suit that had to have been custom made to fit his enormous frame. He looks more like a giant businessman than a hockey player. But players like to dress nice when traveling for away games. Playoffs are apparently no exception.

From about twenty feet away, the woolly mammoth, as Audrey referred to him, makes eye contact with me, then the guard, then his dark eyes return to me. There's not a hint of emotion on his scowling face. Not that you can see most of it thanks to his thick, black beard and long, floppy hair.

"Hi, Preston. You are Preston, right? Could I have just one moment of your time?"

The sports reporters around me scatter like mice, as if avoiding the man's wrath is more important than getting his photo or a sound bite. After watching the GIF of him punching a guy in the face so hard it knocked him out cold, I don't blame them.

But I stand my ground when the brute freezes with his big black duffle bag hanging on his shoulder, his squinty eyes staring at me like I'm a crazy person. And I am, but he doesn't even know that yet. He wouldn't hit a woman, would he? Nah. I have a feeling the dude who got his nose broken did something to deserve it.

That's why I bravely pull my phone from my purse. The Warhawks security guard flips out.

"Are you insane? Don't take his photo!" he hisses at me. "I'm sorry, Mr. Lawrence," he calls out over his shoulder while using his body to block me from his view through the fence. "I'm trying to get rid of her. I'll call Bobcats' security out here to do their damn jobs!"

"What does she want?" his deep, growly caveman voice demands, as if I'm not capable of answering the question for myself.

The guard humphs as if it's obvious, making me grit my teeth and roll my eyes at him. "I'm not a puck bunny! I just want a selfie, or an ussie since I would like for you to be in the photo with me too, of course."

"No."

"No? You won't take pity on a recently dumped, pathetic woman?"

"No. You're wearing Bobcats' colors," he murmurs, narrowed eyes sweeping over my top.

I glance down and realize that the cropped blue, white, and yellow striped tee was probably not the best choice of attire when asking a Warhawk player for a favor.

Desperate times call for desperate measures. "What if I took the shirt off?"

Grinning from ear to ear now, the guard says, "Told you she's a puck bunny."

"I'm not a puck bunny!" I shout. "The only hockey player I've ever been with is Christian Riley."

I didn't know the woolly mammoth could get scarier, but he looks so furious I'm surprised thunder doesn't roll through the sky with a clap of lightning.

"I changed my mind," the big guy says. "The answer is hell no to your selfie request."

"Ah, so you don't like Christian either? Well, join the club, buddy," I tell him. "He loathes you too, by the way. Honestly, I think he's terrified of you, scared of facing you in the playoffs because he actually thinks you may slice his throat with the blade of your skate."

"Thanks for the idea," Preston replies before he's apparently had enough of me wasting his time and starts walking away toward the arena.

"I hope you inflict some pain on him!" I yell to his back.

And okay, that sounded bad. But this is hockey, so bumps and bruises are all part of the game.

Preston stops again and turns toward me in his fancy dress shoes that are so long I could probably use them as paddleboards. "Why is that?" he asks.

"Just your typical bad breakup rage," I say with a wave of my hand. "Anyway, if you enjoy hurting him, then you should know that psychological warfare can sometimes be just as effective as causing someone physical pain."

Okay, maybe I'm getting way ahead of myself. I doubt if Christian would even see my pitiful post trying to look like I'm moving on, much less waste a second being jealous. But a girl can dream. It's the only card I've got up my sleeve to play against him.

Before Preston walks inside, I quickly explain my plan. "All I want is a photo with you to put on Insta to try to piss Christian off. I know you don't do press or photos, but I thought you might make an exception this time since you're rivals or whatever. It probably seems stupid to you, but it may mess with Christian's head if he thinks I'm hanging out with the enemy. Not that you're my enemy. I don't know you. I'm sure you're a very nice man who just scowls a lot..."

My words trail off when he actually starts walking back in my direction instead of running the other way toward the arena. A mobile mountain of fury.

"You were Riley's flavor of the month? Or was it less than a week?" the grump asks.

Ah, so he is familiar with Christian's playboy ways. I really should've known he was too good to be true.

"We broke things off recently, like yesterday. Although, apparently, we weren't ever really together."

"Good. He's an asshole."

"No kidding."

"And you want to use me to hurt him back?"

That sounds so bad when he says it. "I don't want to use you. I just want one photo to try to hurt him back for using me for months. I think you're my only chance to make that happen. He won't care about any other guy."

"But you think it'll burn his bread if it's me with you?"

"Yes. Exactly. Nobody likes burnt bread, right?"

He takes a deep breath that rolls his barrel chest up and down then mumbles something that sounds like, "Fuck it."

"Is that a yes?" I ask to make sure I heard him correctly.

"Do you want your picture with me or not, cupcake?" he huffs.

"Cupcake?" I repeat in a whisper, not sure if I should be insulted or not.

"Yeah, you look all cute and innocent, but I'm not the least bit tempted for a taste because I hate sugary sweets."

"You hate sugary sweets?" I say in disbelief, refusing to think too much about how he basically just said he's not attracted to me. It's not like I care. I'm not asking him on a date, just for a quick picture.

"You've got three seconds to get your ass over here if you want your photo."

"Oh. So, like, you're actually going to do this?"

"If you stop talking long enough to get it over with. I've got a game to get ready for, you know."

"Right. Sorry."

"Let her through, Steve."

"Thank you so much!" I exclaim as the annoyed guard opens the gate to allow me inside the parking lot.

"Move it," Preston says, so I hustle over to stand next to him.

My finger trembles as I press the icon on my phone's screen to pull up the camera app. Then I hold it out, trying to get us both on the screen. But Preston is nearly a foot taller than my five-seven, so it's impossible to get both of our heads in the frame at the same time.

"Ah, maybe you could stoop down or hold up my phone?" I suggest.

"You mind, Steve?" Preston asks the security guard. But the guard just stands there staring at him, frozen in place. "Steve?"

"You're serious? You're going to take a picture with *her*?"

The woolly mammoth growls low and threatening in answer. The sound causes an internal shiver that vibrates deep inside of me.

"You're not gonna punch me, are you?" the guard asks softly, like he knows his life is in jeopardy.

"Just take the damn photo!"

Woo-boy. He gives him a command in a booming daddy voice that I would never, ever tolerate.

Except maybe in the bedroom.

Fine, definitely in the bedroom.

"Yes, sir," the guard finally replies before his daddy sends him to his room without dessert. He holds out his hand for my phone that's trembling more than my own.

"Thanks," I tell him, a little smug that Preston not only agreed to the picture with me, but he also yelled at him.

What I wasn't expecting was for Preston to wrap his arm around my shoulders, pulling me close enough to his side that I can feel his warmth through his suit. He smells good, like, ah, warm laundry right out of the dryer and…sweet vengeance.

"Ah, okay. I got a few," the guard says. I hope my eyes weren't closed in all of them because I was too busy sniffing the man.

"Thank you both," I tell them as I scroll through the images, making sure our heads both made the cut. "Do you mind if I post one of these online?" I ask while trying to decide which one to use.

"I'd be disappointed if you didn't," Preston says.

"Well, thanks again," I say as I drop my phone into my purse. "And good luck with the series. I'm still a Bobcats fan, though, so I hope you lose the seventh game."

"You're a hockey fan, but not a puck bunny?" he asks.

Turning to face him, I say, "Why else would I call in every favor I could until I found someone who had tickets for today's game? It's trophy time, baby!"

I think he almost smiled underneath all his fur. "Right, well, if you really want to piss Riley off, you should hold up a sign that says my stick is bigger than his."

A huge smile stretches my face when the stern-looking

man actually makes a joke. "That is a great idea. He would absolutely hate that!"

"I was kidding. Obviously."

I prop my hands on my hips. "I'm not. I have plenty of time before the puck drop to make a sign. Except..."

Preston's brow furrows like he hates when someone leaves him hanging. "Except what?"

"Except, well, I can't put that sort of declaration on a sign and wave it over my head in front of thousands of people if it's not true."

A gruff scoff. "It is true."

That's a mighty big claim to make. And I can't resist when my eyes lower to the front of his pants as if searching for proof.

Even the guard seems shocked when he does a laughing cough into his fist.

"Of course, you would claim it's true. Any man would. Sorry, but I'm not a liar, no matter how much I hate Christian."

"Trust me, my...stick is bigger."

Christian may be a cheating piece of dogshit, but he is well endowed, that much I do know.

"Again, I want to believe you, Preston, I really do. But without proof, I can't paint those words on a sign and cover it with glitter."

"Glitter?"

"Oh, yeah. There would definitely be lots of glitter over my perfectly spaced stenciled lettering."

"Now I definitely have to see this sign."

"Too bad. I can't make it happen without evidence."

"You want me to give you evidence?"

"Ah…" Is he asking me what I think he's asking? That's the look I give the guard, who is still observing our conversation with his mouth gaping. "Yes?" The word comes out as a question.

Cocking his head to the side, he asks, "Sight or feel?"

"Huh?"

"Do you want to see or feel the proof? Lady's choice."

Do I want to see or feel his…stick. Wow. "You're not serious."

Turning to the guard, who is still silently observing us, Preston says, "Can you take my bag inside and give us a minute?"

"Sure thing. I'll just go wait…" he trails off as Preston hands over his duffle. The guard staggers under the weight of the bag, then stares inquisitively at the hockey player until a glare from Preston sends him scurrying into the building.

Once we're alone, Preston says, "I really do need to see that glitter sign of yours today in the stands, so whatever it takes…"

The way he phrased that comment, using the word *need,* it feels like I'm missing something important.

"Why do you *need* to see my silly little sign?"

"A *big* silly sign. And let's just say I have a bit of a rage problem whenever I see Christian Riley's fucking face."

"No kidding?" I grin.

"Your sign, the meaning behind it, would give me a chance to hold some shit over his head for once."

"He usually holds shit over your head?"

"Something like that." Preston frowns.

"So, we would be helping each other out? You gave me an ussie and I give you a big, glitter sign in the stands?"

"Yes. Only fair, right?"

Knowing it's a two-way street of revenge makes me feel a little better about using the man's photo against Christian.

"Then my answer is both."

"Both?" He looks confused for a moment.

"Yes. I need to see and feel the, ah, proof. Just to be certain." Great, now he's got me using that word *need* when it's really just a want, not a need. I want to feel and see a part of this man that I shouldn't. "How exactly can we make that happen?"

Preston glances around me at the nervous sports reporters and, yes, a few gathering puck bunnies on the other side of the fence. "I think I have an idea if you're willing to play along."

"Trust me. I will do whatever it takes to rattle Christian."

"Whatever?" he repeats as he takes several slow steps toward me. As if on instinct, I retreat backward until I feel the fence behind me.

When his tongue slips out to wet his lips, I figure out his intention. It's way more than a selfie, especially with witnesses watching nearby with phones already in their hands.

"Yes," I whisper, giving my permission and approval.

He reaches up to grab onto the chain-link fence next to my head and leans forward. "What's your name?"

"Elle. Elle Townsend." Crazy how he can make me feel like a twelve-year-old girl towering over me.

"Well, Elle Townsend, I think we're about to go viral."

"Good. Christian specifically told me I could sleep with literally anyone in the league but you."

"In that case, you were the best fuck of my life." That

compliment shouldn't make me feel like I'm glowing. I know it's not true, but boy, does it sound good to hear.

"Agreed. So much better than him…" The words barely escape my lips before his are covering mine.

It's a lover's kiss, nothing shy or awkward about it even though it's our first and we're complete strangers. There's a lot of enthusiastic tongue on Preston's part. And my own, if I'm being honest. My palms press against the cool material of his button down under his suit jacket, feeling his hard abs underneath. Getting more turned on by the second, I grip the fabric to pull him closer until our bodies are touching from chest to…oh boy. As promised, I feel him pressing against my stomach, proving his assertion that he's bigger than Christian beyond a doubt.

An embarrassing moan lets him know that I know. It's followed by a rumbly chuckle that shudders through his chest to my breasts. A bolt of desire stirs throughout my body, making me forget where I am, who I am, until he unfortunately pulls his mouth away, leaving us both panting.

"Sorry. It's been a while," he says as he catches his breath.

Been a while? Since he kissed a woman?

"No…no. It's fine."

"Can't wait to see that sign." His smirking lips barely brush mine again, and I swear I can hear the click of actual cameras snapping photos of us.

Unable to resist, my eyes lower, needing to see the proof of not only his claim but his obvious need for something other than a little revenge.

His need for me.

"It's huge," I whisper, cheeks reddening at my slip of

tongue. "I mean, the sign will have to be huge since I'm in the nosebleed section."

"Then I'll have to find you a better seat."

"S-sure," I agree. "That would be great and all, but I'm with my friend Audrey, and I can't leave her to tend to her nosebleed alone."

"I'll see what I can do. Check with Will Call in half an hour."

"Thanks," I tell him. "For everything."

"I think I'm the one who owes you one."

"W-what do you mean?"

"You may have just saved my ass from free agency."

"Huh?" I mutter, but he's already walking away, reaching for the door to head into the arena.

"If anyone asks, you dumped him for me," Preston says, giving me a wink over his shoulder. "Only an idiot would let you go, right?"

"Right," I say, but the door has already shut behind him and half a dozen people are suddenly surrounding me.

"Are you and Preston Lawrence an item?"

"How long have you been seeing each other?"

"Is it a secret affair?

"Does Christian Riley know about you and Preston?"

Rather than open my mouth and ruin the suspense, I just smile and wave my fingers at them as I head back around to the front of the arena. My phone is out a second later, choosing the best photo of us to post to Instagram.

4

―――――

Preston

There's no way of knowing for sure if the woman, Elle, was making shit up about dating Riley or not. But for some reason, I believe her.

"Thanks for holding my bag," I say to Steve after I walk inside the building. When I hold out my hand, he gives me my duffle back, eyes still wide. The man is probably in shock because he's been working team security for the past two years and never seen me allow a photo or speak to a female fan before. Kids sure, but no puck bunnies. Ever.

Not that Elle was a fan of mine or the Warhawks. Bobcats all the way for her, even after ending things with Riley. Her loyalty to what I assume is her hometown team shouldn't tick me off, but it does. What did I expect? That after playing along with her revenge ploy for a few minutes that she would suddenly switch sides?

29

After all, she only asked me for a selfie. The kiss, well, that was all on me. One hell of a kiss that had me wishing for so much more.

Oh, and I also asked her to lie about her dumping Riley, but that was to her benefit, too.

My phone starts blowing up from notifications before I even make it to the locker room, either from someone recording a video of us or because Elle posted her pic.

I usually hate any sort of media attention, especially when it's about my personal life. But today it feels different. I want everyone to know I was rubbing up on Riley's ex right outside the door of his home arena.

The first equipment manager I see is Jim, so I ask him, "Who do I talk to about tickets?"

His brows reach his thinning hairline. "Uh, tickets for today? Here in Greensboro?"

"Yeah."

"It's a home game for the Bobcats."

"And?"

"And not even the Warhawks owner gets a free seat."

"Well, who can I talk to about purchasing tickets?"

"I'll see what I can find out, but it's the first game of the championships. If I can find any, you'll probably have to pay for them out of pocket and they'll be way overpriced."

"Fine. I'll pay whatever I have to pay for two seats as close as possible to the ice."

"Okay, I'll do my best."

"Thanks, Jim."

"Huh. I didn't know you knew my name. You've never spoken to me before today."

I hadn't? "Oh, yeah? Well, sorry about that."

"No problem, Mr. Lawrence."

When he starts to walk away, I get another idea. "Hey, Jim? Do you have any extra jerseys?"

"Jerseys?"

"Yeah. With my name and number on them?"

"Oh. Yeah. In case yours gets ripped. Why?"

"Could you put it with the tickets you find?"

"I'm not sure I'll be able to get any tickets…"

"Sure, you will," I tell him because I have to see Elle Townsend's sign. "Whatever price."

Elle

"So? How did it go?" Audrey asks when I find her still waiting for me in the front lobby, munching on a giant slice of greasy pizza next to the fan shop.

I flip the screen of my phone around to show her rather than tell. The photo that just went up on my profile is worth more than a thousand words.

Her mouth falls open just before she tosses the rest of her pizza slice in the nearby trash can. "Oh my god! You did it, Elle! You actually did it!"

"He didn't just let me take a photo either," I tell her, still a little in shock. "He kissed me."

"No way!"

"And I think some reporters that saw us in the players' lot possibly got photos or videos of that, too."

"Wow. That's amazing!"

"Now I just need to find some supplies."

"Supplies? Ohhh. Do you need a tampon? I think I have one," she says before she starts digging through her purse.

"No, not those kinds of supplies. Art supplies. I have to make a sign."

"A sign?"

"Yeah, like you know, to hold up during the game. It was Preston's idea."

She blinks at me in confusion. "So, one pic and a kiss later and you're on a first name basis with Christian's nemesis?"

"Apparently. He really doesn't like Christian."

"I wonder what caused the beef between them," Audrey muses.

"No idea. If I had to guess, it was probably a girl, right? I doubt I'll ever find out. I just want to enjoy my quick fifteen minutes of fame and hope it burns Christian's bread to see me with the one guy he told me to never sleep with."

A laugh bursts from Audrey. "Burns his bread? Really, Elle?"

"Who am I kidding, right? Christian Riley won't care if I made out with his rival. He's too busy trying to win the championship trophy and sleep with all the female hockey fans in the world."

"I guess we'll find out soon enough."

"Right. For now, I'm going to need to run to the nearest store that sells posterboard, stencils, markers, and glitter. Then, if we're lucky, Preston is going to leave us better tickets at Will Call."

"Way to go, girl! I'm so proud of you," Audrey says as she throws her arm around my shoulders to give me a hug.

"I'm pretty proud of myself, too. Thanks for encouraging me to go through with this crazy idea for closure."

"Anytime," she agrees with a smile.

"I still can't believe you actually put *that* on a sign," Audrey says as we walk back to the arena from the salon with the biggest piece of posterboard I could find clutched in my hand.

"Is it too much?" I ask with a wince.

"No, not at all. There aren't any bad words, so I bet you'll even make it on camera. Christian is going to hate it!"

"Yes, he is. That's the whole point of making it and waving it over my head."

"Right. If you want to hurt a man, tell the world his penis is smaller than his enemy's. I can't imagine a more painful statement to write in glitter markers."

"This glitter is everywhere! I may never get it all off me," I remark as I glance down at my blue and yellow shirt that now catches the light in the setting sun like a disco ball.

"It's cute," Audrey says. "There's even a little on your nose."

"Crap." I swipe the back of my hand across my nose and face.

"Ah, Elle, you just added, like, a dozen more sparkles."

"Great. I'll have to shower when I get home and scrub with a loofa to get this mess off."

"Not to rush you or anything, but the arena is getting packed. We should probably get to our seats."

"Seats!" I exclaim at the reminder. "I need to go to the Will Call window and see if Preston got us better tickets."

Thankfully, the line for that window outside the arena

only has two people in it. After all, most people have their tickets on their phones nowadays.

Audrey and I wait our turn, and then I tell the white-haired lady at the window, "Hi, do you have any tickets for Elle Townsend?"

"Got ID?" She looks down through the glasses on her nose at us.

"I do. Here, hold my sign," I tell Audrey so I can free up my hands to dig out my wallet from my small, clear, arena-approved purse. I learned that lesson from the first game. Clear bags only. I had to walk my ass all the way back to the salon the first game I came to a few years ago before they would let me in.

I open my wallet and turn it to the lady at the window to show her my license under the plastic holder. "That's me. Elle Townsend."

With a quick glance, she says, "Here you go," shoving a pile of something black through the small hole at the bottom of the window. "Tickets are wrapped inside as instructed."

"Ah, what's this?" I ask.

"Looks like a Warhawk jersey," she mutters. "Traitors."

"Traitors?" I huff indignantly as I turn to Audrey, who is wearing a blue and yellow sundress. It was the best she could do on short notice. "We're clearly Bobcats fans."

"Then why did the Warhawks have the tickets and jersey sent over for you?"

"The Warhawks?" I unwrap the sweater-like material, finding the tickets and hold it up in front of me. The jersey is big enough that it could cover me like a blanket. But no, it's not a blanket. It's Preston Lawrence's black jersey with the big bird on the front, number twenty-two sewn in red all over it; and his long name sprawled across the top of the backside.

"Oh my…"

"God!" Audrey finishes. "He gave you his freakin' jersey! How sweet is he?"

"Like I said, traitors," the Golden Girl behind the glass remarks again.

"It's a long story. I'm still a Bobcats fan." I'm not sure why I feel the need to proclaim my allegiance to our local team, but I do.

"Come on, traitor," Audrey says, plucking the tickets from my fingers. She grabs my elbow and steers me toward the security check-in line. "Wow, Elle. These seats are so close we'll be able to smell the sweat coming off the players."

"Really? How did he get such great tickets at the last minute?"

"Maybe because he has tons of money and was trying to impress you?"

"No. He's just looking forward to seeing the sign I promised him."

"He'll be able to see you alright. Along with the rest of the world," she remarks. Giving me a hip bump with her bony one, she asks, "So, are you going to wear his jersey or not?"

"I guess I have to, right?" I hold it up in front of me in the security line and hear Bobcats' fans groan at the sight. "I can't believe Preston gave me one of his jerseys."

"Christian never gave you one of his, did he?"

"Ah, no." I slip the enormous attire on over the top of my shirt and then have to tie a knot at the bottom to keep it from falling to my knees. "Christian did ask me to wear his jersey once…"

"Let me guess, and nothing else?"

"Ding, ding, ding! We have a winner!"

Audrey rolls her brown eyes and steps forward when the line moves up. "That man's ego knows no bounds, does it?"

"Well, he's gorgeous, and one of the best hockey players in the league, so I guess he had a right to be arrogant."

"A little humility could go a long way is all I'm saying. How about Preston? Did he seem more down to earth?"

"He seemed more…" I try to figure out how to describe his demeanor. "Preston gave off strong I'll-rip-your head-off-if-you-look-at-me-the-wrong-way vibes."

"Wow. Hot."

"How is that hot?" I ask because I'm honestly curious. I couldn't help but think the same thing earlier when meeting him, and it doesn't make any sense. Pretty, clean-cut guys like Christian are my usual type.

"A big, strong man who doesn't put up with any shit is hot. He's a protector. A lot of women are into that sort of thing despite being feminists."

"I guess so…"

"How about this? If there was an apocalypse tomorrow, who would you want by your side, helping you stay alive—a five-foot nothing guy who weighs a hundred pounds or a huge, ripped dude who could carry you to safety in one hand while busting heads with the other?"

"That…that is…when do you have the time to come up with these things, Audrey?"

"I'm single, and I've been single for months. Trust me, I have to figure out some way to get through the nights. While you were screwing a hockey player for nearly half a year, I was alone with my thoughts and a plastic penis."

"Sorry. I guess I shouldn't complain about the great sex, even if it obviously meant nothing to him…"

"It never means anything to men. Women are the ones who attach all the little strings. Men only go along with the strings because they like the sex."

Thankfully, we're next in line, so we place the sign and our clear purses on the conveyer belt of the x-ray machine and let the nice, bald retired man run his metal detector wand up and down us.

5

____

Elle

"These seats are incredible!" Audrey says from beside me. "In that jersey, you stand out like a sore thumb, Elle."

It's nice and warm, so I don't care if I'm wearing the opposing team's colors.

"Yeah, well, my sign is going to do that, too."

"No kidding," she snorts. "I didn't think about it until now, but I bet you're gonna make some Bobcats' fans *very* unhappy by calling out their golden boy."

"Not to mention what they'll say when they see the photo of Preston and I kissing."

"How many likes do you have on your pic now?"

"No idea. I'm scared to look."

"Why? It's a great photo. You look hot and tiny next to the woolly mammoth."

"My phone has been buzzing like crazy, most likely from new comments."

"So have a look. I'll hold up your sign while you check." Lifting it up over her head, she yells, "Woohoo. Let's go boys!" to the men skating around the ice during warmups.

"Which team are you rooting for?" I can't help but ask her.

"Team? I'm just here for the sexy players on both teams, including some of our hottie clients."

Smiling at her, I pull out my phone from my purse. "Oh, wow," I mutter as I scroll.

"A lot of likes?"

"Hundreds. And so many comments. Oh! And there's the photo of us kissing that I'm tagged in somehow. Three thousand people have already liked it! Ugh, but the comments on it are even worse…"

"What do they say?" Audrey sits down in her seat and leans over to see the screen of my phone while I pause long enough for her to read a few. "Ah, trolls. Ignore them, girl. They're just jealous."

"Jealous? They're vicious. This comment that has the most likes says, '*This is the best Preston could do after going five years without a date? He should throw her back and try again, but he'd probably hurt his back.*' Then it's followed up by the laughing until you cry emoji."

"Mean girls never go away. They just get older and more bitter," Audrey says. "Seriously, Elle. Put the phone away and enjoy the game in your new jersey."

The device buzzes again and again in my palm. "It's hard to ignore the comments when a new one comes in every second."

"Put the phone down. Delete the app. Do what you have to

do, but don't let them get to you for one second. They have sucky lives and want everyone else to be as miserable as they are."

"Right." I shove my phone back into my purse and tuck it under my seat. "Give me that sign. It's too late to turn back now."

"That a girl!" Audrey cheers as she hands the sign over.

When a few more of the Warhawks skate out onto the ice for warmups, I get to my feet and hold it over my head, searching for Preston. He's one of the last to come out, probably because he doesn't have to practice shooting pucks or stretching like the goalie. No, his job is to hit the players on the other team, and hit them hard, keeping them from getting near the goal.

Audrey stands up beside me and takes one side of the poster. "So, instead of worrying about the trolls, let's talk about you and the woolly mammoth. What happens now?"

"What do you mean?" I ask as I alternate between watching the two men skating on opposite sides of the ice.

"You got your photo. He upped the ante to include a kiss that the world will see, which makes me think he's on board with the idea of being your fake boyfriend."

"A photo was all I wanted from him, and he was kind enough to do that. I think that means it's over."

"Over? No, it can't just be over!"

"What do you want me to do? Go wait for him by the bus and ask him to come home with me tonight to celebrate his big win?"

"Yes, that is exactly what you should say!"

Shaking my head, I bark out a laugh. "No. That's not going to happen. I just ended things with Christian. And while I felt some sparks from the kiss, that doesn't mean Preston felt them too."

I don't tell my friend about the other part of him I felt while we were lip locked to verify the statement on my sign.

A sign which is probably about to be circulating widely around social media.

Preston

One look at Riley during pregame warmups and I can tell he's already heard about me and Elle. How do I know? His usual smirk is nowhere to be found on his pretty boy face. He looks annoyed, also a little nervous. The cocky shit has never made it to the finals before, and he knows I'm going to be gunning for him every second we're both on the ice.

Elle is right. The son of a bitch does look scared.

"Oh, shit," my teammate Cade says. "I've never seen that psycho smile on your face before, Pres. Whatever you're planning, just don't murder the arrogant prick before we win the championship."

There's a smile on my face? Reaching up, I have to feel around my facial hair to find and trace my lips through my gloves.

I'll be damned. There is a smile.

And for the first time in years, seeing the prick doesn't send me into a completely unhinged, blind rage.

"I'm not gonna kill him," I assure Cade. "I'd rather just make his life hell."

A few moments later, Riley skates around me in a circle, giving me a wide berth before finally saying, "I know what you're doing."

"What am I doing, Riley, other than getting ready to paint the ice with your blood to help the Warhawks get their first of four wins?"

The jackass's face goes pale, and it's not just the reflection from the ice.

"There's nothing going on between you and Elle. There can't be," he says. "We just broke up yesterday!"

"Guess she just couldn't wait to move on with someone who isn't a selfish asshole in bed."

"That's bullshit!" His voice is getting louder the longer we talk, like I'm finally getting to him and not the other way around. God, Elle was right. The psychological warfare is even more enjoyable than hitting him. Bruises heal; words burrow deep into the skin and fester for years.

I give Riley a wink and a grin. "Just wait until you see her sign."

"Her sign? What sign?" he asks. He glances up at the stands as if searching for her. "She's here? How did she get tickets?"

"I hooked her up." Actually, Jim came through for me like I knew he would. Cost me two grand, but it's totally worth it if I win the championship trophy and get a contract extension.

"Fucking hell, Lawrence. You sure are going to a lot of trouble to try to make everyone *think* you're hooking up."

"How else would she know without a shadow of a doubt that my dick is bigger than yours if we didn't hook up at least once?"

I look to the seats I paid for and there she is, white sign held above her head, the gold, red and black glitter filling the big perfect letters glistening under the lights.

THE RESULTS ARE IN: Preston's stick is bigger than Christian's!

Instead of the word "stick" there's a long black hockey stick drawn in the space. It's a thing of beauty, especially since I know how fast she made it. I want it hanging in my bedroom so I can go to sleep with a smile on my face every night.

And hot damn, she's wearing my black and red jersey in the sea of blue and yellow Bobcat fans.

Christian's eyes follow my finger when I point her out to him. His pale face instantly goes Warhawk red, either because of what the sign says about him or because the girl he was sleeping with is wearing my number. Maybe both.

"You son of a bitch!" he yells before he tosses his stick down. Next, he jerks each of his gloves off his hands and throws them on the ice to launch himself at me.

Since I'm several inches taller than the jerk, and therefore have longer arms, I'm easily able to hold him off me with a hand on his forehead while skating backwards. Hell, I'm too busy laughing at him losing his shit to even take a swing at him myself.

When I see a bunch of yellow jerseys heading toward us, I do give his head a push backwards hard enough that his skates slide out from under him, and he lands on his ass. There's no reason for his entire team to jump in and start a fight before the puck drops.

"Can't wait to make you kiss the boards all night long, asshole," I tell him with a smile before I head to the locker room.

"What was that shit with Riley about?" Coach Ramsey asks as he follows me down the narrow hallway.

"Just giving him a taste of his own medicine."

"We can't afford to lose you to penalties, Lawrence. They'll score on every power play they get."

"I know that, and I'm good. I swear I won't throw a punch at him or even retaliate if he tries that shit."

"Oh, yeah? How can you be so sure? I know you've been ejected for brawling with him twice before."

I come to a stop to turn around and face him, towering over the tall, lanky man in his dress shoes since I'm on skates. "How can I be sure I'll get to Riley more than he'll get to me? Because I'm fucking his girl."

I know it's just a rumor Elle and I managed to get circulating tonight. But if enough people believe a rumor, then it may as well be the truth.

"No kidding?" Coach says with a grin. "Good for you, Lawrence. Just don't lose your edge during the finals from too much lovin'."

"Too much *lovin'*?" I can't help but repeat the phrase back to him.

"You know what I'm talking about," he huffs before stomping past me.

Unfortunately, I do know what he means. The buildup of testosterone makes me angrier, more aggressive, which is exactly what my team needs on the ice. It's one of the reasons why I don't date, not even in the off season. I can't afford to have any distractions or waste time on drama with women, especially not with my contract on the line.

So, no matter how badly I may want to make the rumor

about me and Elle a reality, I'm going to keep my big stick in my pants.

6

____

Elle

"This is all your fault!" some middle-aged man wearing Christian's jersey and a Bobcats' hat yells from the stairs next to our seats.

I glance around to see who he's so furious at, but don't see anyone causing a scene. That's when I whisper to Audrey, "Is he talking to me?"

"Yes, I'm talking to you!" the man shouts.

I point at my chest again in confusion.

"You cheated on him with that prick!"

"Ah, I'm not sure who you're talking about. I didn't cheat on anyone," I assure him.

"Even if she did, it's none of your business, buddy!" Audrey yells back from her seat, which is closer to him.

"It's my business, and every other fan's if she ruined our best player!"

"Nobody ruined Christian Riley!" Audrey stands up to shout at him. "If you got a problem with how he's playing, then take it up with him, jackass!"

"Your friend's a traitorous slut!" he calls back before finally taking the steps up and away from us.

"Did he just call me a slut?" I ask Audrey when she retakes her seat.

"Sorry. I didn't mean to escalate things. I was hoping that he would go away if someone called him out."

"It's not your fault."

"And it's not yours either, Elle."

"I think all the people around us wearing blue and yellow would disagree." I slump a little lower in my seat, hiding my face behind the sign. I started to put the stupid thing down in the first period because of all the boos it was getting. Audrey convinced me not to give in to terrorists.

"Between the angry fans here and online, I'm staying away from Preston Lawrence from now on."

"What? No! You said there were sparks when you kissed!"

"Sparks for me, yes, but no spark is worth being the most hated woman in the arena. Possibly the entire city and multiple states. We only have one hockey team in both Carolinas!"

"Nobody hates you. They just need someone to blame for how poorly the Bobcats and Christian are playing. That's on the team, not you."

"Christian can barely stay upright," I note. "He hasn't even taken a single shot! I've never seen him play this badly before."

"He's probably nervous to be playing for such high stakes, that's all."

"You don't think it's about me, do you? What if…what if he's actually furious with me?"

"So? You're furious at him too, remember? He dumped you because he was so certain his team would win the championship, and he'll be a hot shot hero screwing tons of puck bunnies."

"Right. Thank you for the reminder that I wasn't enough, and he needs an army of women to satisfy him."

"Oh, honey. He's a selfish jerk. It has nothing to do with you, or whether you satisfied him. I'm sure you were great. He's just not ready to settle down anytime soon."

"I never once even asked for a commitment, you know? He's right about that. I didn't bring up being exclusive because I didn't want him to dump me for asking him to give up other women. I just pretended he wasn't fooling around on away games. How pathetic is that?"

"It's not pathetic. You should be with someone who would gladly give up other women to keep you around because you are awesome."

"Being tossed aside by Christian doesn't make me feel awesome. It makes me feel…used. But the worst part is that I let myself be jerked around by him for five months because he was a gorgeous hockey star. I was too scared to ask for more because I didn't think I belonged in the same league as him. Turns out I was right about all of that."

"I know it feels yucky now, but things will get better, Elle. I think you have a new hockey star admirer. One who shares a mutual dislike of your ex. That gives you something to bond over."

"But if Preston even agreed to keep this fake relationship up, then we would just be using each other, too."

"It's not the same as how Christian used you. There would be a mutual agreement. Rules to follow. You could probably even throw in no strings attached sex with the woolly mammoth."

"He doesn't date."

"He does now. If he didn't want the attention on the two of you, then he wouldn't have taken it a step further, knowing that kiss would go viral."

"That was just to mess with Christian. I'm surprised he even agreed to a photo."

"Like he was going to turn down a pretty woman."

"I don't think he liked me." I shake my head.

"Then why would he kiss you? He can't possibly hate Christian enough to go around kissing random women. Trust me, Elle. Now that you're wearing his jersey, he's going to gladly keep up the charade."

Maybe Audrey is right about Preston. I'm just not sure if I want to keep up our scheme or not. It feels…wrong.

But it also feels sort of perfectly right in a way that scares me.

Preston

"Good lord, man," Nick says from his seat beside me on the bench. We're both trying to catch our breath, waiting for our line to go back out on the ice. "That sign…damn." He chuckles and holds out his gloved fist for me to bump it. "Best thing I've ever seen."

"Yeah, it is pretty great," I agree. I'm glad Elle's seat is across the arena facing both benches, always in sight. If she had been behind us, well, I would've hurt my neck from all the times I looked in her direction.

"Riley's all messed up about it. How did you manage to steal his girl?"

"It's a long story," I say, not wanting to tell it now when our heads should be in the game. I wasn't sure how to explain it later, really, because it's all fake.

Now, I'm glad I didn't just walk away from Elle instead of hearing what she wanted. If I had ignored her…hell, I probably wouldn't have made it to the second period.

Without the distraction of me being thrown out of the game or making my teammates pick up the slack for me that a penalty would give the Bobcats in a power play, the Warhawks are currently up two goals to nothing. That's right, the Bobcats haven't made a single goal, and they've only taken twelve shots in two periods.

The fourth line comes back to the bench, which means it's time for me and the rest of the first to hit the ice. Riley is already exhausted, ready for his team's change up. When my boy clears the puck and Riley has to stay on the ice, I know I'll still have time to get in a hit on him.

Popping in my mouthpiece, I race toward him as he tries to get the puck away from the wall, slamming into him with all of my momentum and weight, pinning him to the boards.

"Oh, look. You can see Elle's sign from here too," I tell him.

"Get the fuck off me!" he roars.

I don't get off of him. In fact, I keep him smushed like a pancake until Nick swipes the puck from him and hightails it down the ice to the Bobcats' goal.

When I turn to follow him, I make it about two feet before my legs are yanked out from underneath me, causing me to faceplant on the ice. It only takes a second to figure out what happened.

That son of a bitch tripped me!

Thankfully, one of the refs saw it all. He's ready and waiting to call the penalty as soon as the Bobcats touch the puck again.

"Oh, come on!" Riley whines when he goes up to the man in stripes. "Lawrence can't skate worth a shit! He fell all on his own!"

Chuckling, the ref says, "He sure as hell can't skate when you hook his ankle with your stick."

I get up and start skating away, but not before taunting the asshole. "Riley's just jealous my stick is bigger than his!"

Since Riley has to go to the penalty box, our team has the Bobcats outnumbered five on four and take advantage by scoring another goal, making it three to nothing.

In the third period, the Bobcats score once, and their goalie keeps everything the Warhawks shoot out of the goal.

Then, all that's left is celebrating our first win of the series in the Bobcats' arena.

One win down, three more to go until that trophy is ours.

I don't know what it is about Elle, but I can't seem to stop thinking about her for more than five seconds.

At least my infatuation didn't hurt my game. I played damn good tonight. The entire team did.

The Bobcats didn't have a chance, not when their leading scorer couldn't seem to get the puck under control whenever it was passed to him.

But now that the game is over, and it's time to head to the bus, I can't help but wonder if I'll ever see Elle again.

It's not like I have her phone number. I guess I could try to find her on Insta since I at least know her name.

It turns out finding her was easier than I anticipated since her profile picture is the two of us.

I debate whether to send her a private message. First, I'll have to create an account as I'm not currently on any social media platforms. I want my personal life to stay private. But I'll sign up if it's the only way to reach Elle.

I don't want her to think I'm stalking her, but at the same time, I don't want to lose out on a chance to talk to her again.

Maybe it's our mutual hatred for Riley that has me so intrigued by her. I want to know what he did to her, even if I can't ever tell her why I loathe him.

A moment later and the profile for "HockeyLife2222" is set up. Now, I just have to figure out what to say in the message.

Our goalie is closest to me, lacing up his dress shoes on the bench. He's a decent-looking guy who probably gets lots of women.

"Yo, Vincent."

He pauses his tying to point to his own chest with his eyebrows raised. "Me?"

"Yeah, you. Great game tonight."

He blinks at me for a long moment. "Ah, thanks, Preston."

Getting right down to it, I say, "How do you let a woman know you're interested in her without sounding like a creep?"

"How do you…fuck, I dunno. Let's ask, Bryan. Hey, Bryan!" he calls out.

"Yeah?"

"What should Preston say to a woman he's interested in that won't make her instantly block him?"

"Hmm. Well, I guess you could say, 'Hey, baby. When can I see you again'?"

I stare at him, waiting for the rest of his words of wisdom. They don't come. "That's it? That's what I should say?"

Bryan shrugs and winks. "Works every time for me."

I decide to leave off the term of endearment and reword his suggestion to say, ***You look good in my jersey and your sign was a big hit with the entire team. Can I see you again soon?*** I've already hit send when I realize I added the word *soon* subconsciously. I didn't mean to use that word. But still, I don't regret it. I want to see Elle again now, not in a few days, because I won't be here in a few days. After game two, we'll be heading back to D.C. for games three and four. Hopefully that will be all it takes for the Warhawks to win the championship. If so, I won't be coming back to North Carolina again this year.

When I get dressed, I keep checking my phone to see if she's read the message. I stare at it on the way out of the locker room, and when I get outside, standing in the same spot where I first saw her.

And then I look up, and there she is, almost in the exact same spot at the fence, talking to Steve. I swear she's glowing, or maybe that's just a few pieces of glitter getting caught in the parking lot's light.

"Hey," I say when I walk over. "You're here."

"Hey. Great game!" she says with a wide smile.

"Thanks for the tickets!" another woman says, but I can't pry my eyes off the peppy blonde.

"Right. Thank you for the tickets and the jersey. That's all we came by to say," Elle explains in a rush.

That's all they came by to say? Thank you? I find that hard to believe.

"You're welcome." I drink Elle in from head to toe, certain she got prettier during the game even if I'm not sure what's different other than my jersey hugging her curves. Her long blonde hair is now up in a messy ponytail, which is cute. Her cheeks are a little rosy, probably from being crammed into the arena surrounded by fans. But her eyes seem a little red too.

Wait. Has she been crying?

"What's wrong, cupcake?"

"Wrong? Nothing's wrong."

"Are you sure? You look like you've been crying."

"How would you know how I look when I've been crying?" she challenges with her chin raised stubbornly.

"Right, well, did you get my message?"

That seems to surprise her. "What message? How? You don't have my number."

"I sent you one on Insta."

"Oh." Her shoulders slump forward and her face falls. "I haven't had a chance to check all the messages and comments."

"The picture of us getting a lot of attention?"

She nods her head, making her blonde ponytail sway. "It's been crazy. I'm also getting tagged in other pictures of us, you know, kissing."

"Right."

"People are being assholes." When her friend chimes in with that newsflash, I finally glance over at the brunette.

"What do you mean, people are being assholes?" I ask.

"Some people, mostly angry Bobcats' fans and jealous women, are saying shitty things about Elle."

I look back to the blonde, who is definitely less peppy than she was earlier today. "Who was talking shit? What did they say?"

"Some mentioned you should date someone prettier than me, and that I was not only a huge slut but stupid for dumping Christian for someone else."

"Who said those things, Elle?" I practically growl at her.

"I don't know them personally. It's not a big deal."

That's the biggest lie I've ever heard. I grew up with a sensitive younger sister. I know words can cause deeper wounds that won't heal as fast as physical ones. And if being in a damn photo with me is what caused Elle to be upset, then I want to fix it.

"If they hurt you, then I'll hurt them."

Now she gives me a small smile. "You can't beat up everyone on social media."

"I can try," I tell her.

"Most are women. Women who think that you could do a lot better than someone like me."

"Better than you?"

"I appreciate you going along with my stupid scheme, but I'm not sure if it's worth the negative attention anymore."

Shit. She's ready to call our fake relationship quits when it hasn't even been a day. I'm worse at fake dating than I am the real thing.

And while at first, I didn't want any part of her ploy to piss off Riley, now I'm glad I did it. Not just because she helped me get through an entire game against the prick without a penalty or ejection, but also because I like her and want to keep spending time with her.

"Seriously, Elle, don't let those assholes get to you. They're a bunch of blind idiots if they can't see how undeniably beautiful you are. Not to mention brave for having the courage to approach me out of the blue when most men go running when they see me."

"You're just saying all that because you're enjoying tormenting Christian, and don't want to let up yet."

"I promise you, every word is the truth. I'll even pinky promise." I hold up my pinky and wiggle it at her through the fence. She laughs before she wraps her pinky, that's a third of the size of mine, around it. "If you're still not convinced, then you must have forgotten about earlier."

"Earlier?" Elle asks, her brow furrowed all cute.

"The proof you saw and felt right out here," I remind her. "Did that feel like a lie?"

She wets her lips as she looks up at me, obviously replaying the kiss in her head. "No. But, you admitted that it's…been a while."

"What is with you and all your excuses? If you really believe that, then what was Riley's excuse?"

"What do you mean?"

"He's with a different woman every night, and he wanted you."

"I…I don't really know why he wanted me. I was just convenient. Easy. I went down on him whenever he was in my chair."

"Huh?"

"Never mind. Don't you have a bus to catch?" She nods her head, swinging her ponytail toward the open doors of the charter bus. Most of my teammates are already on board. Is she trying to get rid of me or change the subject? Maybe both.

"Right. They're taking us back to the hotel."

"And then?" Her friend is the one who asks that question.

"Then, I guess some guys will go out and celebrate our win."

"Well, have fun," Elle says to me with a smile, like she's assuming I'll be going out too. I don't usually. Maybe I would if she came along. That's doubtful thanks to a bunch of asshats on social media. It doesn't mean I'm not going to try to convince her to not only come, but to keep this plan of ours in motion. She may be the only thing that gets me through the finals and into a contract extension.

"I'm guessing such a true Bobcat fan like yourself wouldn't want to join us?" There, I asked it as a question to give her a chance to let me down easy. No wonder I don't date. This shit is stressful and confusing, not knowing what the woman is thinking about me at any given moment.

"The Warhawks was the first jersey I was ever gifted, so I could probably put aside my loyalty to the Bobcats for one night."

Is that a yes? It sort of sounded like a yes.

"Okay. How about I send you a message with the details when I know them?"

"Sure. If you want."

"See you then?"

"Yeah. Maybe."

Great, now her maybe sounds like a no. But with a final

nod, I force my dress shoes to haul my ass over to the bus steps and climb up them without glancing back at her like a hapless fool.

Once I'm seated on the bus, I have a view of her from the tinted window. And when I see Riley coming at her with all the fury of a pissed off hornet, slitting his throat with my skate's blade begins to look even more appealing.

7

Elle

"**Y**ou have a date tonight with a big, hot hockey player!" Audrey points out the obvious as soon as Preston steps onto the bus.

I'm still staring after him in a dazed awe. "He'll probably forget about me once he's surrounded by women in whatever club they all decide to celebrate in."

"What? No way! He is smitten."

"We just have a common enemy. That's all," I assure her and myself. I will not let myself feel special because another hockey player spoke to me. Just because Preston doesn't like Christian doesn't mean he isn't the same when it comes to being a womanizer.

Except, Christian said Preston doesn't ever date.

Isn't that the whole reason the photo of us kissing blew

up? Because it was so unusual for anyone to see him near a woman?

Despite Preston's claim that it's been a while for him, I still find it hard to believe. If nobody sees him date, that doesn't mean he's not doing it secretly.

"I can't fucking believe you!" a familiar voice shouts, drawing my attention back to the player entrance and exit. Christian isn't just yelling; he's storming over to where Audrey and I are lingering by the fence.

"Of all the people in the world, why did it have to be him, Elle?"

"Uh-oh. Looks like someone is jealous," Audrey singsongs loud enough for Christian to hear.

"Well?" he demands when he's standing in front of me, a tall, angry volcano ready to erupt. I'm sort of glad there's the chain link between us, while also…giddy to have evoked such a reaction from the man who shattered my heart as if it were made of cheap glass.

I would've been happy with getting a glare from him in response to the photo of me and Preston kissing. I didn't think he would care enough to make an actual scene.

But I know the effect on him is more his fear of Preston than his jealousy.

"Oh, I don't know, Christian. Maybe because you said he would never want a nobody like me and I wanted to prove you wrong."

That much is true. While it's highly unlikely that Preston wants me in any way other than pissing off Christian, it would be a huge score to change the mind of the grumpy defenseman who doesn't date.

"What the hell?" Audrey exclaims. "Did you seriously call Elle a *nobody*?"

"That's not what I meant…Anyone but Lawrence, Elle," Christian starts but I roll right over him, furious that he keeps admitting that he doesn't care about me if he's fine with me sleeping with his entire team or every asshole on the planet. The only man who bothers him is the one he didn't think I had a chance with. And while that's true, Preston wouldn't have looked at me twice if not for his revenge plot, I refuse to admit Christian is right.

"You don't get to tell me who I can or can't date. Even if we were still dating or hooking up, or whatever you want to call it, you're the one who said we weren't ever exclusive, remember?"

"Lawrence is a volatile asshole! He broke my arm and gave me a concussion the last two times our teams played each other!"

Wow. Preston actually broke his bones and busted his head? He really does hate him. And Christian is genuinely terrified of the grizzly bear.

"You should probably be careful out there on the ice during the playoffs. An injury like that could hurt the Bobcats' chances and take you out of the MVP running, couldn't it?"

Christian's perfect sculpted jaw clenches. "Stay away from him, Ellie, and burn that fucking jersey."

I run my palm down the big bird covering the front of my chest. "Ah, no freaking way. I like this jersey. You never got me decent seats or gave me one of your jerseys to wear in five months. Oh, well, except for that one night. And it looks like you were wrong about Preston not wanting me, too. He's already invited me out later tonight."

"He doesn't date! Ever!" Christian roars. "And this isn't you, Ellie. You don't sleep around like that! It's fake, isn't it? You're both in on it trying to mess with my head!"

"Think what you want. I didn't come back here to see you tonight. I came to thank Preston for the amazing seats."

"Where the fuck did you even meet him? The I hate Christian Riley fan club?"

"Yes, that is exactly where we met, Christian. How did you know about our secret group?"

"This ends now, Ellie! I'll tell everyone in the next press conference that it's a sham to get back at me because I dumped you yesterday."

"Oh, well, I already told a reporter that I dumped you for him. If you comment now, you'll look like a scorned lover. So sorry about that." It's not true. I haven't spoken to anyone, especially the press or even the fans yelling at me during the game.

"You're going to ruin my goddamn reputation," he grits out through clenched teeth.

"Your reputation as a playboy is still fully intact."

"I meant on the ice! I played like shit tonight!"

"Did you? I didn't notice. The Warhawks were on fire. Especially Preston."

Wow, the oh-so-perfect hot shot hockey player blames a nobody like me for his shitty game? My mind is officially blown.

"You didn't even know who he was yesterday!" His voice is so loud the entire town can probably hear it at this point.

"Well, today I know a lot more about him than just his name." I clear my throat and adjust the sign still hanging in my lowered hand to make my point, then tilt my head to look at the arrogant man who dumped me without an ounce of remorse. "Why are you making a fuss about it, Christian? It's not like you ever cared about me?"

"I don't." I hate that I wince at those two adamant words. "I just...I specifically told you anyone *but* him."

"You can tell me whatever the hell you want; that doesn't mean I'm going to listen," I mutter before turning on my heel and marching back toward the fan parking lot, Audrey whooping in support right on my heels.

∾

Preston

Part of me wanted to get off the bus and beat Riley into the pavement.

But another part of me wanted to watch and see how Elle reacted to him. I needed to know that she's really over him, that getting her payback was out of spite for being dumped and not love or any other feelings for him.

It's stupid really.

It's none of my business if the woman still wants the asshole. Maybe it just feels like my business now because I've found my way into a very public love triangle. I should've thought this through better. If Elle goes back to Christian, I'll look like a goddamn fool, and feel like one too.

Based on the furious look on Christian's face as Elle went toe to toe with him before she walked away, I'm guessing she's not asking him about getting back together.

Tonight, if she shows up to hang out with me, I'll find out what he said. Until then, all I can do is wait.

And while I wait, I go through the hundreds of notifications waiting for me on my phone, and then respond to each and every comment that is rude to Elle.

8

Preston

I keep searching the crowd below the club's VIP section, waiting for the beautiful blonde woman who is a fucking genius manipulator. Most of my teammates are either at the bar drinking or on the floor drinking and dancing. Neither of those things are for me. I only came out because I want to see and talk to Elle for more than two minutes at a time.

When I finally spot a pretty woman walking in alone, her long blonde hair falling over her shoulders, I'm almost certain it's Elle. She changes her hairstyles more than most women change their clothes.

My heart races as I head down the steps of the second floor to greet her.

Her head turns this way and that, searching for me, too. When she sees me approaching, she smiles like I'm her favorite person in the world. Which is ridiculous since we haven't even known each other but for a few hours.

"You came," I shout over the music.

"I did, mostly because you invited me, remember?"

"I know. I just wasn't sure if you would show up. Want to head upstairs where it's a little quieter?"

"Sure."

As soon as we're past the bouncer at the roped off VIP section, I take a seat in one of the purple leather booths and Elle slides in next to me.

"It is quieter up here."

"Yeah, that's why I like it." Already, just by having Elle sitting next to me, I feel calmer. Less volatile. What is it about her that puts me instantly at ease in a way I've never felt before? Right now, I can't take my eyes off the specks of glitter glistening on her cheeks, forehead, and nose. I don't even consider telling her because they're too damn cute. If I had to bet, they came from when she was making my sign.

Suddenly remembering that this is a fake date, I figure I should at least pretend to be a gentleman. "Can I get you something to drink?"

"No, thank you. I drove so nothing but water for me tonight."

"I don't usually drink during the season, either." Or the off-season, I don't bother to mention before I signal the waitress over. "Can we get two glasses of water, please?"

"Sure thing," she says before hurrying off.

Once she's gone, I glance around the room to the people nearby. Everyone, teammates and non-teammates, are either hot and heavy in make-out sessions or close enough to be whispering in each other's ears. I wouldn't mind doing either of those things with Elle, but first I can't help but break the silence by asking what's been festering in my gut for more than an hour. "I saw you talking to Riley after I got on the bus."

"Oh. Right." Elle nods and tucks her hair back behind her ears with a bright, proud smile. "He blamed me, *us*, for how badly he played tonight. Needless to say, he was not happy with me fraternizing with his enemy. He actually forbade me from seeing you again."

I'd love to see Riley try to tell me to stay away from Elle. "And yet, you're here with me now, so you obviously took his decree to heart."

"I told him he doesn't get a say in who I talk to anymore."

"Good. Screw him," I remark. Still, I can't help but point out a discrepancy with Elle's claim to be just Riley's meaningless flavor of the month. "I think you undersold your relationship with him."

"What do you mean?"

"He was furious, Elle. Clearly, you did more than just date a few times."

She shrugs and says with a heavy sigh, "He never cared about me. He said so himself. Our time together obviously meant more to me than it did to him."

"Oh yeah?"

Jesus fucking Christ.

Elle *slept* with Riley.

Probably multiple times.

He's seen and touched every inch of her body.

I don't know why that thought just suddenly occurred to me. Or why I hate the idea of her and him naked together.

Before and during the game, I had so much shit on my

mind that I didn't consider the details of them "dating." Now that I have…well, those thoughts need to fuck right off.

"He just doesn't want me talking to you. He wouldn't care what I did with you if you were anyone else in the world."

"I think he would," I tell her honestly. The normally cool, arrogant asshole was furious tonight. I've never seen him like that before. Well, at least not in several years.

"So, you seem happier than you were earlier," I can't help but remark. She looks stunningly beautiful.

Elle shakes her head and smiles up at me. "And you're not as grumpy as you were this afternoon."

"Really? That must be the effect you have on me, cupcake."

"My effect on you?"

"You're fun. Messing with Christian has been almost as enjoyable as playing in the championships again."

"Tonight, he was angry but also convinced we're faking it," she remarks. That must have been what else he said to her after the game.

"That's just what he wants to believe. The arrogant son of a bitch probably can't fathom why you would want to be with me. Trust me, deep down, he thinks we're legit. He lost it like I've never seen in warm-ups, then again when he got the penalty, a rare thing for the golden boy of hockey."

"I did see him land on his ass when you gave him a shove during warmups. Then the tripping penalty during the game."

"He was furious with me. The first penalty he's been called out on in a long damn time."

"And the Warhawks scored again on the power play while he was in the box, which pretty much sealed the deal on the game."

"One down. Three games to go," I announce proudly just as the waitress returns with our glasses of water.

9

Elle

It feels so incredibly…intimate in this booth with Preston so close and almost everyone else around us busy making out in the dark club. At least that's what they were doing when we first sat down. Now pretty much everyone is staring at us. And holding up their phones to take photos.

I hate being the center of attention. Now I'm really glad I touched up my makeup and decided to take my hair down from the ponytail and style it with waves before coming out.

"You, ah, you don't want to go celebrate with your teammates?" I ask Preston before lifting my sweaty glass of water to take a sip. Preston watches the move intently for some reason.

"Nah. My teammates are all scared of me."

"Scared of you?"

"Yeah. I've been told I'm not the friendliest guy to work

with on the ice, that I'm judgmental, and too violent during practice."

"Why is that?"

"I just call them on their shit when our coaches don't. Apparently, the guys hate being told when they screw up or when I check them too hard in practice."

I nod my head in understanding. Preston is apparently just intense all the time. And he likes to hit his own teammates?

"Have you ever thought about not checking them so hard or calling them out for every little thing?"

"Then how would they get better, or be adequately prepared for our games? The assholes we go up against don't pull any punches. They all just need to toughen up and quit whining like a bunch of babies."

"If you say so," I reply softly. "You seem to take hockey very seriously."

"It's my job, how I earn a living. I have to be the best defensive man on the team, or I'll be replaced with someone bigger, stronger, more violent."

"I'm not sure there are many men bigger, stronger, or more violent than you, Preston."

"Younger then, faster. I don't want to get replaced, so I try to give it my all, even in practice."

"That dedication has obviously paid off." I don't bother telling him that Christian would often wake up late and show up to practice when it was nearly over because he thought he was already the best at everything.

"I may only have another eight good years left in me if I don't get hurt. If I'm lucky. That's why I save as much of my checks as possible now."

"That must be tough, never knowing if one game, one practice, could be your last."

"It's not easy."

After that comment, he glances away, as if he's thinking about all the pressure he's under. When he frowns, I follow his gaze to a man recording us on his phone with the flashlight on.

"Everyone is still looking at us."

"I'm used to it at home and traveling to other cities," Preston says. "Although it's not usually this bad. One growl from me telling them to fuck off and they scurry away."

"Didn't you hit someone for taking your photo?"

"He deserved it."

Okay then.

"Well, all this is because you have a reputation for not dating, right?" I ask.

"Right."

"A reputation you're deviating from today."

"No kidding."

"You really don't date, or do you just keep your relationships quiet?" I can't help but ask.

"I don't date period," he remarks.

"Why not?"

"Like I said, my career could end any day. I've already had five good years in the majors. I need to take every game seriously, play my best until I can't anymore."

"So, what you're saying is that you don't have any time for distractions?"

"Exactly," he answers faster than a speeding bullet. "Dating would just be a huge waste of my time. I'd rather be in the gym, running, or sleeping. Doing something more productive than…well, you know."

Oh yeah. I know exactly what he's saying. Hockey is more important to Preston Lawrence than dating and sex because he only sees both as a waste of his precious time.

Which is super awkward. Lowering my voice, I ask, "Isn't this, us fake dating, a pretty big distraction, especially during the championships?"

"This is a good kind of distraction. A necessary one," Preston says, making me feel a little better. "Nobody thought I could make it through an entire game against Riley without getting ejected."

"Why not?" I ask, my brow furrowed in confusion.

"Because I've never done it before today in the pros."

"Seriously?"

He nods slowly. "Thankfully, since we're in different divisions, we've only met twice since we both went pro five years ago."

"And you were ejected from both games?"

"I didn't even make it through the first period of either of them."

"Wow."

"My team lost both times too, which makes it even worse. I didn't want to let my teammates or the fans down by getting booted out of the first game of the finals."

"No kidding. You must really hate Christian."

"I really do."

"Why? What did he do to you?" I can't help but ask.

"It's…complicated."

"Complicated? Are you just trying to tell me nicely that it's none of my damn business?"

"Pretty much." A corner of his lips lift behind all his facial hair. "Glad you can read between the lines, cupcake."

The nickname for me, while it sounds sort of sweet, still rubs me the wrong way. I'll never forget what he told me, about how he might think I'm cute, but he would never be tempted.

"I get it. That's fine. You don't have to tell me. I owe you for going along with my request for a photo without knowing who I was or if I was nuts."

"What exactly did Riley do to you, Elle?"

"What did he do besides dump me out of the blue? Well, he also, almost in the same breath, told me that I was a nobody, and informed me he had been sleeping with lots of other women when I thought we were together."

"Got it. He was an enormous dick."

"A gigantic dick. And I get it. He's a star. I'm just a woman who cuts hair that he met when he wandered into the salon, after practice one day. I should've known better than to think a guy like Christian would give up other women for me."

"You don't deserve to be treated that way by anyone, especially him."

"Thanks."

"So, you cut hair?"

"Cut, color, style. I share a salon with my best friend, Audrey. She was with me at the game."

"Right, yeah." Preston rakes his fingers through his shaggy black hair. "My hair could use a trim, couldn't it?"

"Yes, it could. And I would be happy to fit you in while you're in town waiting for game two. I'll give you one of my cards with our address on it and you can come by whenever."

"Okay, cool."

My eyes lower to his beard, wondering how he would look without it covering the majority of his face.

"You want to shave my beard off, don't you?"

"I really do."

He gives the bottom of it a tug. "Too bad. It's bad luck to touch the beard during the playoffs."

"That is a big load of superstitious bullshit guys use as an excuse so they don't have to tend to their facial hair for weeks."

"Maybe," he agrees as his hand strokes the long, thick bush. His voice deepens when he adds, "I might be persuaded to shave it off if you can make it worth my while."

A tug in my lower belly instantly responds to the offer hanging in his rich, rumbly baritone.

"Oh yeah?" I ask nervously, as his dark eyes hold mine hostage. "H-how might I be able to persuade you?"

"That kiss today was pretty hot."

Wow. I guess I wasn't the only one who felt the sparks. Maybe he was tempted after all…

"Yes, it was," I agree.

"Hot enough for a repeat?"

He wants to kiss me again?

Yes, please.

Wait. No. I shouldn't.

But I want to, I really do. However, I'm not going to cave without getting a little something from him in return.

"Hot enough for a repeat, *if* I could see the face I'm kissing."

Again, he tugs on the pointed end of his facial hair. This time it's a harder tug, as if he might pluck it all out himself, right then and there. "I'll think about it."

So, no kiss tonight? Did I just kiss-block myself with a silly little demand from the man who doesn't date that he shaves his face? What is wrong with me?

Oh, I remember now. I need to think before diving into more than kissing with any man, especially another hot shot hockey player. One with a major temper and ulterior motives.

"I'm glad you came out with me tonight," Preston says into the silence.

"Me too."

"Do you think we could keep up our game? Keep pretending for a little longer?" he asks.

All those hateful comments at the game and on social media have me wanting to say no and run for the hills. But it's nice having a little male attention after crashing and burning with Christian. And seeing him furious for consorting with his enemy, even if he's not jealous. I think I'm also flattered that the man who is known for not dating women wants to even pretend with someone like me.

"Well, our fake relationship wouldn't really look authentic if we weren't seen together after one night."

"Very true," Preston agrees. "The longer we keep it up, the better. I can't get thrown out of any games or the Warhawks won't extend my contract. Not to mention I don't want anyone thinking Riley stole you back from me."

"Oh."

Why didn't I think of that explanation? Preston needs to keep his temper down to win games and stay on with the Warhawks next season. And it makes sense why he wouldn't want our fake dating to fizzle out too fast. It would make him look bad, lose ground on messing with Christian, defeating the original purpose of our scheme.

Preston wants to keep up our fake dating for a million different reasons, none of which have anything to do with me personally.

"You know, I have an early appointment coming in tomorrow," I tell him as I slide out of the booth.

"You just got here. You're leaving already?"

He obviously only wanted me to come tonight for more photos or videos to be spread online. Mission accomplished.

"Yeah, it's late. I should get home."

"Let me walk you out." Preston gets up and follows me since I can't exactly stop him from going downstairs. I remind myself that everything he does is with a bigger purpose in mind—winning games and getting his contract extended.

A few moments later and we're outside on the busy downtown street, people going from one bar or club to the next since it's a Saturday night.

"Well, congrats again on the win and goodnight," I turn around, looking up to tell the tall man.

"Oh, no. Save your goodbye, cupcake, because I'm walking you to your car."

"You don't have to do that."

"Yeah, I do. Which way?"

"I left my car over at the salon."

"Good. Now I'll know where to go tomorrow since you forgot to give me a business card."

"Oh. Right." I dig into my purse and pull out a card from my wallet as we start walking.

"Thanks." The card disappears into his jean pocket as we make our way across three more blocks.

"Well, this is me."

Preston turns to look over the darkened front windows

with our logo on it and the black awning. "Cute place. I'll see you here tomorrow."

"Only if you decide you want a trim. No pressure," I say, giving him a half smile, the most I can manage after the long, crazy day before heading to my car parked in the alley.

"I do want one. And Elle?" Preston says, following behind me.

"Yeah?"

"I'd be willing to bet that Riley wasn't with you because you were convenient or easy. He wanted to be with you for the same reason I do—because you're beautiful and sexy. Christian Riley may be a lot of things, but he's not blind."

"Thank you, Preston." Now I give him a real, honest smile before I open my car door and slide inside.

What a day indeed.

10

Preston

The morning after our big win, I see a missed call from Tommy after breakfast. I'm in such a good mood that I actually call him back while sitting in the hotel's restaurant. After all, I'm sitting alone, none of my teammates, coaches, or staff willing to approach me during a meal.

"Preston, my man!" my agent answers.

"What's up, Tommy?"

"Last night was insane! How did you pull off nailing Riley's girl?"

Speaking quietly to ensure nobody overhears, I tell him, "That's not…it's just a few photos to make him think we're sleeping together."

"Well, it was a genius idea because it worked. I've never seen Riley go off like that. He played like absolute shit."

"Yeah, he did. It was fun to watch."

"And you kept your anger in check, making it through the entire game without even a penalty!"

"Guess there's a first time for everything."

"Congrats on the win. Keep doing what you're doing and offers are going to start rolling in. The Warhawks office seems to still be holding their breath, hoping last night wasn't a fluke with you."

"It wasn't a fluke. From now on, I'll be fine playing against Christian."

"All this PR about you finally having a girlfriend is good for your image, too. I've been getting calls asking if you want to do talk shows and shit."

"Hell no."

"I figured you wouldn't be up for any of that. That's why I turned them all down. But if you want to give me a few quotes to pass along about this mystery girl of Riley's, we could keep the buzz going through the playoffs."

Elle didn't seem too thrilled about keeping our fake relationship going last night. I doubt if she'll want to keep pretending through the playoffs. That's at least three more games, possibly as many as six.

"No quotes for now," I tell Tommy. "Let me know if you get any offers."

"I will. Stay focused and keep winning," the man says before ending the call.

For the rest of the morning, I try to come up with a way to convince Elle to keep putting up with me.

I don't think she's the type of woman to accept money. There has to be something, though…

～

After a team meeting to watch the film from the night before, I'm in a damn fine mood when I head to Elle's salon.

The Beauty Boutique.

I only saw the outside in the dark last night, the name painted on a window next to the door with the logo of a comb and scissors, or shears, on it. When I walk inside, a bell overhead chimes letting them know they have a customer. Not that they probably heard it over the sound of hairdryers running.

There are six black and silver salon chairs, three on each side of the place, with room to walk down the middle to a tall desk that backs to a wall. One of the chairs is upright in front of a mirror, another is where they must wash hair in the sinks. And the third chair is in front of a helmet looking thing.

Didn't Elle mention something about going down on Christian in one of her salon chairs?

I try to mentally scrub that image from my head as I wait for the beautiful blonde to look up from the head of white hair she's brushing and drying at the same time. Her friend, who is putting some foil on some woman's hair on the other side of the room, smiles and gives me a wave.

I don't mind standing there waiting, since it gives me a chance to ogle every inch of Elle. With her blonde hair tied up in a messy topknot, her bare neck looks absolutely delectable. Her flowy, knee-length green dress unfortunately doesn't hug her curves like the jeans last night. It does give me a nice look at her tan legs. And the things it does to her breasts, pushing them up from the low-cut neck…

"Preston." I didn't even notice the hair dryer cutting off. "Hey. I can squeeze you in as soon as I finish up here with Ms. Crawford."

The mention of squeezing me in has my mind going straight to the gutter. Maybe having a fake relationship after going years without sex is a bad idea. I try to refrain from even self-love during the season, but if I stand here much longer, I'll have no choice but to go stroke one out. Or two or three.

"Do you mind waiting?" Elle asks, when I didn't respond. It takes me longer than it should to realize she's not asking me to delay keeping my hand off my dick.

"I can definitely wait."

For her and a much-needed release. Like Coach reminded me, there's too much on the line to lose my edge now.

"Good. There are chairs, a television, and some magazines in the back. I'll come get you in a few minutes."

"Okay," I agree. I'd rather stand around and keep staring at her, but she probably doesn't want me lurking. Or scaring her customers who all watch me with wide eyes. Still, just seeing her again has me feeling lighter, like the air goes in and out of my lungs a little easier. It's as if her close proximity has the heavy pressure lifting from my shoulders for a little while.

That's probably just my dick temporarily taking over all bodily functions from my head.

I walk to the back, not even sure if the cute little pink and black chairs can hold me, so I choose the black bench seat instead.

And wouldn't you know, the television is on the local mid-day news, replaying the highlights from last night. They even show a quick shot of Elle in the stands with her sign.

About five minutes later, I hear Elle's voice setting up an appointment two weeks out, then saying goodbye before the front door jingles.

"Are you sure you want a cut?" Elle asks when she appears in the open doorway, her hands on her hips ready to get to work.

"Yeah, I'm sure." I follow her back to the first chair. She has to lower it in order to reach my head.

"So, this is the inside of your salon, huh?" I ask like an idiot as she drapes a cape over me and fastens it at the back of my neck.

"This is it. How short do you want your hair? And have you reached a verdict on the beard?"

Is it just me or does she seem to be all business today? Maybe she's just busy and doesn't have time for small talk since I walked in without an appointment.

"I'm gonna leave all those decisions in your hands."

"Really?"

"Really. I trust you," I tell her in the mirror's reflection.

Brows high, she doesn't look convinced. "You trust me? After one kiss?"

"And hanging out last night."

"Did you see the photos of us from the club?"

"I did. There were quite a few tagging us on social media."

"My phone is still blowing up because of the kiss and the sign. And about that second kiss you mentioned..."

"Yeah? What about it?"

"Would it be done in public as another photo op?"

"Sure. Why not? It'll be adding more fuel to the fire before game two tomorrow night."

"Right." Elle visibly deflates, as if that's the wrong answer.

"You are coming to the game, right?" I ask her.

"I don't have any tickets. Audrey and I pulled a lot of

strings for the ones last night that we didn't even end up using."

"I can find you seats again," I assure her.

"Okay, if you can find me a seat, I will be there."

Showing up at the game and spending time with me are, sadly, not even close to the same thing.

"Will you wear my jersey again?"

"Absolutely."

"Then what?" I ask her.

"What do you mean?"

"After game two, I'll have to leave to go back to D.C. for games three and four."

"If that's all it takes for the Warhawks to win the championships," Elle points out.

"What happens to our fake relationship once I leave town?"

"We can pretend we're making the long-distance thing work at first," she suggests, wetting my hair down with a spray bottle of water. Grabbing a comb, she runs it through my hair. "Then, either you'll be back for alternating games five and seven or you won't. The attention dies down once someone wins, preferably the Bobcats."

"Agree to disagree."

Smirking while combing back my hair, she says, "Either way, we could tell anyone who asks that we couldn't make long distance work, not when I have my business here and you play in D.C."

"Not even during the summer for the off-season?" I throw the idea out there. Hypothetically, of course.

She waves her hand through the air. "We'll be old news by the summer."

"Sure. Yeah. Old news." Guess that's a no on hypothetically seeing her after the playoffs.

"So, are you ready to get started?" she asks.

"Do your worst."

Her fingers slide into my thick mane, soothing and arousing as hell. She's not even tugging on it and I'm thinking about her grabbing it when my face is between her thighs.

"You have…a lot of hair. Do you know what Audrey calls you?" Elle asks, forcing me to push down the dirty thoughts.

"Don't you dare, Elle!" the brunette shouts from the other side of the room.

Arching an eyebrow, I say, "Now I have to know what she calls me."

Ignoring her friend's continued pleas, she whispers loudly, "Woolly mammoth."

"Damn. That's harsh. I don't even have any tusks."

"Well, you are going to be a handsome, groomed mammoth when I'm done with you."

"And when I get cold out there on the ice without layers of fuzz?"

"You can think of kissing me," Elle says with a smile. "You said that was hot, right?"

"It was crazy hot."

"Besides, I seriously doubt you have a moment to get cold when you're constantly skating back and forth the entire game."

"True enough."

Elle wets my hair a little more with the spray bottle, then takes a comb and shears to get to work while I try to sit as still as possible.

As the chunks of hair fall away, I ask her, "Is this what you always wanted to do?"

"Own my own business?"

"That and be a, what do you call it, hair stylist? I don't know what you call a female barber."

"Stylist is fine." She flashes me a smile in the mirror. "And yes, I cut off all my dolls' hair by the time I was five, so my parents stopped buying them."

"What did you do then?"

"Cut my own hair, of course."

"Of course. Bet they loved that."

"They eventually bought me a mannequin head along with a few cheap wigs after I nicked my earlobe with the scissors and bled all over the place."

"Wow."

"But then when I got older, and I was allowed to practice on actual people, the reason for cutting and styling changed. It was no longer about being creative. It became a way to help people feel a little bit better about themselves, to walk out of the salon with more confidence than they came in with. It's stupid that women especially put so much stock in their physical appearance, but we do. And when we look good, we feel good. Even if it's only for a day."

"Only for a day?"

"My clients tell me they can never recreate how I style their hair at home. The same goes for me, too. My hair never looks as good as it does when Audrey styles it."

I consider her words for a long moment. "It's bullshit that those assholes were saying awful things about you last night when you work all day, every day, to help others feel good about themselves."

"You're pulling out all the stops today, aren't you, big guy?"

That wasn't a line. I meant it. Still, I tell her, "Just because we're fake dating doesn't mean I shouldn't get in some practice on how to talk to women without getting blocked, right?"

"Sure. May as well get your practice in while you can, since I'm a sure thing."

"How about having dinner with me tonight?" I blurt out.

"Is that an actual request or just more practice?"

"Why can't it be both?"

Elle shrugs. "I don't know."

"You don't know why it can't be both, or you don't know if you want to have dinner with me?"

"I have appointments until about seven tonight."

"My bedtime isn't that early."

"Then…I guess I could call you after I finish up and freshen up?"

"As late as you want. Let me have your phone and I'll put in my number so we won't have to go through social media."

"Okay," she agrees, reaching into her front dress pocket and offering me the device unlocked.

Is it normal for women to be so free with letting someone see their phone? Since I haven't been on a date in years, I would have to delete a few porn sites before I hand over my phone to anyone. Despite my adamant attempt to avoid self-love, I sometimes slip.

After I add in my contact to her phone, I pull up Instagram and my thumbs get busy.

"What are you doing?" Elle asks, seeing the screen over my shoulder.

"Deleting all the hateful shit on your post."

"There are tons of messages and comments!"

"Saying negative things?" I ask, watching her in the mirror's reflection.

Elle shrugs. "Well, not all of them. Some are very nice. But there are a lot of shitty comments."

"Why haven't you deleted the ones from jerks yet?"

"Because I figured they were like gray hairs."

"Huh?" I ask, brows furrowing in confusion.

"You know, if you pluck out one gray hair, two grow back."

"Then you pluck every single one out and be done with them."

Sighing, she says, "I wish the bad comments didn't hit so hard that it takes at least a dozen positive ones to even try to negate it, but that's how it goes."

"That's why I don't even bother reading anything about the team or me in the news. I've had enough criticism for one lifetime after how bad I played my rookie year."

"Yeah? It was tough making the adjustment to the pros?"

"Something like that."

It's not like I can tell her, or could've explained to my teammates at the time, that I barely got any sleep at night because of a crying baby.

I've kept my private life out of the spotlight for almost five years, and I have no intention of revealing it now, not even to Elle.

For the next half hour, I enjoy Elle's fingers running through my hair, especially when she scrubs my scalp with shampoo in the sink. I can barely hold in my groan. This is so much better than the barber shop.

And while Elle is trimming my beard, I get to stare at her amazing breasts that are right in front of my face.

She does a great job too. Honestly, I barely recognize myself when she's finished. I look years younger and probably less like a homeless thug.

"Well? What do you think?" she asks when I don't comment.

Rubbing my fingers over the now neatly short, tidy beard I won't have to worry about getting food in, I tell her the truth. "I like it."

"And the hair?"

I thread my fingers through the shorter locks that she put some product in to make it look messy, but in a good way. At least, I guess that was the goal. "Less to wash and drip with sweat, for sure."

"A glowing recommendation," Elle says. "Mind if I put that quote on our salon's social media page?"

"Go for it."

"Seriously, though, would you mind taking another selfie for me, like a before and after?"

"You sure? I thought the comments yesterday upset you."

"This photo will go on the salon's account for the good of growing our business, getting in new customers in the area. Hopefully, they won't be jerks."

"Then let's do it on one condition?"

"What's that?"

"We keep up our act until the finals are over."

"You want to keep seeing me through the finals?" she repeats, not the least bit enthusiastic. She's not having second thoughts about getting back with Riley, is she?

"I want to keep seeing you, Elle."

"While you're in town for game two and when you're back in town for game five?"

"While I'm in town for tomorrow's game, and *if* I have to come back for game five," I amend, because I hope the Warhawks can win four straight games to take the trophy.

"So, we'll keeping seeing each other until you stop coming to Greensboro, whenever that may be?"

"Yes." When she doesn't instantly agree, I tell her, "Come on, Elle. It'll be fun. And it'll drive Riley fucking crazy."

Now she bites her bottom lip, before finally saying, "Deal."

I'm glad she agreed, even if I had to bring up Riley to seal the deal.

Since I'm about her height sitting, Elle takes a few snaps of us with her phone and then I'm out of excuses to lurk around the salon any longer.

"How much do I owe you?" I ask after she removes my cape and blows the loose hair from my neck with a hairdryer.

"Nothing. It's on the house."

"Are you sure?"

"A friend doing another friend a favor."

"Friends. Right. Well, thank you."

"Thanks for coming by."

"Hope to see you tonight."

Nodding, she says, "I'll let you know when I get finished up."

"Can't wait."

After I walk out of Elle's salon, it's like the world is too quiet, too empty without her next to me, her fingers no longer running through my hair.

I'm obviously developing stalker tendencies since I have

her Instagram up, probably before I make it half a block to my car.

Only this time, I also look for *The Beauty Boutique*'s page. It's got a decent following already, and there my face is, front and center next to the picture from yesterday. What I don't like is that Elle cropped herself out of both. We're gonna have words about that at dinner.

Before I can send her a message asking for a copy of the original pictures, I recognize a few other men scattered through the client photos underneath mine.

Of course, Riley's smug ass face appears several times. That one I don't care for but was at least expecting. It's the other men, at least half a dozen other Bobcats hockey players, all freshly cut and facial hair shaved or trimmed.

Elle was adamant yesterday that she wasn't a puck bunny, but these photos tell a different story. She's been up close and personal with at least…seven.

Before I can stop myself, my feet turn around to stomp right back to the salon. Thankfully, Elle is alone, sweeping up my black hairs that are all over the floor, her friend somewhere in the back.

"Hey. Is everything okay?" She frowns when she looks up and sees me.

"You said you weren't a puck bunny," I remark, holding up my phone to show her the photos instead of trying to name them all.

Elle blinks up at me as if waiting for me to say more. When I don't, she just shakes her head and lowers her gaze to the broom that's sweeping the floor once again.

"Well?"

"Are you seriously asking me if I slept with all those players? Wow, Preston. Now who sounds like an asshole? I'll give you a hint—it's not Christian or those jerks online."

Damn. Her comment puts me in my place, making me feel about two feet tall.

What the hell is wrong with me? It's bad enough that she had to deal with all the strangers bad-mouthing her and slut shaming her yesterday. Did I really just come charging back into her salon to basically call her a liar and infer she's slept with men before she even knew my name?

Yes, yes, I did.

"I'm sorry, Elle. That's…I'm not sure what I was thinking. I just got irrationally jealous, which is stupid since we just met yesterday…"

"And we're in a fake relationship," she adds.

"Fake. Right," I agree. "And I know there is no excuse for me acting like a possessive dick, but it has been years since I dated a woman. Guess I'm out of practice on what's appropriate…"

Elle slowly bends down to sweep the hair into a dustpan then dump it into the trash can before facing me again. "Slut shaming isn't that new of a concept."

"I wasn't…that wasn't…the problem wasn't that I thought you had been with them as much as it was thinking that they had been with you."

Frowning even harder, she crosses her arms over her ample chest and huffs, "That doesn't make a lick of sense."

"I guess I just feel sort of protective of you. I know you can take care of yourself. It's just, if any of them used you then hurt you like Riley did, I would kick their asses." When Elle winces at the term "used" I immediately want to take it back, swallow it down my throat. Too late now…

"Preston, I think you should try to figure out how to resolve conflicts without resorting to violence, even if it's figurative and not literal."

"I know. You're right. I should. But growing up, my parents and coaches encouraged me to use my size and strength to be a bully on the ice. That's what I was good at, not skating, not scoring. Just being scary, hitting people, and hurting them so I could one day go pro."

"You are good at it, and it pays you millions of dollars a year, so I get it. Maybe you could just try to keep your temper on the ice. No, not just on the ice, but in the games."

"What do you mean?"

"You said your teammates aren't fans of you always roughing them up."

"That only happens in practice."

"Since they're your teammates and not your enemy or opponents, you can't take it a little bit easier on them in practice?"

"No. I'm trying to prepare them for the hits during games."

"Have you ever hurt any of them?"

"Nothing major."

Shaking her head, she says, "I don't think you're supposed to hurt people on your team, Preston. That could be one of the reasons the Warhawks haven't extended your contract."

"How do you figure that?" Elle's a sweet girl, but she doesn't know anything about the behind-the-scenes politics with agents and owners and shit.

"All those guys in those photos are Christian's teammates, and they actually like him. It's why they let him convince them to come here for haircuts to help me and Audrey out, as a favor."

"Yeah, I'm aware of how they all worship the ground that prick walks on."

"It's not just because he's a good player, the leading scorer in their games. He's actually friends with them. As arrogant as he can be, he always gives them the credit they deserved for assists or blocking goals or whatever else. They hang out together several times a week. They're almost as close as a family."

"Are you telling me I should be more like Christian fucking Riley?"

"Only as a team player. Not in your personal life, obviously." Elle rolls her pretty hazel eyes that look a little more green and less gold today. "He could definitely learn a few things from you about being a better man when it comes to relationships. Or at least a lack of wanting the distraction."

"How long did you two…date?" I ask rather than use the more indecent term.

"Five months."

An actual whistle of surprise escapes me. "That's a long damn time, Elle."

"Long enough that I thought we were together, as in not seeing anyone else, since he came over most nights. All the nights he was in town."

"But when he went out of town…"

"He couldn't keep it in his pants. Or didn't want to keep it in his pants. He should've at least told me. He assumed I knew he was with other women. It was crazy for me to even give Christian Riley the benefit of the doubt that I was enough for someone like him."

Fuck. I hate Riley just a little bit more for making Elle feel that way.

"You are enough, Elle," I assure her.

"Not for him, I wasn't."

"Riley's a stupid fool who ruins everything."

"What do you mean, he ruins everything?" she asks.

"I just meant that he can't help but get in his own way because he's an asshole who only thinks about himself."

"That we can agree on. I don't think he ever once considered how I felt about him. To him, I was just a warm body whenever he wanted it, but for me, he was more than that…"

"Did you love him?"

Her lips twist as she seems to consider my question for a long moment. "I don't know. I don't think so. I wanted to, but it was like I knew deep down that he was holding back part of himself from me, so I held back a part of myself, too. He still broke my heart, but I'm not going to waste weeks or months mourning a love that wasn't ever there."

Thank god she doesn't love him. He still broke her heart, though. I don't even know what to say to that.

I don't want to say anything. I want to do something, to lash out and punch the son of a bitch in his smug face.

Both of my fists clench by my sides as my temper tries to break free again like before. Before I met Elle. But I push it all down. Getting angry at Christian or hitting him yet again won't change anything for her.

All I can do is try not to make things worse.

"Sorry I was a dick who assumed the worst about you. I…I guess I have trust issues with people. But I promise I won't flip out like that again on you."

"Good. Because of that macho bullshit, I'm this close to being done with you, Preston." Elle holds up her finger and thumb about an inch apart. Shit. I really am fucking things up with her.

I haven't seen this tougher side of Elle, and it's hot, even though I know she means every word. I'm on seriously thin ice with her.

"This is my place of business," she reminds me. "If a client had been in here when you started roaring…"

"I'm sorry," I say again. "I'll go. Wish I could press rewind and leave for the first time again."

"Yeah. Me too." Elle lets out a heavy sigh. It's a sigh that says that she didn't sign up for me calling her a liar or demanding to know things about her past that aren't any of my business.

My trust issues come from an ugly, fucked-up history of having the people I loved, the people I trusted more than anyone else in the world, hurt me. That's another reason why I haven't tried to date anyone in years.

And even fake dating a beautiful woman is turning out to be even harder than I expected.

11

Elle

"What was all of that about?" Audrey asks when she walks out of the back. No doubt she was hiding while Preston and I argued.

It didn't feel like a fake argument for a fake relationship, either.

"I wish I knew," I admit as I stare out the glass where he just disappeared down the sidewalk. "He's so…confusing."

"No kidding. But your cut and shave made him like ten times hotter."

Grinning, I tell her, "He has a nice face. It shouldn't be hiding under layers of hair."

"Agreed."

"Ugh, damn these handsome hockey players!"

"You're worried he's just like Christian?"

"He's nothing like Christian," I say confidently. "But that doesn't mean he won't find a way to break my heart too if given half a chance."

"Your fake relationship got awfully serious fast, didn't it?"

"Right?" I agree. I rub my temples. "My head is just all over the place. It's telling me to call this whole thing off with Preston and avoid all things hockey until next season."

"But?" Audrey correctly guesses there's more to it.

"But my gut seems to like Preston and wants me to keep helping him keep his temper in check on the ice. I want to trust him, to keep doing…whatever this is that we're doing for some crazy reason."

"Maybe because he's a nice distraction from missing Christian?"

"Yeah. Maybe. How ironic is it that I need a distraction, and Preston is all about avoiding them in his career? That's why he never dates."

"There's definitely more than meets the surface with the slightly less woolly mammoth."

Unable to help my smile, I tell her, "Stop calling him that."

"How about caveman? He's awfully jealous for a fake boyfriend. I think deep down he wants to throw you over his shoulder, take you back to his cave, and have his way with you."

"I don't know. He called me cupcake when we first met."

"Cute."

"No, he didn't mean it in a good way. He said I might look cute and sweet but that he wouldn't be tempted for a taste."

"Yeah, right," Audrey says with a roll of her eyes. "He's a man. Sex is all most of them want."

"Only until they find someone new and better to have their way with."

"Christian did a number on you, girl. Don't let that arrogant asshole hold you back from anything or anyone. He's like the worst of the worst players."

"You knew that from the beginning, didn't you?" I ask her.

"Of course I did! You knew it too. And yet, you couldn't resist his perfect athletic body, gorgeous face, or rapt attention."

"I only had his attention when he was in town. When he got lonely or horny every night."

"But he made you feel special. I get it. Sometimes we need that feeling more than we need to be smart and protect our hearts."

"I really did think it was just fun and flattering with Christian at the beginning," I admit. "But after the first month when he kept wanting to see me, I thought it could be more."

"So did I. And I do think it was more. As much as he was capable of offering himself. Christian Riley still has some growing up to do. Preston though…"

"What about Preston?"

"He is a grown-ass man. I think he's the type to go after what he wants and stick with it, you know? Not squander it away with an eye always looking for something else on the side."

"That's exactly what Christian was doing! Looking for someone better while stringing me along."

"I didn't say someone better. Just someone else because he hasn't figured out what the hell he wants."

"And you think Preston has figured out what he wants?"

"Yes, I do. He doesn't date and yet he's willing to go along with this scheme with you."

"Only to make Christian angry, to avoid hitting him so he doesn't get thrown out of a game. Preston's main goal is to get his contract renewed."

"And the plan is working. But I think it's also a little more than all of that."

"I don't."

I think the reason that Preston hates Christian goes way deeper than the two of us can even imagine.

Nobody holds a grudge like that without a damn good reason.

Preston

I feel like crap for how I lashed out and treated Elle earlier when she's been trying to help me. And while I apologized, I wish there was more I could do for her. She's already putting up with enough shit from Bobcat fans as it is. Then I had to go and pile more shit on her to make her feel bad.

Pulling up the photos we were tagged in by sports sites online, there are tons of rude comments about Elle and Christian. I guess a lot of people knew about them being seen occasionally together for months, while I didn't have a clue.

Too bad there isn't a way for me to delete that crap from sites and other people's Insta, but I can't.

Maybe there is something I could try to do to help.

Pro athletes get way too much attention whenever they speak out, even when they have nothing important to say.

After avoiding it for so long, here's hoping I can get some of that attention too…

Spencer Williams is staying in the hotel room next to mine, so I knock on his door first to ask for his help.

"What's up?" the short, stocky backup goalie asks. Then his eyes bulge. "Holy shit, you cut your hair and your beard? During the championships? Are you insane?"

"It's just hair," I assure him as I rub my hand over the closely shaved beard along my jaw. "Could you help me record a video?"

"Ah, sure. What's it for?"

"To call pricks out for being assholes."

"Ah. Sounds fun." I offer him my phone that he takes gingerly, holding it like it's made of glass. "So, just record you?"

"Yeah."

"Okay, tell me when you're ready."

"I'm ready."

Once he gives me a nod, I stand there and launch into what I would like to say to each and every asshole out there.

"So, I've seen and had to delete some comments from my girl Elle's page that really piss me off. That's why I'm saying knock it off before I start knocking out some of ya'lls teeth. Stop this shit and leave Elle alone. Say whatever the hell you want about me, I don't care. Just leave my beautiful girl out of it from now on. Thanks."

I slice my finger across my neck for Spence to stop recording. "Did you get it?"

"Yeah, man. I got it," he says when he hands the phone

back to me. "And I think that's the most I've ever heard you say in years," he remarks.

"I don't like to run my mouth unless it's important."

"Like telling us all how much we suck in drills?"

"Some of ya'll have been slacking off at practice and you know it, staying up too late, partying. We're professionals. The few lucky SOBs that get paid to play a game we love. But our job is still to show up and train hard so we can win games."

"Right. Yeah. But some of us like having a life outside of the arena."

"I have a life outside of hockey," I huff.

"You do?" he asks, not sarcastically, but as if he's genuinely asking. "You come to practice, games, then leave. Last night was the first time you even attempted to hang out with us, and you left as soon as that girl did."

"Yeah? So?"

"So, give the guys a break. Everyone handles the pressure of the game differently. Some drink, some fuck, or some, like you, are all work and no play. That's a good way to burn out."

"I'm not even close to getting burnt out," I tell him. "That will never happen."

"Hopefully not. Will you at least go easy after we take the trophy home?"

"I've already won a championship with Wisconsin," I remind him.

"Well, other than Nick, the rest of us haven't, jackass!"

My eyes narrow, jaw and fists clenching at the insult.

Spence puts up both of his palms in front of his face and says, "Hit me if you want, but it's the truth. You act like you're the only one on the ice who has people counting on you. The first thing I bought when I signed last year was a house for my mom. She stands around for twelve hours a day in a fucking nasty ass poultry plant, six days a week. If I could become a starter, maybe she could finally leave that damn place behind."

"Sorry, man. I didn't know."

"That's right, Pres, you don't know what the rest of us have riding on us to succeed, especially the backups. You were lucky enough to become a starter your first season. You don't know what it's like wishing and hoping for a chance to prove yourself, and feeling like shit because you know the only way you'll probably get a chance in the spotlight is if another teammate gets hurt."

"The spotlight isn't all you think it is," I mutter.

"At least you've experienced it. Most of us haven't. Only you and Nick have ever held that damn trophy we've only dreamed of. The rest of us want our chance just as much as you do, if not more."

"I get it," I tell him. "I'll...try not to be such a dick."

"Seriously?" he asks, blinking at me in surprise. "Are you just saying that shit to get me to lower my guard so you can hit me?"

"No. Although, your face came close to meeting my fist when you called me a jackass."

"I get why you're the way you are, man," Spencer remarks. "You want us to all to play our best. That's what we want too. But it's damn hard to find the determination to do that if all we hear is how much we suck or are riding the bench because you knocked us on our asses."

I'm suddenly reminded of what Elle said earlier, about how it takes a dozen positive comments to negate one negative one, and realize I may be the jackass Spencer thinks I am.

Coach Ramsey can be a hardnosed jackass, making us bust our asses, but he always gives two compliments for every criticism, like, "*Nice check, Lawrence, but let's try to keep our men's brains all in their heads. God knows they need every bit of it. Drive your shoulder into our opponents' backs with that kind of momentum, and the fuckers will leave the puck to run in the other direction the next time you come barreling into them.*"

"Thanks for the feedback," I tell Spencer who lifts his brow in shock. "Keep it up, since you're the only one who isn't afraid to get shit off your chest."

"Yeah. Okay," he replies, swallowing so hard it's audible.

"And don't give up on starting. Keep practicing. It won't necessarily be an injury that takes Vincent out of the game. His reflexes could slow."

"Great, so I should hope for my teammate's injury or failure in order to get a shot?"

"Not hope for it. Just be prepared to step up if either of those things happen, and not be a shit goalie."

"Right. Okay."

I turn around to leave, but add over my shoulder add, "Don't tell Vincent what I said. I don't want him getting the y-i-p-s when we're so close to the trophy."

"Get the hell out of here with that godforsaken word! It's fucked up to even spell it out loud, man! You fucking know that!" Spencer says as he shoos me out of his room before I jinx our goalie with the Y-word. "And find yourself some joy, Pres, from something other than hockey. Like that hot blonde…"

"Don't even start," I growl the warning at him before I walk out into the hallway. "You don't talk about her, and I won't use the Y-word ever again."

"Deal," he says with a grin when he sticks his head out as I walk to my hotel room. "It was awesome seeing Riley flail last night. He looked like a terrified little rookie instead of a hot shot MVP."

"He was definitely off his game. Here's hoping he doesn't find his balls before game four," I reply.

12

Elle

"Have you seen the video?" Audrey asks me as soon as Mrs. Waverly is sitting under the loud dryer.

"What video?"

"Oh, just the one everyone in the world is talking about!" When I continue staring at her blankly, she scoffs, "You haven't seen the video Preston posted online?"

"Preston posted a video?"

"Yep."

"About what?"

"You."

"Me?" I exclaim. "Show me. My phone's on the charger in the back."

"Then you probably have a ton of notifications on it. Here," she turns the screen around and presses the button on the side of the phone to increase the volume. Then Preston's deep, gruff voice fills the room, and I am left stunned.

"Well?" Audrey asks once it's over.

Throwing my arms up in the air, I say, "I can't believe he did that. Now there will be even more haters and trolls."

"You think so? Because I don't. Who would go against anything that scary dude says?"

"He's not as scary now that I cleaned up his beard and cut his shaggy hair."

"True, but he's still big as hell. Look at the comments. Not only do women think he looks amazing with the trim, but even Bobcats fans are commending him on standing up for you. Here's what one person said: *People are assholes, sorry they said rude shit about your girl. Good on you for coming to her defense and calling them out.* That's you, Elle! You're his girl."

"I'm his fake girl."

"But that is a real video threatening everyone on social media to behave when it comes to you."

"That's just…it's all part of him pretending we're dating or whatever, so he can beat Christian and get his contract extended with the Warhawks."

And maybe he also felt a little guilty about storming in and calling me a puck bunny earlier.

"All that may be reasons that Preston's in this fake relationship, but he posted the video because he cares about your feelings. He doesn't want people upsetting you. It's sweet."

Biting my bottom lip, I confess to her, "He asked me to go to dinner with him tonight…"

"Yay!" she exclaims with a clap of her hands.

"And I was going to go with him until he stormed back in here and basically called me a slutty puck bunny. If he cared about my feelings, then why would he do that? What he assumed, he's not much better than the jerks on Insta."

"Girl, I'm not excusing his behavior. He was definitely out of line. But I think he was mostly just jealous. He did not like the idea of you cutting all those guys' hair."

"Because they play for the Bobcats and are Christian's teammates?"

"No, silly! Because they were men."

"We have lots of male clients."

"Yes, we do. And we don't sleep with any of them ever. Well, before you and Christian, so it was bullshit for him to assume such a thing. Still, the fact that he even got upset suggests that he's catching some feelings."

"No, he's not."

"And what about you? Are you still feeling-free when it comes to Preston?"

"Of course. I know where the two of us stand. Yes, the kiss with him was hot, and he's pretty fun to hang out with, but he's only talking to me to irk Christian. Preston will be gone in a few days, never to be seen again."

"D.C. isn't that far away..."

"It's too far for me to even think about, even if Preston was actually interested in being with me. Christian lived literally blocks away and it was still too far. If he would cheat on me after being away from me for one day, then how could I trust a man who lives hundreds of miles away?"

"Not every man is a whore like Christian Riley. Someday, you're going to have to buck up and trust a guy if you ever want to have a serious relationship."

"Well, that's a future problem. Not one I need to worry

about now because Preston is not a real relationship, much less a serious one."

"Fine. But I think you should go to dinner with him."

"Really? Why?"

"Because you're still not over the pain Christian caused you. It's not fair that he's probably going out and having fun while you stay home alone. You don't have to do anything but eat a meal with Preston. Let people take a few photos and post them while you chat him up. Then go home. It'll be better than sitting home all night missing that asshole, right?"

"I don't know. It's crazy, but I thought I could really like Preston, you know? Before he went all 'roid rage. Now, I think it's for the best that he acted that way."

"Because now you don't have to worry about actually crushing on your fake boyfriend?"

"Yes."

"In that case, what do you have to lose by having dinner with Preston? If you're not going to fall for him, then it's all good. Go enjoy a free meal with a hot hockey player and make Christian crazy jealous before tomorrow's game."

Cringing, I ask my best friend, "Is it wrong that I don't want Christian to win?"

Audrey gasps and dramatically clutches her chest. "That's blasphemy in these parts!"

"I want the Bobcats to win the championships; I just wish they could do it without that gorgeous bastard helping them."

Preston

. . .

When I sent a time and place for dinner reservations to Elle, she agreed, but her responses to my messages since have been short, to the point.

She's still upset with me.

Hopefully, I can make up for being a dick during dinner.

I'm standing on the sidewalk outside the Italian joint Vivace, that had great reviews online, when I see Elle walking toward me from the direction of her salon. Her hair is different from all the other times I've seen her. Guess that's one of the perks of being a hair stylist. Tonight, her blond locks are sleeked back into a low bun-thing at the nape of her neck. I think I like the hairstyles when there's unobstructed access to her neck the best.

After I allow my gaze to lower to the snug black dress showing off her ample cleavage and every single curve, I have to quickly try to recall our team's shots on goal stats and percentages from the past few games to prevent a noticeable bulge in the front of my pants.

"Hey," Elle says softly with her approach, eyeing my dark suit. "I thought this was the type of place that I needed to dress up for."

"You've never been here before?" I ask in surprise.

"Nope. Some of us don't make big bucks playing professional hockey," she replies with a small smile.

I'm just glad she's never been here with Riley. If I had to bet, their dates were probably not usually done in public.

Gritting my teeth together to ignore that thought, I grasp her bare upper arms to lean in and give her a brief kiss on her lips. When I pull back, I hold her gaze and tell her, "You look gorgeous, Elle. Thank you for agreeing to come tonight."

She quickly glances away toward the windows of the restaurant, to the people seated inside. "Just don't expect me to go Dutch. I have rent due next month."

"Absolutely not," I assure her with a grin. It doesn't escape my notice that she completely ignores my compliment. "Do you live close to the salon?"

She nods her head. "Yes, I have an apartment just four blocks away."

"That must be nice."

"What about you? Do you live near the arena in D.C.?"

"Ah, not really. I wanted a house outside the busy city. The traffic sucks, though, so maybe I should've found something closer to the arena within walking distance. Doesn't matter now, though, since I may be moving to another city before next season."

Elle frowns. "You're that certain the Warhawks won't renew your contract with them?"

"I wish I could stay on, but the odds aren't great if they haven't put it in writing by now. I thought making the championships would be enough to earn a renewal, but I guess not. At least I lasted longer with them than I did in Wisconsin."

"How long did you play for Wisconsin?"

"Only two years of the five in my contract before they traded me."

"I'm sorry. That must be awful, not knowing when you might have to up and move."

"You have no idea," I mutter, dreading that conversation so damn much I've been ignoring Maya's phone calls for the past two days. I did cave and text back short and sweet responses to her as required, knowing I would want the same if she were away. When I get back home, it'll be time to face the music, and she's going to be fucking distraught.

My go-to when I'm dealing with bad news is to stress eat the shit out of comfort food. It's usually greasy shit, like entire pizzas, bowls of pasta, and pans of garlic bread. I try not to think about the reasons why I crave that kind of shit from my childhood.

"Ready to go in and eat?" I ask Elle as my stomach growls.

"Sure. This doesn't look like the type of place where we'll have to worry about a lot of phone cameras taking photos."

I'm not so sure about that, but I don't comment as I reach for the door and pull it open for Elle.

Rather than step inside, she asks, "Why did you post that video?"

The video? Oh, right. "Because I didn't want anyone saying shit about you anymore."

"Well, you don't need to swoop in and save the day. I can handle the negative comments."

"Can you? Because you were upset last night and earlier today about them."

"I'm trying to just ignore them from now on," she says before she finally walks inside.

After giving my name to the hostess, she leads us right to a table for two against the wall thankfully, and not by the windows facing the street.

As soon as we get seated, I ask Elle, "Do you need me to go through and delete the bad ones?"

Pulling the device from the purse on her shoulder, she unlocks the screen, then hands it over. "Sure, you can do that while I run to the restroom."

Elle's barely out of view when I start scrolling.

There are significantly fewer negative comments on her personal account, but I quickly delete the ones that are there before checking the salon page, then her messages.

Not all that surprising. Most DMs are men hitting her up, but a few are women calling her names or telling her she's crazy for "cheating" on Riley. Those are deleted and blocked.

Then, I come upon the message thread between Elle and Riley.

Shit.

I didn't mean to open the log; it just sort of happens. Curiosity gets the best of me. Even after I tell my eyes to stop reading or I'll gouge them out, but they don't obey me.

The first message was from Elle reaching out to Riley saying, ***I thought you were lying about being Christian Riley, so I looked you up***. Then she asks him to tag the salon if he posts a selfie with his new haircut. He agrees, and offers to tell his teammates about her salon, to send her more business, which he, of course, did.

It was actually decent of him, and it explains all those photos of hockey players I flipped out about earlier. It was none of my business, but now I'm certain that Elle didn't hook up with any of those guys. I shouldn't have assumed the worst.

Not that her having sex with other men is a bad thing. She's a grown woman who can do whoever she wants.

I just wish I could make it onto the list of men Elle invites to her bed, even if I know I shouldn't.

I'm incredibly relieved that there aren't any dirty photos being passed between Elle and Riley. Stressed or not, seeing any part of that asshole would've ruined my appetite.

13

Elle

Vivace, the restaurant Preston picked tonight, is one that Audrey and I have walked past plenty of times and looked at with longing. Despite how good the ratings are, neither of us can afford to pay hundreds of dollars for a meal while running our own business.

It's the type of place men save up for to bring their wives on Valentine's Day or take their sweetheart to propose. A night, a meal to remember. Not the kind of place a guy wastes money on for a fake girlfriend he just met.

Even though I feel completely out of place, I leave the restroom to make my way back to the table.

My phone is sitting innocently beside the silverware on my side when I take a seat.

I guess Preston made quick work of deleting messages, and hopefully didn't respond to any of the trolls.

I'm about to ask him when he blurts out, "I fucked up again."

"Oh?" I ask in confusion, glancing around to see several patrons now watching us, but thankfully not snapping photos.

"I read your DMs."

"There were some mean messages, but it's fine," I assure him.

"No, Elle, I mean, I read the ones between you and Riley."

"Oh." I try to recall what we may have said to each other. I think I only teased him about actually being the pro hockey star he claimed to be when I cut his hair the first time. Then I asked if he would tag the salon for free promotion.

"He, uh, did a decent thing, tagging you and encouraging the teammates to become clients."

Preston looks like he would rather have all his teeth knocked out than admit something decent about Christian.

The waiter comes over before I can respond, placing menus in front of each of us.

"Good evening. Would you like to hear today's specials or sample our featured wine?"

Preston doesn't look at the man in his fancy server tux. He just stares at me. "If you want to leave, I won't blame you."

"I'm not going to leave," I assure him, then give the waiter a smile. "Could we have a moment?"

"Of course," he says before bowing and turning away.

"You're not going to leave?" Preston asks as soon as he's gone.

"No. I gave you my phone voluntarily. It's not like you peeked at it without my permission. I don't have anything to hide."

"Okay. Good," he says, exhaling a relieved breath.

"I went through Christian's phone a few times without him knowing," I confess softly.

"You did?"

"Didn't find anything except messages from his teammates. I think he deletes chat logs he has with women after he dumps them and blocks them, or when he decides he doesn't want to see them anymore."

"Fucking asshole," Preston grits out.

As if on cue, my phone lights up with a new text alert. "Speak of the devil and he shall appear," I remark.

"What do you mean? Riley just texted you? Like just now?"

I nod, then pick up my phone to toss it back into my purse before placing it on the hook on the side of the table. My bag may not be an expensive designer, but I don't want it getting dirty on the floor.

"What did he say?" Preston asks.

"I don't know. Don't care either," I tell him as I pick up the menu. "Let's not talk about him anymore tonight."

"Deal. I wish I didn't have to think about him for the rest of my life."

I glance up at the angry man across the table, wanting to ask yet again what caused him to hate Christian so much. But I remember Preston's response last night that it's "complicated." Meaning, it's none of my business.

So, I drop it, and instead focus on choosing which item on the menu to eat tonight while enjoying the company of my fake date.

I've just finished my salad when the buzzing starts up from my purse. Preston eyes it, then me. "The suspense is killing me."

"But I thought we were going to avoid talking about him for the rest of the night," I remind him.

"Like usual, the self-centered asshole refuses to let that happen."

"He'll stop eventually."

Preston gives me a look that says he knows an easy way to stop it. I know I could easily block Christian's phone number and that would be it. Why haven't I done that yet? I have no freaking clue.

"Just read them, Elle. We don't have anything else to do while we wait for our entrees."

"Fine," I mutter before retrieving my phone from my purse. Opening up the message log, I read them aloud for Preston without even knowing what they say. "*Why are you avoiding me?* Then, he says *I know you want to talk to me, or you would've blocked me already.*"

Preston grunts his agreement with that statement.

"I have a reason," I assure him. "And it's not because I want him back."

Preston arches an eyebrow, waiting for me to give him the explanation.

"Is it wrong that I like seeing him squirm? After months when I could barely get a text response from him after waiting hours, it feels good to have our roles reversed."

"What does he want, Elle?"

"Ah, well, he says, *I'll just come over if you're not going to respond to my messages.*"

"Asshole can't take a hint."

"I haven't…" I pause, unable to help reading ahead.

"He hasn't what?" Preston asks.

"He says he hasn't been with anyone since he saw me in the arena wearing your jersey."

"You know he's lying, right? The prick can't go an hour without finding someone to inflate his ego a little more."

Before I can respond, the phone begins buzzing in my hand. Then it keeps buzzing. It's not incoming text messages, it's an actual phone call with Christian's name flashing on the screen.

"I don't think he's ever called me before," I remark in shock.

"May I?" Preston asks.

He wants to answer my phone? That would really tick Christian off. And since I don't have anything to say to him, I gladly hand it over to the grumpy man.

He answers with, "What do you want?" Preston's dark eyes hold mine through the long silence before I hear Christian's voice. It sounds like he asks, *"Who is this?"*

"Who do you think it is, genius?"

"Preston? You have got to be fucking kidding me." That response is shouted loud enough for me to hear it clearly.

"Stop bothering Elle. We're trying to have a nice dinner."

"Bullshit!" he grits out.

"See you on the ice tomorrow," Preston responds before ending the call and offering the phone back to me.

"Thanks. And nice job. Not a single curse word. Well, at least on your part. I could hear what he said since he was shouting. I'm surprised he took time out of his busy schedule of dicking around to actually call me."

"He obviously misses you and wants you back."

"No, he doesn't," I assure him. "And he can't want me back when he never had me. Not really."

Neither of us say much through the rest of dinner. Thankfully, my phone remains silent in my purse.

Preston pays the check and then we walk outside into the mild May night.

"Thank you for a delicious dinner," I tell him.

"You're welcome, but I wish you didn't say it like that."

"Like what?"

"Like you can't wait to get home and be rid of me."

"That's not…I didn't mean it that way. I like hanging out with you, more so when we're not talking about Christian the whole time. Besides, you have a big game tomorrow. I don't want to be a distraction."

"If I promise not to speak of the devil, could we keep hanging out?"

"I don't know. What did you have in mind?" I ask him curiously.

"Well, I'm not sure," Preston says while running his fingers over his newly trimmed beard. "We could go back to my hotel room."

I'm so stunned at his suggestion that it takes me a moment to recover. "I-I don't think that would be a good idea."

"Why not?" he asks. "Think about how furious Riley would be if he sees a photo of you coming back to my hotel room or hears about it."

"That's…he would assume that we…you know."

"Yes, he would," Preston quickly responds.

Going back to Preston's hotel room would be foolish. I know that. But at the same time, it would feel so great to let Christian assume we slept together — a feat that the arrogant bastard was certain would never happen. He was so sure that Preston wouldn't want a nobody like me.

"Let's do it!" I blurt out, then immediately slap my palm over my mouth. "I mean, let's go back to your hotel room."

"Elle, you know I don't expect anything, right? That's not why I asked," Preston rushes to add.

He just wants to get under Christian's skin a little before tomorrow's game. I shouldn't be hurt that he doesn't want to have sex with me. It's ridiculous. I don't want to have sex with him, either.

Not now, at least.

"Good, because I'm still angry at you for storming into the salon earlier."

"I don't blame you for that, either," he agrees, giving me a half grin. "But seriously, we could just hang out and watch a movie, or do whatever you would do if you were at home."

"Okay," I agree. "Lead the way." I wave my arm in the direction I assume is his hotel, and Preston grabs my hand when it flies past him.

"This way," he says, pulling me in the other direction.

"Oh."

His hand is strong and warm, and he doesn't release mine as we begin the walk across the street.

"So, cupcake, what would you be doing at home tonight if you were all alone?"

I glance up at his face, wondering if he intentionally made that sound dirty or not. And while I have plenty of toys, it's not like I use them every night I'm without male company.

In fact, I rarely used them while Christian and I were dating. He may have been a huge player, but he knew all the best positions to get me off.

Shaking my head to clear those thoughts, and assuring myself that Preston's question wasn't about that sort of thing, I tell him, "Ah, I would usually grab takeout on the way home from the salon. Eat, then have a nice, long bath before throwing on my comfiest pajamas to curl up on the sofa and watch those cooking competition shows. Which is ironic since I can barely boil an egg, but I just like watching others create magic in the kitchen."

"I've watched some of those shows too, but I'm always appalled by how small their pretty little finished dishes are, no more than two or three bites for me. Let's watch and order dessert from room service."

"Sounds good to me," I agree with a smile.

14

Preston

Women are so damn confusing.

Or maybe it's my lack of experience that's making me confused.

When we got back to my hotel room, which was thankfully documented by several fans in the lobby, Elle asked if I had a shirt she could change into since her dress wasn't the most comfortable for curling up on the hotel room sofa. A small loveseat that we both squeeze into, after she's wearing one of my black Warhawk tees that comes down past her knees.

It shouldn't be so hot seeing her wearing my shirt that swallows her whole, but it is. Mostly because it's mine, but also because I know she's only wearing her panties underneath. No bra since it's hanging with her dress. And that knowledge is driving me crazy since she insists on sitting on her knees, knees that are touching my leg, with the cotton tee riding up to reveal the majority of her legs.

She said she was still angry at me from earlier, but if she wasn't, would she let me pull her onto my lap and kiss her?

I shouldn't be thinking about anything but the game tomorrow, and here I am, wondering what kind of panties Elle is wearing. What color, what style, what texture? Is she the type of girl who wears thongs? If so, I may combust just thinking about how amazing her ass would look in one.

Then, as if her wearing just my shirt wasn't enough torture, our slices of chocolate pie came and I had to watch as Elle savored each and every bite, moaning around her spoon, then licking it clean.

I was a sweaty, nervous wreck eating my own slice, then having to go wash it down with a big glass of water.

When I come back to the loveseat, the side of Elle's head is resting against the back of the leather, her eyes closed, sound asleep.

I can't leave her sitting up like that all night, and I sure as shit can't put her in the king-sized bed and contort my big-ass body to sleep on the loveseat either.

We can both sleep comfortably in the bed without even touching. Even if I want to touch her more than I want to breathe at the moment.

Scooping Elle up with my arms around her bottom and neck, I take her over and lay her down gently on the pillow. She doesn't so much as twitch as I tuck her in with the bedding.

Elle

I wake up with an awful crick in my neck, sleeping on a flat pillow that isn't my own, in a bed more comfortable than my own.

Popping up, I tug down the enormous tee, that had ridden up to my stomach, back down over my knees to survey the bedroom. It's a nice hotel room dusted with the light of the rising sun peeking through the gap in the heavy blinds.

And beside me, the biggest man I've ever seen is flopped out on his stomach. His broad, bare back takes up more than half of the enormous bed.

I must have fallen asleep watching TV with Preston last night, and he tucked me into bed before joining me.

Not that I blame him. I could've managed to tuck my knees and curl up on the small loveseat, but even if he threw his legs over the rolled arm, he would've been squished.

Easing slowly out of bed so as to not wake the hockey player, I peel back the covers and then sneak a glance over at Preston's lower body, relieved and a little disappointed that he's wearing black and red plaid pajama pants.

Tiptoeing to the bathroom, I use the facilities, wash my hands, then swallow a gulp of minty green mouthwash. I swish it around to get rid of my morning breath while undoing my chignon to run my fingers through the tangled strands and redo it into a messy bun.

Figuring my best bet is to get dressed and slip out to avoid any awkwardness, I head back to the bedroom to grab my dress from where I hung it up in the small closet. Since

Preston is still out cold, I quickly tug his shirt off to slip the dress back over my head.

It's just covered my ass when a deep, rumbly voice says, "Good morning."

Startling, I spin around to find Preston's head still resting on his folded arms, bleary eyes staring right at me. He looks grumpy and sleepy at being woken up, and yet, somehow, still stupidly hot.

"Hi. Good morning. I was trying to be quiet so I wouldn't wake you. I should have…I should've changed in the bathroom."

"Glad you didn't. And I didn't see much."

"Oh, well, good," I say in relief, just before he adds, "Just all those cute little rosebuds on your sheer panties and bra. Now I'm wide awake."

"Preston!" I exclaim.

Throwing his tee at his face, I tug my dress the rest of the way down my thighs, my face flushing in embarrassment. "First you tuck me into your bed, then you sneak peeks at my underwear while I'm changing?" Although I can't blame him for the second part. I really should've taken my dress back to the bathroom and changed there.

Chuckling, the grizzly bear sits up, revealing his hairy, muscular chest and hard stomach as he stretches his arms above his head. "You fell asleep. I couldn't leave you kneeling on the loveseat all night. Well, I could have…" he trails off, eyes darkening as they remain locked on me as if he's thinking about a less innocent type of kneeling. "And you know I couldn't sleep on the loveseat and chance my back aching before the big game tonight."

"Oh, I know there's no way that all of you would fit into

such a tight space."

"Not that kind of tight space," he replies with a grin.

His quick response makes me begin to wonder what's wrong with the two of us. Last night was completely innocent, just two friends sharing a meal and watching shows together. How is it that everything coming out of our mouths this morning sounds like innuendo?

"I should go," I say, gathering my purse and shoes I'll put on in the elevator.

"You sure you're okay, Elle?" Preston asks, sheets rustling as he gets out of bed. "With last night, I mean?"

"Oh, yeah. It's fine. I've never slept with a man before last night. I mean, never just slept with a man. You know what I mean. Anyway, it was…fun," I say in a rush while undoing the deadbolt on the door.

"Yeah, it was fun," Preston says from right behind me. I try to open the door, but it won't budge but an inch. The big man behind me reaches up to push the door shut so he can unlatch the metal bar. Ah, that's what I forgot. "Do you really have to leave so early?"

"I have an appointment at eight-thirty," I lie.

Preston's palm flattens against the door. "Do you really?" he asks softly, his minty breath blowing across my neck makes me shiver.

Minty breath?

Turning around to face him, I ask, "How is your breath so fresh right out of bed?"

"I woke up an hour ago."

"Oh."

We're standing so close that only a few inches separate our faces. I take a step back, leaning against the door, which is when I notice the obvious, impressive tenting of Preston's pajama pants. I tell myself that it's just how all men his age wake up, raring to go. God knows, I lost count of how many times Christian poked me awake. Since we both slept in the nude, he had easy access to push right on inside.

When I look back up at Preston's face, his dark, heavy-lidded eyes are staring at my mouth when he says, "Were you lying about an early appointment?"

"Yes," I whisper, since I'm obviously a horrible liar.

"Will you stay long enough for me to kiss you goodbye?"

"Wh-why? There, um, aren't any phones recording us here in your room," I remind him.

He leans forward, rubbing his nose along my throat… sniffing me. "No, there's not."

"So then why…"

"Because I liked kissing you." His damp lips brush the side of my neck, making me instantly get wet for him.

"But…"

"But what? You don't want me to?" This time his open-mouthed kiss on my neck has me biting my lip to keep from moaning.

"No, no. I do, it's just, I could use a shower, and you…you said you wouldn't ever be tempted for a taste."

"Huh?" he asks, his tickling lips and tongue leaving me breathless and dizzy.

My hands grab his thick biceps to keep myself upright, and well, because they feel really nice.

"When…when we first met outside the arena, you called me cupcake," I remind him.

"That was before I knew you, before I kissed you and didn't want to ever stop." Between his mouth and words, I'm melting into a puddle, aching, and more turned on than I think I've ever been in my life.

"I thought you weren't attracted to me," I explain.

The space between our bodies vanishes in an instant, the hardness of him pressing into my stomach, causing me to gasp.

Preston chuckles at my reaction and says, "How could you possibly think I'm not attracted to you when you can see and feel just how badly I want you?"

"Doesn't that, um, usually happen first thing in the morning?"

"I've been aching for you since we met, Elle. All day yesterday. Last night. I couldn't sleep for wondering what you were wearing underneath my shirt. And now that I know..." he growls against my neck and my leg is suddenly curled around his hip to pull his lower body closer to mine.

Even after Preston's low groan at the contact, I ask, "So, you do want me?"

"God, yes." He pushes himself against me harder, the soft fabric of his pants rubbing against the crotch of my damp panties. "You have no idea how much I want you. Every time I see you, I get so damn hard. Touching you, tasting you, it's all I can think about."

With that confession, I grab the sides of Preston's face to bring it to down to mine. As soon as our lips connect, his tongue seeks mine, thrusting deep, mimicking the movement of our lower bodies.

Preston grips my thigh, holding it tightly to his hip. When he must be confident that I have no plans to lower it, his big, warm palm slides down, grunting into my mouth when he grabs a handful of my bottom. "I need to see more of this perfect ass." He squeezes it a few times before a thick finger slides underneath the strip of fabric running between my cheeks. He moves lower and lower until… "God, you're soaking wet," he murmurs against my lips.

"Since the second your lips touched my neck," I confess.

His lips leave mine to find that spot underneath my ear again while his hand runs back up, over my hip, to shove down the front of my panties.

"Oh god!" I cry out when his thumb brushes my clit. Grabbing Preston's arm, I clutch it tight while squirming as much as I can against the door, seeking more contact. His thick finger teases lower before it wiggles inside of me, making me gasp.

"This…*oh*…this was supposed to be…fake," I remind him and myself as the warm, liquid pressure builds in my lower belly.

"I know. Fuck, I know that," Preston agrees. His mouth sucks on my neck hard enough to leave a mark. "I can't keep my hands off you."

"And…you're leaving…tonight after the game."

Not even that truth can chase away my release that's at this very moment barreling toward me like a bullet train. I'm going to come on his fingers and then…then what happens?

Those thoughts fade away as my muscles tighten around his finger and I explode. I hold his arm tight, keeping it where I need it as I cry out through the pleasurable waves.

Preston's lips tug at my neck as if trying to draw out the ecstasy longer.

All too soon, the intense sensation begins to fade.

I want more. Need more.

I reach for the front elastic of Preston's pants, but his hand slips from my panties to grab my wrist, stopping me.

"You don't want me to..." I trail off when his mouth and his tongue returns to duel with mine.

"I want it all," Preston says when he finally pulls back to look at my face. "But I'm leaving tonight. I would need more than one time with you, cupcake. You deserve so much more than one fucking time."

And while his words soften the blow, it still doesn't change what Preston's doing.

He's rejecting me.

~

Preston

God, I want to be inside of Elle so damn bad. My dick is weeping at the thought.

But my head is putting on the brakes.

I don't want to have a meaningless, one-time romp with Elle. That wouldn't be fair to her, even if she says it's what she wants right now.

So, despite how badly I want more, I have to stop this before things go further than a kiss and an orgasm for her.

Elle is still hung up on Riley's sorry ass. They just ended things, so I don't want to rush her into something with me. Not to mention that I'm not sure if my ego is ready for the comparison.

I don't have any recent practice in bed. What if it's not

good for Elle? I don't want her to compare me to that son of a bitch.

Of course, Riley's probably great at sex since he's been with hordes of women while I've not been near a woman's body in years. That I remembered where the clit was is a miracle.

"I wish I could rip your dress off and throw you on the bed," I tell Elle honestly. "You have no idea how much I want to do that. But…I can't."

"You can't?" Her eyes lower to the erection jutting out of my pajama pants, proving I very much *can*.

"I, we, shouldn't. I've got the game tonight and have this thing about not…indulging right before."

"Oh," she says. The disappointed in that one word has me rethinking everything.

No. That's just my dick trying to take over control of my entire body.

Trying to explain myself better, I tell Elle, "While I would love to spend the rest of the day worshipping you, if I get on my knees, I know I'll get too excited and there won't be any stopping my dick from exploding. I need that…edge in the game if we're going to win."

"Then, I guess I should go."

I nod my head, even if I wish she would stay and…what? Stay on the other side of the room so I'll keep my hands and other body parts to myself?

"Thanks for dinner and dessert, and that…" she trails off, her face flushed.

"You're welcome for all of it."

There's a pause for a long moment and we just look at each other.

"Ah, Preston?"

"Yeah, cupcake?"

"I can't leave until you let me."

That's when I finally realize that I'm still pressing her to the door, my chest brushing her luscious breasts.

"Sorry," I mutter, forcing my bare feet to take two steps back so she can go.

"Good luck tonight. Try not to get ejected," Elle says softly, giving me a small smile before she turns around, opens the door, and slips out.

15

Elle

I can't believe how stupid I am.

Letting things go so far, nearly sleeping with Preston, after sleeping in the same bed with him, wasn't smart.

I should be happy that he stopped things before they went any further. He's leaving tonight. If things had gone any further, I probably would've regretted it as soon as he stepped on that bus and disappeared from my life for good.

I definitely should not be thinking about how Christian never had any rules about not having sex right before a game while staring at the salon windows and drinking a giant cup of coffee.

"Morning!" Audrey says cheerfully when she strolls through the door.

"Morning," I mutter from where I'm slumped in my salon chair, spinning in slow circles between sips.

"So, how was your dinner date?" she asks while flipping on all the lights in the building that I forgot.

"Fine."

"Fine? That's a lie if I've ever heard one. How was it really? And why do you look like something the cat dragged in?" Audrey asks when she returns to the front.

"Do I look that bad?" I ask, glancing down at my three-quarter length white and pink dress.

"You look adorable, as always. I was referring to your drooping shoulders, frown, and the constant chair spinning. You look sad. Did Preston upset you? If so, I will figure out a way to kick his big ass all the way out of town."

"No. Well, yes, he's sort of responsible. I was irre-sponsible."

Audrey's steps are loud as she marches over to my chair and grabs the armrests to spin it around to face her. "Spill, Elle. What happened?"

"We went to dinner at Vivace."

"Ooh, fancy."

"Yes, it is, and I felt completely out of place, like everyone in there knew I couldn't afford a salad. For once, it actually made me appreciate Christian's preference for takeout..."

"Bzzz. Wrong answer," Audrey says before spinning me in a complete circle so fast that I nearly spill my coffee. "Time for you to forget that fool's name."

"Okay. Sorry. So, anyway, dinner was going fine, then Chr...*the fool* started texting me. My phone was buzzing like crazy. Then he actually called me!"

"Wow. What did he say?"

"He asked in texts why I hadn't blocked him and threat-ened to come over if I didn't respond to his messages. Preston answered the call and told him to leave me alone because we were having dinner."

"Wow."

"So, we made it through our meal without any further interruptions. Then, when we were outside saying goodbye, I did something stupid. Something very stupid and very public."

"What did you do?"

Trying to cringe and hide behind my mug, I whisper to her, "I went back to Preston's hotel room. People saw us and took photos."

"Seriously? I thought you were still mad at him for being an alphahole!"

"I am. I was! I just went back to his room to watch TV, not for sex."

"Uh-huh. Did you stay all night?"

"Yes, but we only just slept. I fell asleep on the tiny sofa. Preston tucked me into bed at some point, then he slept on the other side. No touching at all."

"Okay. That doesn't explain why you look like a sad puppy this morning."

"Well, when I woke up this morning, I got dressed to leave…"

"What do you mean, you got dressed?"

"My black dress was so tight I couldn't sit in it any longer. Preston gave me one of his shirts to wear."

"Uh-huh," Audrey murmurs with a grin, as if it's a bullshit excuse.

"Anyway," I huff, waving a hand in the air to move on. "He was awake when I changed back into my dress this morning."

"Why didn't you change in the bathroom?"

"Trust me, I've been asking myself that same question."

"You *wanted* him to look, you little hussy!"

"No, I didn't. I thought he was sleeping."

Crossing her arms over her chest, she tilts her head to the side and says, "Come on, Elle. Be honest."

"I really didn't think it through. I was just in a hurry because I couldn't believe I fell asleep, that I slept next to him in nothing but a T-shirt and panties all night."

"Did he see anything?"

"Yes. He saw my bra and panties in the brief second it took to put on my dress."

"A matching set?"

I roll my eyes. "Of course."

"You don't wear a matching set unless you intend for someone to see them."

"Whatever. Fine! I wanted to be prepared for our date just in case I stopped being angry at Preston for his alphahole move of asking me if I slept with the Bobcats players."

"Okay. That's all understandable. So far, I haven't heard why you look all fuck drunk, ashamed, and sad while rocking a mean hickey on the side of your neck."

Gasping, I slap my palm over my throat. "Crap. I forgot about that."

"So, are you going to tell me how that happened? I'm assuming it occurred sometime after the hockey player saw your underwear."

"Right. Preston followed me to the door when I was leaving, and he was blatantly…turned on, you know? We kissed, then his hand was in my panties, his mouth was on my neck, and I got off."

"Whoa, whoa, whoa. Back the truck up. How are you

going to give me all the details of everything except for the hookup?"

"It happened nearly that fast," I admit. "Over and done. And then Preston was done."

"You mean he got off too?"

"No, I mean that he stopped me, us, when it was his turn."

"Oh. Why in the world would he do that?"

"He gave me some excuse about not *indulging* before a game, and how he was leaving tonight, so I took off. Now, I feel yucky because those seem like ridiculous excuses. Christian never had any sort of rule like that."

"First of all, he should only be referred to as the fool from here on out."

"Right, sorry."

"Two, stop apologizing!"

I open my mouth to apologize for apologizing, then purse my lips together and give a nod of agreement instead.

"Good. And third, you didn't tell Preston that part, did you?"

"What part?"

"The part about the fool!"

"Oh, no, of course not. I try not to bring up his name around Preston."

"So, to sum up last night and this morning, you went on a dinner date, Preston ripped the fool a new one on the phone, then you went to Preston's hotel room to fuck with the fool before tonight's game?"

"Yes. That was stupid, wasn't it?"

"You've got it bad for the woolly mammoth, Elle. There's nothing stupid about that."

"He's leaving tonight after the game! That's the other

reason why he didn't want to take things further this morning."

"That excuse at least makes a great deal of sense."

"What?"

"You just broke up with the fool. Do you honestly think that you're emotionally ready to be with someone else, someone who is leaving town in a few hours?"

"No. I know it was for the best to stop. I just feel so…blah about it." I swallow the rest of my coffee in one gulp, savoring the burn down my throat.

"Could that blah feeling have anything to do with you thinking that Preston, being the voice of reason, means he's not attracted to you?"

"Well, yeah. What if that's the basis for all of his excuses?"

"Elle, didn't you mention he was standing at attention?"

"Yes."

"Then you have your answer! Don't go to the dark place, convincing yourself his stoppage has anything to do with you personally. He wants you, but he has a championship game on the line and knows that you're still vulnerable from a recent breakup with his nemesis."

"When you say it like that…"

"It all makes perfect sense, right?"

"Yes, thank you for talking me off the insecurity ledge."

"That's what besties are for," Audrey says as she leans down to wrap me in a hug. When she pulls away, she stares at me seriously. "Now, on to the most important question — do we have tickets to tonight's game?"

Smiling, I tell her, "I think so. Preston said he would try to get us tickets because he wanted me to come."

Grinning like the cat that ate the canary, Audrey nods and says, "Yes, he certainly did."

I roll my eyes at her innuendo. "You know I meant the game!"

"I didn't. At least tell me if it was good?"

Huffing out a laugh, I tell her the truth, "I came so fast, I momentarily forgot how to speak."

"Atta girl! Don't let all your crazy assumptions ruin your buzz."

"Easier said than done."

16

Preston

Even hours later, I'm still distracted by my morning with Elle.

A growing part of me regrets stopping. A part that's been aching for her for hours, unable to forget how sexy Elle was in her lacy panties and bra. The sweet taste of her neck. Her cries when I found out how hot and slick she was.

I walk into the locker room in a damn daze. The shout of one of my teammates has me finally coming up for air.

"Dude! Where the hell did your beard go?" Saul asks and the entire locker room goes silent.

"On the floor of the salon," I say as I drop my bag on the floor and plop my ass onto the bench.

"Why, man? What were you thinking?" Vincent asks softly.

"I wasn't thinking. I let the woman cutting my hair decide what to do with the beard. She left the roots so…"

"So, we're going to fucking lose now!" our goalie exclaims.

"Hot damn! If Pres kills Vinnie, I'll finally get to start," Spencer says with a chuckle, causing Vincent to flip him the finger.

Our goalie isn't cowed, though. He, and some of the other guys, look…distraught.

"Oh, get the fuck over it," I tell them. "Not shaving during the playoffs is just a bunch of superstitious bullshit and you all know it. Grow a pair and let it go. The amount of fur on your face tonight isn't what's going to make or break us. It's how we fucking play."

"That makes sense," Saul mutters. "I should really wash my lucky socks."

"Yes, you definitely should," I tell him. "We've got this, gentlemen. There's no amount of superstition that's going to stop us from kissing the championship trophy this year."

"Still, there's no denying that you don't look as intimidating without most of your face hidden behind blackness," Nick remarks when he comes over for a close look.

Getting to my feet, I tower over him, even though he's already in his skates. "She cut my hair, not my balls off, asshole."

"She may as well have. You don't scare me half as much as you did before. Same will go for opponents," he remarks, even though he's backing away.

"Then I guess I'll have to hit people twice as hard to make up for my appearance," I respond. "You just worry about scoring, Reeves, and let me handle the intimidation."

I try not to let the concerned glances from my teammates, and hell, even the coaches, bother me during warm-ups.

It's time to get my head in the game. Nothing else.

Well, maybe a little something else when Riley comes out of the locker room to take some practice shots.

As I skate up to him, he turns as if sensing my presence, and shoots one of the pucks in his pile right at my face.

Thankfully, my quick reflexes have me ducking to dodge so it doesn't hit me in the damn head.

"I don't buy your bullshit about dating Elle for a second," he grumbles.

I don't even like hearing him say her name.

"You don't buy it, huh? Even though I'm intimately familiar with her pink bra and panties with the cute little rosebuds on them? They are hot as hell, and so sheer, you can see right through them."

"What the hell, Lawrence? You been snooping through Elle's underwear drawer like a perv?"

"No, I saw them when I peeled them off her sexy body last night in my hotel room."

So, that only happened in my dreams, but it felt real enough after I got Elle off on my fingers.

Rather than get angry, Riley chuckles. "Nice try, but I know you haven't fucked her. You wouldn't risk nutting before a game this big with so much on the line."

"I didn't say we fucked, did I? There are plenty of things I can do for her—not that you would know because you're a selfish fucking prick."

"Maybe I am selfish," he agrees. "But I don't have a stupid rule about saving up a load before a game. If anything, I always had the best luck if I came down Elle's throat right before the puck drop."

This son of a bitch…

"All I had to do was sit my ass down in her chair and she would gladly swallow every drop I gave her."

The rage I had tried to push down comes boiling up like a volcano ready to erupt.

But there are more important things than knocking the asshole out cold on the ice before the game starts.

Winning the championship trophy for my family, my teammates, the fans, getting my contract renewed, those are all more important. I'll take all my anger at Riley and use it for good—hitting all the Bobcats who got to feel Elle's fingers in their hair. I'll spread the hate around, do my job to keep the Bobcats from scoring, and help my team score enough goals to win game two.

So, before I skate off, I simply tell Riley, "Is the lack of Elle's mouth going to be your excuse when you lose again tonight? Let's see if my good luck comes from getting on my knees for her."

It's another fantasy, of course. I would love to get my tongue between Elle's legs…but I'm leaving tonight after the game.

After we win.

I don't even know if I'll see Elle again before the bus loads up.

When I get back to the locker room, I send her a text, making sure she picked up her tickets at Will Call. I also ask her to come say goodbye after the game, as hard as it will be, so I can see her one last time.

17

Elle

Today's game feels...different.

Nobody calls me names or even gives me the evil eye when I walk into the arena with Audrey, wearing Preston's jersey.

The tickets he got for us today are almost as close as the first ones, which is insane.

"There they are!" Audrey says before we can even sit down.

I follow her pointed finger to the ice where Preston is skating toward Christian casually, and Christian, well, he pops one of the pucks up and then shoots it right at Preston's head. He dodges it easily, though, and then they talk. Or yell at each other.

"I wonder what they're talking about," Audrey says as we finally squeeze past a few people to get to our seats.

"I'm not sure if I want to know. Hopefully, Preston stays calm."

"He doesn't look like he's going to choke the life out of Christian, so that's a good sign."

I let out the breath I was holding when Preston skates off toward the tunnel leading to the locker room. Christian resumes shooting pucks toward the goal, one right after another, making about one in every three.

We watch him until my phone buzzes in the pocket of my jeans. Pulling the device out, I'm amazed to find a text from Preston when he should be preparing for the game.

Did you have any trouble getting your tickets?

Then another message quickly follows the first. *Will you come say goodbye before we leave the arena?*

I quickly text back, *These seats are great! Thank you <3 And yes, I'll come see you off. Now, shouldn't you be listening to the coach giving the team a pep talk?*

He says, *Coach's pep talk was short and sweet – Go kick their asses.*

Good luck, I tell him along with a four-leaf clover.

Moments later, both teams are on the ice, the announcer introducing the Bobcats starting line. Then the National Anthem singer barely gets off the ice before the puck drops.

"Do Preston's hits look even more vicious tonight?" I ask Audrey during the first period as another Bobcat gets plowed over.

"Oh yeah. He's hangry. And I don't mean hungry and angry."

"Then what…"

"He's obviously horny and angry," she remarks, causing a burst of laughter to escape from me.

"Oh my god."

"Well, it's true, right? No Os for him. That man looks like he could really use one."

"You're ridiculous. He's just determined to win the championships."

"And determined to mow down every single one of our Bobcat clients."

"Our clients?" I repeat before I look closer at the numbers of the home team being targeted. While I never really paid much attention to the guys who come and go from the salon, there are some familiar faces being smushed into the boards by Preston.

"No way," I mutter.

"I guess he figured out a way to spread his rage around to multiple players. There go our clients. But at least it seems to be working for him," she says just as the Warhawks score the first goal of the game.

Preston

"Another great game tonight, Lawrence," Coach Ramsey says to me on the walk to the bus.

"Thanks, Coach."

"Guess the rest of the guys will shave now that you proved facial hair doesn't decide who wins or loses games."

"Maybe so."

"I like this change I've seen in you on and off the ice this week. Too bad it took so long for you to loosen up."

I train hard, work hard, and play my heart out on the ice. That's why we've won the last two games, right?

It can't be because of Elle. That doesn't make any sense. The idea that she could cause a positive outcome is just as ridiculous as believing in any other silly superstition.

Except, I actually feel different since I met her. Better. Not just a better player, but a better human. My only regret is talking shit to Riley about Elle.

I shouldn't have mentioned her underwear or anything else about what we haven't done together. If Elle found out I made up lies to try to cripple Riley, she would probably punch me in the nuts. And I would deserve it.

It's not fair that, other than fooling around with her this morning, the rest of my fantasies about being with her will remain fantasies.

I'm glad to see her blonde hair glowing in the dark back lot when I walk outside.

"Great game tonight," Elle says when I approach where she's waiting by the fence.

"Let her in," I tell the Bobcats' security guard who quickly obliges.

"Hi," I say when she's finally in front of me, no chain-link between us.

"Hi," she replies. "It's just a coincidence that some of my and Audrey's Bobcat clients got roughed up by you tonight, right?"

"No clue what you're talking about," I lie.

"Seriously?"

"Do you really think I would go to all the trouble of compiling a list of names and looking up jersey numbers of men who have had the pleasure of your fingers in their hair?"

"I would hope not. They're just clients, you know."

"And I just want your hands in my hair."

"But it's sort of my job to touch people's hair, even men. And you're leaving."

"Fuck. I know," I grumble. "The bus is waiting…"

"So, I guess this is goodbye," she says. "I can give you your jersey back."

"No. Keep it," I tell her, grabbing her upper arms as if to keep the material on her beautiful body.

"Are you sure?" she asks.

"I'm sure. Thanks for everything, cupcake. It turns out shaving my beard down didn't cause us to lose."

"I'm glad I didn't jinx you," she replies with a dazzling smile that makes me forget how to breathe. "Even if a tiny little part of me was hoping it would."

"Evil woman," I huff, giving her shoulders a light shake, mostly to pull her closer. "I should've known you had ulterior motives for wanting to cut my hair and shave me."

"I'm still a Bobcats fan underneath the Warhawks jersey. But now I'm also a Preston Lawrence fan."

That makes me grin at her like a fool. "I'm a pretty big Elle Townsend fan myself."

Letting my duffle slide off my shoulder and to the ground, I lean down to cover her lips gently with mine, once, twice, as if testing the waters on a goodbye kiss. Wondering how far she'll let me go in a parking lot surrounded by people.

Thankfully, Elle doesn't pull away. She swipes the tip of her tongue over my lips, causing them to part on a groan, setting me off.

Sliding my palms down her back, I cup her bottom and lift her up my body. Elle's arms wrap around my neck at the same time her legs wind around my waist.

The lift makes it so much easier to kiss her, not to mention that it lines up our lower bodies in that delicious way, like they're meant to fit together despite the drastic difference in our sizes.

I ignore the whoops and whistles coming from the bus as I try to memorize every inch of Elle's mouth, her taste, her fancy salon shampoo scent, the way she feels in my arms.

Being connected to her is everything, as if I could kiss her like this forever and never get enough. The tight hold Elle has on me makes me think she feels the same.

Until a persistent ringing interrupts.

Elle pulls back panting. "I think that's your phone?"

"Shit, sorry," I say as I lower her feet to the ground again. "Could be my agent."

I slip my phone from my suit pocket and immediately answer when I see the name on the screen. "Hey, everything okay?"

"Just calling to say congrats!" Maya and Finley both shout so loudly through the phone I have to pull the device away from my ear.

"Thanks. Can't talk right now. The bus is waiting," I tell Maya. "I'll see you both soon."

"Have a safe flight!" she says before I end the call.

"Sorry," I tell Elle as I slip my phone back into my pocket, right before Coach Ramsey yells, "Let's go, Lawrence! We've got a plane to catch."

"You…you should go," Elle says when I grasp her waist to pull her closer.

"Fuck. I know," I tell her. Why is saying goodbye to her so damn hard? "I can't believe it was just two nights ago that we met right out here."

"I know," she agrees, bracing her palms on my chest. "Thank you for everything. Good luck with the rest of the games. I hope you get your contract renewed."

"Thanks, cupcake."

I give her one last swift kiss on the lips before I pick up my bag and reluctantly head for the bus.

18

Elle

"It's weird how much I already miss him, even though I barely knew him, right?" I ask Audrey on our walk back to our cars that are parked at the salon.

"I think he was good for you. A nice distraction. And that kiss was hot as hell!"

"It was. It didn't feel fake, but it still felt like goodbye."

"Didn't look fake either," she agrees. "I just hope that now that Preston's leaving town, you won't give in to the fool."

"That is not going to happen. I promise. No giving in to the fool ever. And maybe it's for the best that Preston left before we got any closer."

"Why do you say that?"

I bite down on my lip, worried about telling her, but wondering if I'm overreacting. "Preston got a call right before he got on the bus."

"Yeah, I saw. What about it?"

"Well, I got a peek at the screen before he answered."

"And? Who was it?"

"The screen said 'Maya?'"

"That's it? Just Maya?"

"Yes. It obviously was a woman. I could hear her voice. And Preston smiled when he was talking to her. He ended the call with, 'see you both soon.'"

"Does he have a sister?" Audrey asks.

"No clue. He never mentioned any siblings."

"Give me a second." Her phone is in her hand a second later, the screen's light illuminating her face. "I can't find anything online about his personal life. But it was probably his mom or sister."

"She sounded young."

"So, then it could've been his sister."

"But why wouldn't he have mentioned her before? And you know how there's like so much tension between Christian and Preston. Sorry, I mean the fool and Preston. What if the reason they hate each other is because of this girl?"

Audrey considers that silently for a moment. "Then why would Preston have beef with the fool if he got the girl?"

"Ugh. I don't know," I mutter as I yank my hairband out to smooth my hair back into a messy bun.

"Does it really matter who she was since Preston is gone now? You weren't planning to see him again, right?"

"When we first started our fake relationship, he asked me about continuing it through the championships, then pretending like it fizzled out in the summer when we couldn't do long-distance. But he didn't mention it again. If he wanted to keep seeing me, he would've asked tonight, wouldn't he?"

"Maybe he wanted to, but he doesn't want it to be fake anymore, which makes it confusing."

"I don't know. I'm probably stressing over all this for no reason."

"I much prefer you stressing over Preston and your fake relationship to you stressing over whether the fool was going to message you, or come over, or break your heart."

"I'm so over him."

"Are you really?" Audrey asks, staring at me with her brows raised.

"Yes, or at least I'm getting there."

"Thanks to Preston?"

"Yes. Thanks to Preston. It was nice spending time with him, taking my mind off being dumped. I enjoyed messing with Chris...the fool, more than I should have."

"That jerk deserved every second of misery. Besides, it's not like Preston permanently maimed him or anything."

"At least not yet. There are still at least two more games to go," I remind her.

Preston

I think about Elle the entire plane ride home. She's probably just glad that I'm gone, out of her hair, so the attention on us will die down.

Although, that goodbye kiss felt like it meant...more. Like it was just for us, not the cameras or the press.

It's late when I get home, so I try to be quiet when I sneak into the house. Of course, my phone dings loudly with a message just as I unlock and open the front door, dropping my bag inside the foyer.

Still, I can't be mad about the noise, not when I see that it's a text message from Elle asking if I got home safe.

She wouldn't ask that unless she cared, right? Or she's just a nice woman who is worried about a friend, nothing more. A friend who seems to like kissing me as much as I enjoy kissing her. Touching her. I already miss just being in the same city as her.

The anxiety of the championships and this fake arrangement make me want to stress eat. Since we won both games, there aren't any loser brownies waiting for me on the kitchen counter. A good thing, I guess.

I'm digging through the refrigerator, eyeing the leftover pizza, when the overhead kitchen lights flip on and Maya hugs me from behind. "You're back! Two games down and two to go!"

"Are you drunk?" I mutter with a shake of my head.

She scoffs indignantly. "No, I'm not drunk."

"Is Finley asleep?"

"Of course he is."

"Then you should keep it down," I remind her.

I pull out some leftover spaghetti instead and shut the fridge door to finally face her.

Her chocolate eyes narrow at me. "Shouldn't you be in a better mood after winning the first two games of the championship finals on the road?"

Yes, I should. Why don't I feel good? Oh, right. "I met someone."

"No kidding," my sister snorts. "I was wondering when you were going to mention her. Elle is it? You didn't respond to any of my texts about her!"

"Guess that means you've seen all the photos of us?"

"Everyone in the world has seen the photos, Pres. Even Finley."

"How did he see them?"

She shrugs. "Some kid at preschool told him he saw his uncle on the news. Finley was furious that he didn't get to miss school to come to the games in North Carolina."

"There was no reason for him to miss school for just the second game of the series."

"I know that. But we both wanted to be there in person cheering for you. He wouldn't have missed school Saturday."

"It's too dangerous for the two of you to be wandering all over a strange city alone, being surrounded by Bobcat fans."

"Well, at least the next two games are home. There is *nothing* that will keep us from missing those games."

"Of course not. Best seats in the house."

I remove the lid on the storage container and pop the spaghetti into the microwave, punching in the time.

While we wait, Maya says, "So...did you tell Elle the whole history?"

"What do you mean?"

"Did you tell her the reason why you try to murder Christian whenever you see his face?"

"No."

"Why not?"

I lean my back against the counter and shrug. "Because it's nobody's business, not even hers."

"A word of advice, big brother. You can't have a relationship with a woman if you're not completely honest with her."

Good thing Elle and I are not in a relationship. It was just to make Riley jealous, get him off-kilter for the finals. And it worked. Better than we even expected. But I don't tell my sister all of that. She wouldn't approve of pretending.

"You already miss her."

"Why the hell do you assume that?"

"Because you're moping around after winning back-to-back away games for the championship, stress eating old leftovers! What else could it be?"

"Fine. I miss her. I wish I had invited her up to D.C."

"Why didn't you?"

"Because I'm not sure if she would come. She has a business to run, and it would be asking too much of her to drop everything to come here for three or four days."

"It's only three or four days. And I bet if she's here, you will be less likely to lose your temper on the ice."

"There are a lot of reasons why I wish she were here. Still doesn't change the fact that it's not going to happen."

"You won't even ask her?"

"No."

"Have you spoken to her since leaving town?"

"She sent a text asking if I got home okay."

"That's a good sign. Have you responded yet?"

"No." I was going to as soon as I saw the message, but I knew that once I sent a response, the communication between us would likely stop. I wanted to think of something to say to get her to send a response back.

God, I feel like an idiot teenage boy again.

"Then ask her to come up here when you respond. She'll need time to prepare."

"She's not going to come to D.C."

"You won't know if she will or not unless you ask her. Did it occur to you that she was maybe *hoping* you would ask her to come?"

"No."

"It's the freaking championships!" she exclaims, reminding me of Elle's enthusiasm for the sport. "And it's a good thing you have a sister knowledgeable about how women think. They want men to make the first move to avoid looking clingy."

"You're probably wrong."

"If I'm right, then you have to do dishes for a month. If I'm wrong, I'll do them."

"Deal. But you can't trick Finley into doing them for you."

"Fine," she mutters. "He just loves making a sudsy mess anyway."

"Back to Elle…"

"Cute name for a cute girl."

"Back to Elle," I start again. "Do you think it would be better to ask her on a phone call or by text?"

"Phone. She'll be less like to turn you down on the spot like that, or to think too long and talk herself out of coming."

"Good," I say, since I wanted to call her anyway.

19

Elle

I'm not able to sleep a wink. No, I keep looking at my phone, flipping between two different text logs.

One is with Preston, waiting for him to tell me he had a safe flight. My sent message shows as "Read" but no dots have appeared to show him typing back a response.

The other texts, well, those are from Christian. The most recent one came in about an hour ago, asking if he could come over. Obviously, it's a booty call. I guess his options aren't as plentiful after losing the first two homes games of the championships. He must need some…comforting, and I was the first person he thought would be desperate enough to agree.

Thankfully, I can't even think about anyone but Preston after that crazy hot kiss that felt more like foreplay than a goodbye.

If we had been at my place or his hotel room, I have no doubt about how it would've ended.

I wanted him so badly, right then and there. But then his phone had to ring, showing a woman's name, and his coach yelled for him to get on the damn bus to get to the airport.

I think the reason I'm so disappointed is that I know a night with Preston would mean something, unlike with Christian.

Texting me was probably more about competing with Preston anyway, trying to get me to choose him as soon as the Warhawks left town just so he could rub it in Preston's face at the next game.

So, while I wait for Preston's response, I type out a careful response to Christian that can't be construed in any way but the one.

No, I don't want you to come over. I don't want you to text me again, either. Goodbye, Christian.

I really should block his number. I'm about to do just that when my phone dings with a new message from Preston.

Are you still awake?

Okay, that doesn't answer my question about getting home safe. I still answer it.

Yes.

Before I can ask him if everything is okay, my phone buzzes in my hand with an incoming call from Preston.

"Hey," I answer right away. "Are you okay? Did you and the team make it back safely?"

"Oh. Yeah. The flight was fine. I should've mentioned that."

"Yes, you should have," I tell him with a smile he can't see. "I stayed up waiting to hear from you."

"Good. I'm glad, even though you'll hate me for it tomorrow," he says, making my smile widen.

"So, what's up? What was so important you had to call?" I ask him.

"How would you feel about seeing me this week?"

"Seeing you? I'll see you on television."

"No, in person. I…I miss you and I want you to come to our two home games."

"You-you want me to come to D.C.?" I skip over the part where he said he missed me, wondering if maybe I misheard him. He just saw me a few hours ago.

"I know that you have the salon to run and probably a bunch of appointments booked, but I would really like to see you here in town, cupcake. Is there anything I can do to convince you to come here for both games?"

"Both games?" I ask in surprise, since there will be a day off in between.

"Yes."

"Why is it so important that I come up there?"

"Because if you're in the arena, I'll have a good reason not to hit Riley."

"Oh."

"That not a good enough reason?"

"I don't know," I admit honestly. And while I'm being honest, I tell him, "He just texted me a few minutes ago."

There's a long pause. "Riley texted you tonight?"

"Yes."

"What did he say? What did he want?"

"What do you think?" I mutter. "He wanted to come over."

"That son of a bitch!" Preston exclaims. "Did he forget he

hurt you and walked away? Or that I warned him to leave you alone? If I were still in town, I would whoop his ass."

"It's not a big deal."

"Could you…will you tell me how you answered him?"

"I told him I didn't want him to come over and not to text me again, either."

I can hear the whoosh of Preston's relieved exhale through the phone line. "Good. I'm glad you told him that."

"Did you expect me to say yes after that kiss tonight?"

"God, I need to stop kissing you in public. If we'd been alone…the things I would do to you, Elle."

Now it's my breath that catches. "We were alone the other day," I remind him. "In your hotel room."

"I remember," he grumbles, his voice lower than moments before.

"And you only kissed me."

He sighs heavily. "You're still not over him, Elle."

"What?"

"Riley. You're not over him. I hate it, but I'm pretty sure it's true. So, until you are, I don't want to be a rebound…puck."

"A rebound puck?" I repeat, a smile on my face, even though I know he's right.

"You know, when someone aims for the goal, but it bounces back off the goalie so someone else gets to take the shot while he's distracted and score?"

"Right. I thought you meant a rebound as in the first person you date after a breakup just to try to bounce back."

"I guess both of those would work. Or a revenge…puck. Either way, I don't want to be that guy. I want to be the clear shot you make on purpose."

"And if I could move appointments around to come to D.C. would there be a chance of a clear shot?"

"I don't know, Elle. I want to say yes, but I think that has to be left up to you."

"How good would the seat be in the D.C. arena?" I tease him.

"The seat? Oh, it would be so fucking great."

"Then I guess I have to come and make another sign. Let me check with my clients and Audrey tomorrow to see if she can cover for me."

"So, just one seat for you?"

"Yeah, just one seat this time."

Going alone to a rival team's city for a man I've only been fake dating for a few days but would love to real date sounds a little scary.

Still, I really want to give it a shot.

20

Preston

I can't believe that son of a bitch is still texting her, still begging for another chance. And since I'm so far away now, I can't help but wonder if Elle might give in to the asshole.

At least I get a response from Elle bright and early the next morning. She's definitely coming to D.C., and she wants to know when to arrive and for how long.

I jokingly text back to ask if now was too soon.

Her response, ***I should work for most of the day tomorrow, catch an afternoon flight, and be there for the puck drop.***

Sounds good, I tell her. ***I can buy your plane ticket.***

Elle: ***No, thank you. The tickets for tomorrow and Friday's game are more than enough.***

Preston: ***So, you are staying through Friday?***

Elle: ***How long did you want me to stay?***

Sunday, I instantly respond.

Elle: *Since I don't have any appointments this Saturday and the salon is closed on Sundays, I guess I could make that work.*

Preston: *Great. Wednesday through Sunday. We'll spend the weekend celebrating the Warhawks winning the championship.*

Elle: *Ha! You wish!*

As soon as I find out Elle is coming, I start speed cleaning the entire house from top to bottom. Maya and I keep it pretty tidy and clean, as much as we can with a four-year-old running around with about a million toys. Still, the whole place could use a late spring cleaning.

"You're dusting the freaking ceiling?" Maya asks from the entryway when she returns home from taking Finley to preschool.

"Yep," I reply while running the duster head over the ceiling fan. "Going to clean the whole house today."

"Oh really? Does this mean Elle is coming?"

"Yep."

"Yay! I can't wait to meet her!"

Lowering the duster, I point it at her. "Be nice to her during the games. And please don't give her the whole history."

"Why not?"

"Because..." I trail off, seeing a cobweb in a corner that needs to be knocked down.

"Do you trust her, Pres?"

"Yes."

"Then why not tell her the truth?"

Shrugging, I mutter, "I don't know."

"You're a stubborn jackass, that's why," she huffs. When I

ignore her and start wiping down the baseboards, she says, "So, she's coming tomorrow and staying here with us?"

Shit. "I assumed she would stay here. I mean, if that's okay with you?" I finally face my sister again. "I should've asked you first."

"It's your house, Pres. You can have guests whenever you want."

"It's our house," I correct her. "And that includes Finley. If you think it would be weird for him if Elle stays over, then I'll book a hotel room."

My sister rolls her brown eyes while going over and fluffing the pillows on the sofa. "You don't have to get a hotel room to hook up with you girlfriend or whatever she is. If Elle's going to stay over, I can just schedule a sleepover for me and Finley to get us out of your significantly shorter hair. It'll be fine."

"You don't have to leave."

"Trust me, it's for my benefit more than yours. I don't want to stay and hear you two going at it all night."

"That's not... we won't be going at it. She just broke up with fucking Riley."

"Poor girl. How long were they together?"

"Five months. He didn't think it was serious, but she did."

"And he dumped her?"

"Right before the championships started."

"Now you have another reason to hate him," she murmurs while folding the blanket neatly and hanging it over the ottoman. "But you're smart to give her time, to avoid being a rebound."

"That's exactly what I told her. I'm not sure if she agrees."

"Well, it's still for the best."

"Actually, Elle didn't mention where she would be staying. We only talked about dates."

Pulling out my phone from my jogging pants pocket, I send her a quick message to ask if she wants to stay with me, adding that I have two guests rooms, so she doesn't think I'm trying to pressure her into anything.

Her response comes instantly.

Elle: *I think it's best if I book a hotel room while I'm in town.*

"Dammit," I mutter after reading her response.

"What?" Maya asks, coming over to try to peek at my phone before I put it away.

"Elle's getting a hotel room. I told her she could stay here..."

"Well, maybe that's for the best too, so you don't rush into anything when emotions are high after a win."

"I don't like it. The thought of her staying somewhere else in the city alone every night."

"Then let her stay in the hotel the first night, then bring her over to the house to visit the next day. Let her see the place before you ask her if she wants to cancel her room and sleep here."

"Yeah, okay. I can do that."

Really, the only person I have to blame for Elle not wanting to share a bed with me is myself. Even though I know it's best, it still sucks.

"Riley's still texting her as of last night," I confess to my sister when she starts to head to the kitchen.

She stops in her tracks and says over her shoulder, "Probably only to hurt you because he thinks he can win her back."

"Do you think she'll go back to him? They live in the same city. The asshole is being persistent, and they have a history..."

"No clue, Pres. That's another reason why taking things slow is a good idea."

"True enough. But I hate it. I hate him."

"I'll leave you to your cleaning," she says with a sigh.

"Will you clean your room and Finley's?" I ask before she leaves.

"Sure, thing. Even though I doubt Elle is going to spend much time in either," she answers with a smile.

Preston: *Let me know when your flight gets in. I'll try to pick you up from the airport.*

Elle: *No way! It'll be so late I'll have to get an Uber straight to the arena. All you need to think about is losing game three.*

Preston: *I believe you meant 'winning' game three. And I wanted to see you before, but if your flight comes in late...*

Elle*: I'm sure. There will be plenty of time for me to see you after you lose.*

Preston: *Your ticket's at Will Call. I'll call you after our win to see about where to meet up.*

Elle: *Deal. Good luck. Don't get into any fights.*

Preston: *I'll try my best.*

Game day in our arena takes some of the pressure off my shoulders. The home crowd cheering gets all the guys hyped, myself included.

And when Riley and his teammates skate onto the ice to warmup, the familiar rage feels further away because Elle will be here any minute. She changed her schedule to come to my hometown, to support me tonight.

When Riley comes up to me, like I knew the prick would, I

tell him, "Stop texting Elle. She doesn't want anything to do with you. How many ways do we have to tell you?"

"I'll win her back eventually, just like I'll be winning the championship trophy. Just wait and see."

Ignoring his bullshit confidence, I say, "I can't wait to see her in my seats tonight. Did she ever travel to any of your games? I'm guessing no, since having her there would've stopped you from being able to fuck around behind her back."

"Elle's coming here?" he asks, his eyes widening in surprise. He glances around to where he knows my seats are, where Maya and Finley are already seated next to an empty one. After a long moment, he asks, "Then where is she?"

"Her flight must be running late."

"Yeah, right. Maybe she's just bored and had enough of waiting because of your stupid rule. She's insatiable. Trust me, I would know."

I don't respond to that taunt, just flip him off and get my head back in the game.

21

Elle

My flight thankfully doesn't have any delays. I have an hour to get checked in at the hotel and drop my luggage off, then get to the Warhawks arena with my new sign with barely ten minutes to spare.

The incredible center ice, front row seat ticket is waiting for me at Will Call as expected.

And while I assumed I would feel like an outsider as I head inside the arena in Preston's jersey, several people wave and smile at me like they know me.

I guess they may have seen me in photos too, but unlike the Bobcats' fans, they're all friendly and supportive of the two of us together. A few even tell me how great Preston's been playing thanks to me. I refuse to take the credit for his hockey performance, but I tell them thanks.

Not a single negative comment is made to my face as I take

my seat right in front of the glass, directly across from the benches. My seat is on the end of the row again, thankfully, and the raven-haired woman in the seat next to mine is staring and grinning at me so intensely it freaks me out.

"Hi," I say to be nice as I lower my butt down and prop my sign against the wall in front of us.

"Hi!" she replies cheerfully, lifting her hand to even give me a little wave, which is when I notice the number twenty-two on her sleeves of her Warhawks jersey.

"You're a Preston Lawrence fan too?"

"Oh, the two of us are his entire fan club right here," she says, throwing an arm around the shoulders of the little boy in the seat on the other side of her. "Isn't that right, Finley?"

"Uh-huh." He absently gives a nod as he tosses popcorn into his mouth from the big bucket on his lap while watching the rival mascots do a skit on the ice.

Preston's fan club, huh? Is she a puck bunny? And why does the kid sort of look like a tiny Preston with slightly lighter hair color?

"You're Elle, right?" she asks when she turns back to me.

"I am."

"It's so nice to finally meet you! I'm Maya, Preston's sister, and this is my son, Finley."

"His sister!" I exclaim in relief. "I should've known since you two have the same raven hair." So, the name on his phone, the woman he said he would see soon, he was talking to his sister and nephew.

Now I feel silly for even assuming the worst about Preston. But what I can't figure out is why didn't he ever mention her?

"Yep, little sister. Which is how we acquired the best seats in the house for the finals. I'm glad you could make it up from North Carolina."

"He told you about me?"

"Well, yeah. I couldn't get him to talk until he got home from Greensboro, but it's hard not to discuss you since everyone in the world knows about the two of you."

Oh crap. Did Preston tell his sister that our relationship is fake or not? I have no way of knowing and don't want to say the wrong thing. Not that I think he would care if his sister knew it wasn't real…

"I haven't had a vacation in a while, so my best friend and business partner told me I should come up here for the next two games."

"I'm glad you could make it. I can't believe the difference in Preston since he got back from the first two games. I wanted to bring Finley to them too, but Preston worried about us being the only Warhawk fans surrounded by nothing but Bobcats fans."

"Well, as a Bobcats fan myself, I'm sure you and Finley would've been fine."

Pointing at the turned away posterboard, she whispers, "Is that the sign that caused so much drama?"

"No, I made a new one." Turning it around, I show her my glittery handiwork.

Maya reads it aloud. *"Don't puck with my man*! I absolutely love it, almost as much as the one about Christian!"

"Yeah?"

"Seeing that sign about his…stick on television made my year, even if it's more info than I needed to know about my older brother. I couldn't believe it when Preston said you two were dating. I haven't seen him with a woman since before the minors."

"Really? That's not just what he tells the press?"

"Trust me, Preston hasn't looked at a woman in years. I would know too. Finley and I live with him."

"You do?"

"Yeah. He's been so great, taking us in when…well, I don't know what I would do without him."

"That's sweet. I had no idea he even had a sister or an adorable nephew. He didn't tell me anything about you."

"I'm not surprised. He doesn't like sharing his personal life and knows I don't want the attention on Finley."

"Right, that makes sense," I agree. And Preston barely knew me, so I shouldn't have expected him to tell me about his personal life, his sister's life, after we met and began our fake relationship. I wouldn't want photos of my kid all over the place either. People can be so vicious.

"Preston said Christian dumped you after five months together," Maya remarks.

"Yep, he used me, then dumped me right before the championships started. He also made me feel like crap about myself. I didn't even know he was with other people while we were…anyway, it didn't end very well."

"Well, you lasted longer than I did."

"What do you mean?" I ask, my brow furrowed in confusion. Preston's sister knows Christian? Is she the reason they have a beef with each other, why Preston can barely get through a game without hitting the other man?

Maya turns to the boy, and says, "Headphones." He dutifully slips what I'm assuming are noise canceling headphones hanging around his neck on over his ears.

Turning back to me, Maya says, "Preston doesn't like for me to share this with many people, but he trusts you, so there's no reason not to tell you the truth."

"Yes, of course you can trust me," I assure her. "I'm a hair stylist. Everyone tells me their secrets."

"I bet so," she replies, giving me a small smile. Then she takes a deep breath and says softly, "The last time I spoke to Christian was when I told him I was pregnant."

"Pregnant?" the word comes out of my mouth way too loud, so I slap my palm over it. When I am certain I can keep my volume down, I ask, "You were pregnant...with his... his..." I lean forward to glance around her again, getting a better look at the boy who I'm guessing is four or five. His hair is a chestnut brown, lighter than his mom's and Preston's. And while he reminds me of his uncle, he has a little dimple in his chin that's just like Christian's.

"Please don't tell anyone." She clutches my arm and whispers even lower. "Finley doesn't know, either."

"No. No, of course not," I promise her. "I just...Christian never mentioned him."

"That's because when I told Christian I was pregnant, and wasn't sure what to do, he said he was sorry, then sent me money through Venmo to 'take care of it,' and that was that. Once I made my decision, I wanted to let him know but his number wouldn't even take my messages, so I think he had, um, blocked me."

I remember Christian mentioned that he usually breaks things off with women by blocking them, that he only told me in person because he wants me to keep cutting his hair.

"Wow, Maya. I am so, so sorry. I can't believe he would do that..."

"Preston assured me we were better off without him in our lives. I know he was right, even though it's…never mind. We just met and already I'm getting word vomit all over you."

"No, it's fine. Thank you for telling me. And no wonder Preston hates him so much!"

"Preston has always blamed himself," Maya leans over to tell me softly. "He and Christian were friends, best friends actually, hockey teammates and roommates in the minors. He introduced me to Christian when I came to Raleigh for my freshman year of college at NC State. Pres even gave his blessing for the two of us to date…"

"Then you got pregnant, and Christian ghosted you."

"Yep. Christian got signed with the Bobcats and left town without looking back. Preston never forgave him. I've tried to convince him to let it go, but every time the two have met in a game during the pros, Preston goes berserk on him. Well, until the other night. Not that I think Pres is using you just to piss Christian off or anything."

"Right," I say, even though I'm starting to realize that's the *only* reason Preston agreed to the photo, the kiss, the sign, and giving me one of his jerseys.

Now it all makes sense, why he was more than happy to help me get back at Christian. I knew he had his reasons for wanting revenge, even if Preston refused to tell me what they were.

I get it now.

He wouldn't tell me because he was protecting his younger sister.

His nephew, Christian's son!

The arena erupts into cheers and applause when the lights go down as the Warhawks come skating out onto the ice.

Seeing Preston again, even from this far away, my stomach turns flips. I'm getting way too invested in this whole mess with him. And if I'm not careful, it'll become more than just fun or fake.

Maybe it already has.

"There's Uncle Pres!" Maya says, removing her son's headphones and pointing him out. They both stand up and whoop, the boy cheering with his popcorn container tucked under his arm.

Preston's been like a father to Christian's son because the boy has never had a father of his own. It's so sweet of him and so…responsible. He's obviously protective of them both.

At the same time, it feels like this enormous secret that he's been hiding from a father if Christian doesn't realize Maya's son is his. How could he not? Either way, now here I am, causing drama between the two men all over again years later.

"I, um, I think I need to go get some fresh air," I tell Maya as I get to my feet, leaving my sign against the wall.

She looks over at me with a frown. "Are you okay?"

"Yeah. I'm fine," I lie. "I'll be right back."

And I was planning to go back.

I really was.

But once I make it outside in the cool night air, I just can't stop my feet from walking further and further away from the arena.

22

Preston

I search the stands for Elle during the singing of the Star-Spangled Banner, but the seat next to my sister is still empty. Damn. Guess her flight was late.

The Warhawks start off the game hot, with Nick scoring a goal within the first two minutes. But then Christian scores a goal right after, and his teammate does as well at the end of the first period, leaving the score two to one. It feels like all the air in the arena is sucked out on the way to the locker room for first intermission.

Again, I look at the front row, but there's no sign of Elle yet. Not then or before the second period begins.

In the second, our goalie is able to stop every single puck. But on offense, we can't seem to get a decent shot off.

When Elle doesn't show up by the beginning of the third period, I start to worry incessantly.

Did something happen on her flight?

Did her Uber get in a wreck?

God forbid, did she get hit crossing one of D.C.'s streets?

Late in the third period, the Bobcats score again. We lose all hope of making up two scores, ending the game one to three. Now we're two wins to their one in the damn series.

It sucks, but it's rare for a team to sweep the finals in the first four games. Maybe we'll do it in five.

I'm just glad it's over so I can finally check on Elle.

There are no calls, voicemails, or texts from her on my phone, which has me even more concerned.

A text from my sister pops up while I'm holding the device.

Tough loss. You'll get them in game four!

After a quick shower in the locker room, when I see that I still haven't heard a word from her, I send her a message.

Preston: ***Is everything okay?***

Elle: ***Everything is fine.***

Fine? That's all she's going to tell me. Of course, I know it has to be complete bullshit.

Preston: ***Where were you tonight? I thought you were coming to D.C. for the game.***

Elle: ***I am in D.C.***

What the hell?

Preston: ***Where? You weren't at the game.***

Elle: ***I'm at the hotel now.***

The hotel? She's being vague on purpose. I just wish I knew why.

Preston: ***You're not going to tell me which one?***

Preston: ***Elle, what's going on with you?***

Dots appear and disappear over and over again. Finally, she hits send.

Elle: *I talked to your sister.*

She talked to my sister? Why does that sound like such a loaded response?

And the only way she could've talked to Maya was in the arena. She came, but she must not have been here for long. I know because I spent way too much time looking for her.

Preston: *Okay. So, you were at the game? And talked to my sister, then left?*

Elle: *She told me that Finley is Christian's son.*

Oh fuck.

What was Maya thinking? I told her not to talk about that shit! I barely know Elle and my sister doesn't know her at all. Yet, she just blurted out her most confidential secret to her within minutes of meeting for the first time?

Preston: *She shouldn't have told you all that, but now you know why I hate that asshole.*

Elle: *Yeah, I finally get it. And don't worry, I will never tell anyone.*

Again, I get the feeling there's more to those words. That's why I give up on texting and call her.

Elle

When my phone rings in the middle of texting with Preston, I debate whether to answer it. But if I just start ignoring him, I'm no better than Christian.

"Hi, Preston," I say, my voice heavy with reluctance.

"I thought you would sound happier since your Bobcats won tonight."

Did they? I haven't even turned the television on or looked at updates on my phone. I just walked around D.C. for hours, lost in my thoughts. I went so far, and my feet hurt so bad that I had to get an Uber to come pick me up to get me back to the hotel.

"I'm sorry the Warhawks lost," I tell Preston. "Did you get to play the whole game?"

"I did."

Whew. That's a bigger relief that I expected it to be. If he had been thrown out, I would've blamed myself. Would Preston have blamed me, too?

"Losses happen," he adds. "We're still ahead in the series, so that's all that matters."

"That's true."

"Why did you leave the game so early, Elle?"

"I...I just went to get air and ended up walking."

"You walked alone at night in D.C.? Are you crazy?"

"It was fine," I hedge.

"What's up with you, Elle? Why did you come all the way to D.C. and not stay to watch the game?"

Squeezing my eyes shut, I blurt out the conclusion I came to during my long stroll. "I don't think we should keep up the fake relationship."

There's a long pause before Preston says, "Why not?"

"Because...because now I know why you hate Christian,

and I've got this secret to keep from everyone. It's all just too much."

"I'm sorry Maya put that burden on you. She shouldn't have told you. I can't believe she trusted you enough to run her mouth."

"I won't say anything to anyone," I assure him.

"I know you won't."

"Good," I say, glad that he trusts me that much. "Then, I guess this is goodbye."

"I want to see you," he says, making my breath catch. "I hate knowing you're in my town, but not where I can find you."

"I'm sorry, I just, I don't feel like pretending in public to piss off Christian tonight."

"That's why you think I want to see you? To piss him off?"

"Well, yeah."

"Elle, tell me what hotel you're staying at or come to my place. I won't let anyone see us together, okay?"

"That's impossible."

"No, it's not. I live outside the city with only a few neighbors."

"It's late and I don't have a car."

"Now you're just being stubborn."

"Goodnight, Preston."

"Elle, wait!" he says, but my finger presses the button to end the call.

I have to get out of this fake relationship fast before I do any real, permanent damage to my heart when it hasn't even had a chance to heal from the last break.

23

Preston

"What the fuck did you say to Elle?" I ask Maya as soon as I walk into the house and drop my duffle with a loud thud.

"Excuse me?" she asks from her seat on the sofa. Her eyes narrow at me when I move to tower over her. "I know you took a big loss tonight, but I don't appreciate your tone or use of the f-bomb. You better be glad Finley's gone to bed."

I replay the words that just came out of my mouth and… yeah, I would knock out anyone who said that shit to my sister, especially in front of my nephew.

"Sorry, I'm just…I don't know where Elle is staying, and she won't tell me what's wrong."

"Oh wow. You really do care about her," she remarks while crossing her legs underneath her.

"Of course I care about her! It's why I hate whatever this shit is that's coming between us."

"Well, I think I may have an idea about why she left the game now."

"What do you mean?"

"Sit." She nods to the nearby chair, so I grumble a swear and fold myself into it. "Could it be that Elle was hoping that you were going along with pretending to date her for her sake and not just for your own revenge?"

"How do you…how did you know we were pretending?"

"Because you would do anything to mess with Christian, including stealing his girl or pretending to steal his girl, and bragging about having a bigger stick."

"Yeah, well, everyone else thought it was real."

Nodding, she says, "Right. They did. What if Elle was starting to think it was real, too?"

"What do you mean?"

"Come on, Preston. She likes you, and not just in the let's-just-screw-over-Christian-together way."

Shrugging, I huff, "Good. I like her too."

"Now that she knows the depth of your hatred, though, what Christian did to me when I got pregnant, Elle thinks you hate him more than you like her."

"Oh shit." I scrub my palm over my face, beginning to understand what she's getting at.

"Exactly!" Maya says triumphantly. "Now, how are you going to prove to her that you actually care?"

"No idea."

"Then you better come up with something fast before she hops on a plane out of here first thing in the morning."

"That's not going to happen. I have to find her. Tonight."

"But how?"

"I guess I'll have to call or visit every damn hotel in town."

"I'll help!" Maya offers.

"Thanks. And sorry for snapping at you, I'm just…"

"Yeah, I get it," she replies with a sad smile. "What do you need me to do?"

"Could you find Elle's salon on Insta and track down her friend Audrey something? She probably knows where Elle's staying."

"You got it," she says, phone already in her hands.

"Let me know what she says. I'll be checking with hotels until I hear from you."

"She probably booked a hotel near the arena, right? Start there."

"Yeah, okay. I will," I agree.

∼

Elle

Even though I'm still wide awake, the hard knock on my hotel door a little after two a.m. scares the crap out of me.

I wasn't even going to see who it was through the peephole, until I hear his voice through it.

"Elle, I know this is your room."

"How?" I say aloud before I realize he probably can't hear me through the door.

I finally get out of bed to go unlock the door, but I leave the chain in place. It'll be the line I need to keep the addictive hockey player on the other side, to not get any deeper into this mess I'm in.

And despite Preston's "rule" about no sex before a game or during the season, there's only one thing a man wants when he shows up begging to come in this late at night. I can't count how many times Christian showed up out of the blue, not caring if I had early appointments the next morning and woke me up.

Seeing Preston standing on the other side of door, even knowing he has ulterior motives, still gives me those nervous butterflies in my stomach. Again. I absolutely hate those fluttery bastards.

The big grumpy man looks good in his jeans and a black hoodie that's pulled up over his head. He would be a scary sight to see on the street in the middle of the night, or knocking on my hotel room door, if I didn't know him. Or at least I think I sort of know him.

"You sleep in my jersey?" is the first thing he says as his eyes lower to where the material ends just above my knee.

Shit. I should've changed before answering the door. Now he probably thinks I'm pathetic and pining for him.

Which is the truth, but I didn't need to be so obvious about it.

"It's nice and warm," I lie. Quickly changing the subject, I ask, "How did you know which hotel, which room, I was staying in?"

Preston shrugs his wide shoulders. "I called and asked around."

"Asked around?"

"I stopped by a few hotels and asked if you were a guest."

"How many hotels?"

"All the ones from here to the arena."

"Oh my God." I rest my forehead on the door. He must be really desperate for that booty call.

"Maya sent Audrey a message on Insta. She told her which hotel but not the room number…"

He walked around looking for me? Had his sister message Audrey? Why didn't she tell me? Not that I've had a chance to tell her how this whole thing blew up in my face. I didn't feel like talking to anyone tonight, not even my best friend.

I can't believe Preston would go to so much trouble after a grueling hockey game. I also can't believe the hotel would rat out my room number.

"And the front desk just told you which room I was staying in without my permission? What if you were a criminal coming up here to rob me?"

"Since the man at the front desk and his manager recognized me, I don't think they were too concerned about me robbing you."

Shaking my head, I mutter, "Oh. Right. We're in your hometown."

He uses every inch of his height and size to crowd the small opening. "Is there any way I can talk you into letting me come in?"

"Why?"

"So that we don't have to talk through the crack in the door?"

"There's nothing to talk about." *And I can't sleep with you.*

I don't say that last part to him. It's not that I don't want him. I do. It's that he was right. I'm not over Christian, or at least the pain he caused. Until I am, I shouldn't be intimate with Preston or anyone else yet. Especially when my feelings are one-sided in this situation.

"Oh really?" he asks. "Maya seemed to think there was some confusion that needs to be addressed."

"No, there's no confusion. I get it, Preston. Really, I do. What Christian did to her, you have every right to hate him."

"Agreed. Please tell me you don't feel guilty about making him jealous, Elle."

"No, I don't feel guilty about that."

"Then what's going on?"

"I...I think I got the wrong idea about us. I thought maybe it was real. And I shouldn't be upset with you. From the beginning, you told me you don't date, that you don't want any distractions. It was stupid to think I was an exception."

"That's true, I don't date. I haven't dated anyone since I made it to the pros."

"I know, and I understand. You've been so focused on helping take care of your sister and your nephew. They depend on you, on your paycheck. I get it. You have to avoid letting anything mess up your career at all costs. I don't want to cause any problems for you either. Even if this doesn't count because it's not real..."

"Elle, I want you to be the exception to all my rules. I want it to be real, too."

"Why?" I whisper.

"I know it's probably hard to believe, but I like you more than I hate Riley."

Trying to purse my lips together rather than smile like a lunatic, I say, "If that's true, then you must like me a whole hell of a lot."

"I do. Why else would I have spent an hour searching the city for you in the middle of the night?"

"I-I don't know."

"Trust me, cupcake, wanting to see you doesn't have anything to do with making Riley jealous."

"It doesn't?"

"No. I meant it when I said I missed you. You, not the rumors or the publicity or whatever. I asked you to come to D.C. so I could see you in the stands wearing my jersey, and so we could spend time together after the game. Preferably alone."

"Oh."

"Now, will you please open the door? I just want to be in the same room with you for a few minutes. I know it's late and what this may look like, but I swear I'm not here for anything else. I know you're still not over him." When I don't confirm or deny that statement, Preston says, "He always came by late at night too, right?"

"He did. The only time I usually saw him unplanned was in my chair for a haircut or, um, late at night. At least he would bring over a late-night snack…"

"I hate him even more for treating you like you didn't deserve his days, too."

That comment finally has my fingers reaching up to undo the chain on the door because it's exactly how I feel. Like I was Christian's part-time hookup when I wanted to be with him all the time. At least Preston gets that.

And how ironic is it that now, with Preston, it's the complete opposite?

"Hi," he says with a smile that makes me nearly melt when I open the door wide enough for him to walk in.

"Hi," I reply before shutting and locking the door behind him. "I really am sorry you lost tonight. And that I didn't stay for the game."

"I get it," he replies. "I should've told you the truth from the beginning. Maya told me to when I got home from Greensboro, but I was being stubborn. I've got serious trust issues…"

"You're protective of her and Finley and want to keep them out of the media frenzy. I don't blame you. If I had a sister and a nephew, I would feel the same. People online can be so cruel."

"They can. I hate the shit they've said about you. They're just jealous morons, you know that, right? They don't deserve a second of your time."

"I'm trying not to read the comments. At least the Warhawks' fans were nice to me at the arena. Only smiles, no screaming assholes."

"Really?" Preston says in surprise. "That's good. I'm glad. I didn't think about how the crowd would treat you, but I should have."

"The home team seems very supportive of you and I dating. But after tonight, when I left the arena and the Warhawks lost, they could all be blaming me."

"Nobody can blame that loss on you. Our whole team was off, playing like they thought game three would be a piece of cake after winning the first two away games," he says with a sigh. "But seeing you, knowing you were sleeping in my jersey, makes the loss a little more bearable. Do you have on shorts underneath?"

I shake my head no.

"You are killing me, cupcake," he growls before fisting the sides of it to pull me closer to him. Flush against his body, I can feel exactly what he means. As my fingers grip the tops of his wide shoulders, a rush of liquid heat warms my lower belly, making me wish he didn't have that stupid rule.

And when Preston's lips lightly graze mine, that heat has me nice and slick for that particular activity.

He kisses me like he's pouring every second we were apart into claiming my mouth. This goes on for so long my knees are weak.

When he finally pulls back, our mouths are a hair's breadth apart, our breath mingling, Preston says, "Give me one little taste, and I'll never ask you for anything again."

I nod my head in agreement, even if I'm not entirely sure what he means by "a taste." That could encompass several possibilities...until Preston sinks to his knees in front of me. His large palms slide up the sides of both of my thighs, heading underneath the jersey until they come to the waistband of my panties. With his gaze locked on mine, Preston slowly peels them down my legs, only breaking eye contact when he reaches my ankle. He looks down to help me step out of them.

He dangles my navy-blue thong on a single thick finger while he examines the growling head of a yellow feline on the front triangle. "I didn't even know they made Bobcats' panties."

I have to clear my throat to respond. "Those are obviously my lucky panties if they won tonight. I told you that underneath the Warhawks' jersey, I'm still a Bobcats fan."

Still studying the panties as if they're the first he's ever seen, Preston says, "If they're lucky panties, then you're definitely not getting them back."

When he balls the panties up and shoves them into the

front pocket of his jeans, I gasp indignantly. "You dirty pervert!"

Grinning up at me with his palms sliding up my legs again, this time taking the hem of the jersey with them, he tells me, "How about this? Let me stay here with you tonight. I promise to keep my hands to myself, and I'll give them back to you in the morning."

"I don't know," I reply, causing his hands to pause just an inch before exposing all of me to him. "What if I don't want you to keep your hands to yourself all night?"

Just because I'm not ready to have sex with Preston, doesn't mean I don't want him to touch me.

"Deal," he quickly agrees.

A second later and his face is pressed against my sex, lips kissing me softly in an incredibly intimate area. When he tries to lift the material up my stomach, I cover his fist to stop him.

"Can the jersey stay on?" I ask. His dark eyes peek up at me before he nods. His fist releases the material, leaving his head to hold it up high enough to keep it out of the way, while his hands slide underneath, up over my hips, my waist, and ribs, before reaching their destination—my bare breasts.

Preston cups them and groans against my flesh before squeezing them and flicking the pointed tip of his tongue over the bundle of nerves at the apex of my sex.

"Oh my god!" I cry out at the warm, wet sensation, my fingers sinking into his soft hair.

One of his palms releases my breast to lift my right leg, draping it over his shoulder. The move opens me to him, allowing his tongue access to every sensitive inch. His palm moves around to squeeze a handful of my ass while the other holds my breast, his thumb brushing my nipple.

"God, yes," I moan as he tastes me frantically, furiously, as if he can't get enough. Preston's tongue dips and swirls, making me crazy. The pressure in my core builds and builds until it explodes within me, setting off fireworks behind my closed eyes, and tremors through my entire body.

When the pleasurable waves begin to ebb, I realize that Preston's hands tightly gripping my waist are all that's keeping me from falling on my ass.

Pressing a chaste kiss to my mound, he gets to his feet, lifting me off mine to carry me to bed.

Once I'm lying down, my head on the pillow, he joins me. Spreading my thighs apart, he lies down flat on his stomach between them, looks up at me, and says, "I lied. I need more than one taste. Call a timeout if you want me to stop."

My lust hazed mind can't even process his comment before his head disappears underneath his jersey, and he begins devouring me yet again.

24

Preston

I spent a record-breaking amount of time with my face buried between Elle's thighs last night. My hands roamed her sexy body the whole time underneath the jersey that's hiding her from my sight.

While I love seeing her in nothing but my jersey, she insisted on keeping the damn thing on all night. She didn't seem to mind my hands or mouth, which makes me think she's self-conscious. I hate that she feels the need to hide even an inch of her skin from me.

More than that, I hate that Riley has most likely seen all of her; that he's touched her, kissed her, done all the things I want to do but haven't yet.

God, I want her.

But we both agreed no sex yet. That's probably for the

best, since, as turned on as I get whenever I'm near Elle, I know I wouldn't last five seconds inside of her.

Which is why I made last night all about Elle and her pleasure. My dick has waited years. It can wait a few more days or weeks.

After the finals are over, when I know that she's getting over Riley and we're not together for any ulterior reasons, I may be ready to cross that final line with Elle. Until then, I don't mind suffering as long as she isn't.

I need to prove to her that wanting to be with her doesn't have anything to do with that prick. I want her because she's gorgeous and sweet and sexy as hell.

Those thoughts, along with all the others in my head, disappear as soon as I feel Elle's lips press to my bare pec. Her fingernails glide through my chest hair, then down the length of my happy trail before moving back up. Lying flat on my back and shirtless, my abs tighten in response, while another part of me swells in anticipation.

"Morning," Elle says with her body curled up on her side in the crook of my arm.

"Morning. How did you sleep?"

"Like the dead. Did I even say goodnight?"

Chuckling while trying to ignore the persistent ache in my lower body, I tell her, "The last thing you said to me was, *"Oh crap! My toes are cramping but don't you dare stop...don't...yes! Yes! OH YESSS!"*

Her palm playfully slaps my belly, sending a jolt of need lower and making me groan.

Elle lifts her tousled blonde head to look at my face. "I didn't hit you that hard."

"No, I know," I assure her. "But something is so hard it's about to burst."

"Oh. I would be happy to help you with that." Her fingernails circle my belly button, then slide lower at the same time her damp tongue flicks over my nipple. "Your next game is still thirty-six hours away..."

Game? What game? My brain can't comprehend anything right now except needing Elle's mouth and hands on me.

"Preston?" she eases her small hand underneath the waistband of my jeans that I slept in to keep things from going too far. The denim was an extra layer of clothing to use as a barrier. If I had slept next to Elle in just my underwear, knowing she wasn't wearing any panties underneath my jersey, it would've been too much temptation.

But this isn't sex. It's close, but not the same. And Elle offered...

Reaching down, I pop the button and lower my zipper. "Make it stop hurting, cupcake."

"Yes, sir," Elle replies and then she's moving. Straddling my lower legs, she tugs my open pants down my thighs, then my boxer briefs that have an embarrassing damp spot on the front. My erection pops up between us, demanding all of her attention.

And Elle obliges. She wraps her small fingers around the base to hold it still, then leans forward to lick it like a lollipop. She teases up and down my length until I'm nice and wet, and so close to coming I'm shaking all over. That's when she glances up at me, her green eyes holding mine as she opens her mouth nice and wide to welcome me inside.

"Fuck!" I shout to the ceiling, my neck muscles tightening as I savor the slide of her hot tongue, her muffled moans, and sweet, blessed suction. My fists clutch at the bedding, refusing to touch Elle's head for fear she'll stop.

Years. I haven't been inside a woman's mouth in years.

It's even better than I remember. Or maybe that's just Elle.

I'm in a tortured state of agony trying to make it last as her head bobs faster, as she sucks me harder, deeper. So deep, I feel the back of her throat, the walls constricting around my shaft, and I. Am. Dead.

"Wow," I mutter once I'm able to speak the English language again. "Wow." I scrub my palms over my face that feels numb. My entire body is still buzzing.

"Do you regret it already?" Elle ask from where she's moved back beside me.

Removing my hands, I look at her like she's crazy. "What? Why would I ever regret that?"

"If you don't win tomorrow…"

"I'm not going to blame you if we don't win tomorrow," I assure her. Wrapping an arm around her back, I drag her closer to me. "I needed that. More than I realized."

"Good."

We both lay there in silence, Elle's head resting on my chest, her fingernails lightly drawing circles on my stomach while my palm slides up and down her spine, between the numbers of my jersey.

"What are your plans for the day?" I finally ask her.

"I don't have plans. What are yours?" she asks.

"I have practice…" I glance over my shoulder at the hotel alarm clock's glowing red numbers. "Shit. Soon. It shouldn't be a long one, just mostly yelling at us for all our mistakes last night. After that, would you want to come over to the house with me? I could bring you back to the hotel tonight if you don't want to stay over."

"Okay. But I think I would like to stay over, if that's all right with you and Maya."

"Of course it is. She helped me clean the whole place just in case you stopped by."

Lifting her head to see my face, she asks with a smile, "You cleaned for me? That's so sweet." And it earns me a kiss. "And definitely wasn't to make anyone jealous."

"Have you heard from him since the other night?" I can't help but ask.

"Yes."

"Why?"

Elle rolls her eyes and lays her head back down on my chest. "Why do you think?"

"I meant why haven't you blocked him and be done with him?"

"I-I don't know," she stammers. "Seeing him miserable, or at least pretending to be miserable, makes me kind of happy."

"You aren't thinking about taking him back?"

"God, no! And could we please try not to talk about him anymore?"

"Sorry. I just wish he would stop bothering you."

What I mean is that if Riley stopped contacting her, then it might be easier for her to move on, to get over him, and fully be with me.

Kissing the top of her head, I tell her, "I should get dressed and get going."

Slipping my arm free and climbing out of bed with Elle

there is harder than it should be, but I make it to my feet. After fixing my pants, I look for my shirt and hoodie while Elle sits up in the pile of sheets, hair messy, lips pink and swollen, looking so sexy it hurts.

"I'll text you when practice is over and then come pick you up. I left my car at the arena last night while I walked around the city."

"I'll be ready," she agrees.

Once my shirt, hoodie, shoes, and socks are on, I lean over the bed to give her a kiss goodbye. "See you soon."

When I start to pull away, Elle grabs my hand to stop me from walking away. "Thank you for last night. For tracking me down."

"Thank you for letting me in." I lean down to give her another kiss, and while I'm distracted, she strikes. Her quick fingers fish her panties from the front pocket of my jeans.

"Got them!" she announces proudly, waving the Bobcats thong like a flag. "You did promise to give them back."

"Fine. Just don't wear them tomorrow night. Or any panties. That'll be my good luck," I tell her with a wink, before I make myself walk out the door.

25

Elle

As soon as Preston leaves, I hop up to take a shower, then pack my things so I'll be ready when he finishes up with practice.

Last night was…I don't even have the words to describe it. But I decide to try around noon when I know Audrey will be taking her lunch break.

"Beauty Boutique," she says when she answers the salon phone.

"Hi!"

"Hi yourself! You want to tell me why I got ten messages last night from Maya, Preston's sister, just as I assured you she was, asking me the name of your hotel?"

"It's a long story." I flop down on the foot of the bed with a sigh.

"And I've got an hour to listen."

"You have to eat."

"I can hold the phone on my shoulder and eat my chicken salad sandwich just fine."

I fill her in on the parts of the story that I can tell without giving away Maya's secret. When I'm done, Audrey says, "So, you freaked out about catching feelings, left the game, and refused to tell the poor man where you were?"

"It was stupid, I know! But I didn't think Preston felt the same way I did, that this…thing between us is real. Being around him, pretending it was all fake in public, it would've been too hard."

"You were trying to protect your heart by ending things with him?"

Swallowing around the lump in my throat, I admit the truth to her and myself. "Yes."

"Did he figure out which room you were in? I didn't want to text you and ask in case it was supposed to be a good surprise."

"Yes, he found my room. The clerk and manager told him since they recognized him."

"Of course they did."

"We talked at the door and then I let him in, and he stayed the night."

"Now we're finally getting to the good stuff! Give it to me."

Getting to my feet, I pace around the small space while remembering every second. "We did some things to each other and cuddled. It was nice."

"Multiple orgasms nice?" she asks.

My feet freeze. "How in the world did you know that?"

"Your voice is peppier than usual. You sound like you had a very good night."

"I did."

"And? How many?"

Biting my bottom lip, I tell her . "Several."

"Several? As in more than two?"

"Yes."

"Holy shit! Go Preston!" she yells through the phone, causing me to pull it away from my ear. "The woolly mammoth has some moves."

"Oh my god," I mutter. "I'm hanging up now."

"Wait! What happens next?" she asks in a rush.

"Oh, well Preston had to go to practice this morning, then he's going to pick me up so we can spend the day and the next few nights at his house."

"Yay! Text me details. I want to know everything!"

"I'll try," I agree. "Thank you so much for squeezing in all my clients this week."

"Girl, you are living the dream, caught in a love triangle with two hot hockey players. As long as you give me details so I can live vicariously through you, we're totally even."

"Okay then," I agree with a smile she can't see. "Talk to you soon!"

Preston

Practice was brutal, physically, and emotionally, since Coach Ramsey ripped us all a new one about letting up when the stakes are highest.

When it's finally over, and I've grabbed a quick shower, I text Elle to let her know I'm on my way finally, and then I call Maya while I walk to my SUV.

"Hey! I take it you either found Elle or spent the night in the locker room?"

"I found her. We're good." Better than good. We're fucking amazing.

"That's a huge relief. I'm so glad I didn't mess everything up by running my mouth."

"Me too," I agree. "So, the reason I'm calling is that I'm about to pick up Elle from her hotel, and then we're coming to the house. She's probably going to stay the night."

"Good! I'll start making sleepover arrangements."

"You don't have to leave…"

"Finley will love spending time with Joey, and his moms are cool. They'll probably let me crash in their spare room in exchange for some season tickets."

Fuck.

"I'll see what I can do for next season," I agree. What I don't tell my sister is that I may not be playing for the Warhawks in the fall. Maya would just freak out about shit neither of us can control, so there's no point in stressing her out until I know for sure if I'll have to relocate over the summer.

"Thanks, Maya. See you in a little while," I tell her, knowing that my sister will lurk around all afternoon to talk to Elle before her and Finley head out later tonight.

When I pull up to the hotel, Elle is standing outside on the sidewalk next to her luggage. Wearing a pair of snug, curve hugging white jeans, and a frilly sleeveless shirt with red and white swirls, she looks like an actual, edible cupcake. And I like that she looks so eager to see me.

"Hey," I say when I put the SUV in park and climb out. "You didn't have to wait down here on the curb. I would've parked and come up to get you."

"It's fine. I know how tough parking can be in D.C. And I guess I was a little excited."

"Glad to hear it." I give her a quick kiss, hopefully fast enough for any cameras to catch, then nod my head to the passenger seat. "Hop in while I load up."

As soon as we hit the highway, I reach over and grab Elle's hand.

"How was practice?" she asks.

"Awful. All the coaches were pissed off. Coach Ramsey called us a bunch of two-toed sloths who better wake the fuck up before tomorrow night's game."

"Harsh," she replies with a grin. "You'll get them next time. Maybe the Warhawks were a little cocky and got too slack last night."

"That's exactly what happened," I agree. "These young guys don't realize that you can't ever let up. That's when your opponent will be waiting to swoop in, score, and kick your ass."

"You should give your teammates that speech. Wake them up. I'm sure they would appreciate your experience."

Chuckling, I tell her, "They would probably ignore anything I say."

"I bet they don't ignore your criticism during practice. Those men look up to you as a veteran. Not many players win the championship their rookie year."

"Guess not," I agree. "I lucked up and landed on a damn good team my first year coming out of the minors."

"How long had it been since Wisconsin had won the championship before you got there?"

Thinking back, I tell her, "I think it was twelve or so years."

"Maybe they won because of you joining the team that year."

"I was a rookie. I barely played."

"You're too humble, Preston. You're a great player and a crucial part of the Warhawks."

"Thanks, cupcake." I glance over at her for a second and give her hand a squeeze.

When her cheeks flush, I can't help but ask, "What are you thinking about?"

"Nothing."

"Liar. Tell me."

"Fine. When you called me cupcake it just reminded me of last night, when you asked to taste me."

"Oh."

"The day we met, you said you would never be tempted for a taste."

"I lied. I didn't want to be tempted by any woman, especially not one who had a history with Riley," I explain to her. "But I was pretty much a goner as soon as I saw you pleading with security to meet me."

"It was a stupid idea," Elle says. "I don't regret it, though."

"Good. I don't either," I tell her with a smile.

26

Elle

Preston's house is adorable, which I tell him.

"It's just a house," he mutters, as if he can't see its charm.

The one-story ranch is surrounded with warm, colorful flowers decorating the front yard and greenery crawling over the tall, wooden privacy fence in the back, no doubt to keep Finley safe. Some of his taller toys can be seen from the drive-away—a treehouse, along with a swing set. It's not what I would've expected for a bachelor. Preston's not really a typical bachelor living alone, though. His sister and nephew live with him, like they've made their own close-knit family with the three of them.

It's a grown-up home for a man who works hard to provide for and take care of the people he loves.

As Preston pulls the SUV into the two-car garage next to a

217

sedan, I realize that he's never mentioned his mother or father. Not that he told me about Maya either before I met her. His parents, however, weren't at the game last night. I don't even know where he's from.

"Do you see your parents often? You've never talked about them, and they weren't at the game," I remark as he puts the SUV in park.

"Our parents are dead to me."

"Dead to you?" I repeat, thinking that sounds a bit harsh for the two people who raised him.

Sighing, he stabs his fingers through his short hair while staring at the garage wall in front of us. "Our father is a strict asshole, and while our mom is a nice woman, she does whatever my father tells her to do. Maya and I grew up going to a Catholic school, church when the doors were open, the whole nine yards because our father is devout. So, while we didn't expect them to throw a party or anything when Maya told them she was pregnant, we thought they would at least be supportive since she was so stressed out about being a teenage mother. I went home with her to tell them, for moral support. Their reaction was even worse than I expected."

"What do you mean?" I ask.

"When Maya told them she was pregnant, our father flipped out. He told her that if she didn't marry the man responsible fast, before anyone found out she was knocked up, she wasn't welcome in his home, and they wouldn't keep paying her college tuition."

"Wow."

"Mom didn't say a word. She just acted like our father's demands were perfectly normal. I knew Riley would never agree to marriage. And even if he would have, Maya was so young. How our father treated Maya, like one simple mistake had ruined her, wasn't right. I told him so. We nearly got into a fist fight before Maya ran out sobbing. After that, I convinced her to move in with me. It was a small, shitty apartment in Raleigh at the time. Christian…Riley had just moved out, so she stayed with me, and I worked part time roofing houses to support us when I wasn't playing hockey."

Wow. Not only were Preston and Christian friends, but they were also roommates, which means they were probably really close.

"I tried to get Maya to keep taking classes at State, but she couldn't. She was a wreck those first few months. Thankfully, a few weeks before Finley was due, I got called up to the pros. It was such a fucking relief, like our prayers had finally been answered. I bought our first house just outside Milwaukee. We lived there for two years until I was traded. Pulling up roots wasn't so bad, since Finley was only two, but now…" he trails off, but I know exactly what he was going to say.

"Now leaving the D.C. area would be tough on him since he goes to preschool," I finished for him.

Preston nods when he faces me again. "He's a little shy, and he's just getting used to his teachers and starting to make friends. It would suck to have to make him move again."

"So that's why you're trying to get a contract extension with the Warhawks?"

"Yes. I'd give anything for them to keep me on."

"You helped get them to the championships, could very well help them win the trophy this year. The Warhawks would be fools to let you go."

"Here's hoping. So far, my agent hasn't heard shit from them about renewing."

"Maybe they're just waiting to see how the season ends so they know how much they'll have to pay you to keep you."

"Guess we'll find out soon enough."

"So, you haven't spoken to your parents since Maya was pregnant?"

He shakes his head. "Our mom still reaches out to me by text on birthdays and holidays. Maybe I should block her number, avoid the trauma that goes along with every occasion when she contacts me but not Maya. It's hard on my sister. She feels guilty for turning me against them, but I could never forgive them for that shit, though. I don't want Finley around that judgmental asshole, either. Knowing my father, he would call him a bastard in front of him, I would kill him for it, and then I would end up in jail."

"You're right. It's best not to go down that road," I tell him.

Taking a deep breath, he looks over and asks me, "What about you? Are you close to your parents? You mentioned that they weren't happy about you cutting your dolls' hair or your own."

"You remembered that?" I ask in surprise, barely able to recall telling him that in our conversation at the salon. "My parents are great. They still live in our hometown of Eden. It's a rural place about an hour away from Greensboro. We try to see each other once a month since they have their own bakery to run."

"And you have the salon to run."

"Right. Everyone is busy. I'm hoping they'll sell the bakery soon. They're getting too old for all that hassle."

"Yeah, owning your own business must be a lot of work."

"It is, but it's worth it to be your own boss," I agree.

"I don't doubt it," Preston replies. His eyes then flicker

toward the door leading into the house from the garage. "Well, are you ready to meet the boss of my house? I know Maya has probably been peeking out the windows, waiting for us to come inside so she can grill you."

"I like your sister. She seems nice. Hopefully, this meeting goes better than our first."

Unbuckling my seatbelt, I reach for the door when Preston grabs my hand. "I don't want you to think you're stranded out here if you decide to run again. Not that I want you to run, but if that's what you want, I'll take you back to your hotel or the airport or wherever you want to go."

"I know. Thank you." I lean over to give him a quick peck on the cheek, then we both get out of the SUV, Preston hauling my luggage up to the interior door, then through it. As he predicted, his sister is waiting for us in the kitchen. Wearing a red Warhawks hoodie and black leggings with her raven hair in a ponytail, she looks more like a college coed than a mother.

"Hi there! I was wondering how long you two were going to sit out in the car." She throws her arms around me, giving me a big hug as if we're friends or family who have known each other for years.

"Told you," Preston mutters. "Elle, you remember Maya. Maya, be nice."

"I'm always nice," she huffs, bracing her hands on her hips. "And I'm so glad that you two worked things out. I've never seen Preston so out of sorts like he was last night. He bit my head off, but I totally deserved it."

"You bit your sister's head off?" I ask him. "Why? Because I left the arena?"

"You heard her," he says. "She admits that she deserved it by overwhelming you."

"I'm used to his temper tantrums," Maya says with a roll of her chocolate brown eyes, so similar to her brother's. "So, come in and get comfortable. Then I want you to tell me *everything* about yourself."

"Maya," Preston mutters in warning.

"What? I'm curious about the woman who made my grumpy brother break his own rules after years and years of refusing to date."

"I think you know everything there is to know about me," I assure her as I follow her to the living room.

"I'll put your luggage in one of the guest rooms," Preston calls out from the hallway. "But don't think that means I don't want you in my bed, cupcake."

"Cupcake," Maya repeats with a chuckle as she flops down on the navy-blue sectional. "He's ridiculous."

"Right, because he doesn't eat sweets."

"Who doesn't eat sweets?"

"I thought Preston said he doesn't like them."

"Oh, honey. That man can't stop once he starts in on the sweets. He tries to avoid them because if he's in for one cupcake, he won't stop until he's gobbled down half a dozen."

Well, now I guess I feel a little better about the term of endearment.

27

Preston

I've barely been home long enough to show Elle around when my phone buzzes in my pocket.

Pulling it out, I see Tommy's name on the screen.

"Hey, ah, my agent is calling," I tell her. "Do you mind?"

"No, of course not. Answer it!" Elle says encouragingly.

When I still hesitate, Maya says, "Take your call, Pres. I'll keep Elle company."

Elle nods her head in agreement, so I tell her, "I'll make it quick" before heading out the front door.

"Hey, Tommy. What's up?"

"Good news," he says.

"What?"

"I have an offer with your name on it. You need to sign ASAP, today if possible."

He's crazy if he thinks I'm going to make a decision this huge in a matter of hours.

"Which team?"

"The Grizzlies."

"California?" I exclaim, then remember why I'm talking to him outside, to keep Maya from overhearing. "I can't go to California. That's literally on the other side of the country!"

"Beggars can't be choosers," Tommy replies. "I suggest you sign this baby now, tonight, before shit goes sideways in the next championship game."

"I'm not…I hope I won't get ejected from any game, but I can't sign tonight. I need some time to think."

"If you don't sign with the Grizzlies then the only hockey you'll be playing is a pick-up game with old men on a frozen lake."

"So, you still haven't heard anything from the Warhawks?"

"Not a peep. And I don't expect to either. If they wanted to keep you, they would've already made an offer."

"Right. Fuck."

"So, it's Cali or bust, my man. Well, there has been some chatter from one another team."

"Which team?"

"The only one who can't exactly let it get out that they want a player from the team about to beat them out for the championship trophy."

"The Bobcats want me?" I say in disbelief.

"Don't worry. I've made it clear that you would *never* play on the same team as Riley. He's a lock with them for at least three more years since he's already got his eight-year contract on their books. Grizzlies are offering significantly more money than you would get out of the Bobcats, anyway."

Playing in Greensboro while it has serious downfalls, like having to put up with Christian Riley's sorry ass every damn day, also has it perks. At least one. Elle. But can I afford to take a pay cut? Not if I have to find another place to live while keeping up this house if Maya and Finley stay here.

Besides, Elle and I just met. We barely know each other. Moving just to be near her and taking a slash in my pay would be crazy long-term.

"So, it's looking like I'm going to have to move to California."

"That's what I thought. I'll send you the contract tonight. Think fast and don't tell anyone about it until the ink is dry. They could change their minds if you drag your feet."

"I'll read over it and give you an answer as soon as I can," I assure him. "But I doubt if it'll be before the end of the week."

Tommy makes a groan of annoyance. "The sooner the better, Preston. I don't think I can stress that enough. One mistake in the finals and you can kiss this opportunity goodbye."

"Yeah. I understand," I reply.

I know he's right. I would be a fool not to sign an offer tonight when my options are so limited. But leaving Maya and Finley in D.C., being so far from Elle, I don't want to think about either of those things right now.

Elle

"So, I'm glad things aren't weird between us, after last night when we met and because of Christian," I tell Maya while Preston has stepped outside to talk to his agent.

"Of course not. I don't waste my time on thinking about that jerk anymore."

"Were you together long?" I ask.

"We only dated a few times. Nothing serious, but I thought I was special."

"I know the feeling. He apparently has that effect on women."

"Yeah, and I found out the hard way. His first reaction to me telling him I was pregnant was to ask if I had been screwing around with any frat boys on campus." She rolls her eyes. "He was my first. The only guy I've ever been with."

"Ever?" I repeat, since it sounds like she means even now he's the only one.

"Dating as a single mother isn't easy. Or maybe I'm just too scared to put myself out there again and get hurt."

"I'm sorry he hurt you, and that you have to raise Finley without his support."

"It's fine. Preston is twice the man Christian is. My brother is the only person I've ever been able to count on."

"He's a good man. I'm really glad that I met him, even if it was under unusual circumstances."

"I'm glad you two met. It's nice to have a female to talk to around here. I hang out with some of the other moms at Finley's preschool sometimes, mostly at kids' birthday parties or school events, but they're nothing like me. They're older with husbands and careers, while I don't have either. I don't have anything in common with them except a son, and I think they look down on me for being single. As if only married couples should have the right to have children. Finley is my entire world. I wouldn't change a thing about my life, despite what those snobs all think."

"That sounds awful. Maybe they're just jealous of you."

"Yeah, right," she says with a soft laugh.

"Seriously, Maya. You're young and beautiful without any restraints, other than raising a son. You don't have to go to a job you hate, or deal with marital issues, cheating husbands, or whatever else. You're lucky enough to have a sweet boy, while they're all probably raising hellions."

"Thanks, Elle. I never really thought about it that way. I shouldn't envy them, not when they're probably not happy. I am, though."

"That's good."

"I get lonely sometimes, but I'm always happy to get out of bed every morning to spend as much time as possible with my amazing son and my super talented brother."

"That's all that really matters," I agree with a smile.

"Soo," she drawls. "What's going to happen with you and Preston after the last championship game?"

Shrugging, I tell her the truth. "I don't know yet. Preston is still waiting to hear about whether his contract will be extended. That's probably what he's talking to his agent about now, so until he knows for sure…"

Maya holds up her palm to stop me. "Wait, what? Are you saying that Preston's contract with the Warhawks is in limbo?"

Oh crap.

"You…you didn't know he hasn't received a contract extension yet? Shit. I'm so sorry, Maya. I shouldn't have mentioned that. Please don't tell him. He'll be furious."

"Why didn't he tell me?" she huffs. "This affects my life too!"

"I'm sure there's a good reason. He probably didn't want to worry you until he knew for sure if he has to relocate."

"Preston!" Maya jumps up from the sofa and yells so loudly I wince but follow her.

Apparently, she was so loud he could even hear her from outside because Preston appears in the doorway a moment later, his phone still in his hand, looking back and forth between us with concern. "What's wrong?"

"I'm so, so sorry. I didn't know that Maya didn't know," I tell him.

"Didn't know what?" he asks, eyes skimming from me to his sister.

"We might be *moving*? How could you keep this from me?" Maya exclaims, hands braced on her hips.

Preston throws his head back and curses at the ceiling before responding to his furious sister. "I didn't want you to stress. But I'm starting to realize that secrets make everything ten times worse. I should've told you. I know that." He pauses for a long moment, looking toward the door, then back to his sister. "Everything is still up in the air right now. I have to go to the team that wants me. As soon as I have more information, I'll share it with you."

"You better!"

"But just because I may have to move doesn't mean you and Finley have to, you know. You could both stay here in the house. I could come visit as often as possible."

Scoffing, she says, "I don't want to have to decide between uprooting my son or losing my brother!"

"You're not going to lose me."

Maya paces away from the foyer, then right back. "Do you…do you not want us to move with you this time?"

"What? Of course, I want you and Finley to go wherever I go, but I can't expect you to leave this place, not when Finley's enjoying school and making friends."

Maya's eyes glisten when she says, "You know he would be devastated if you left us."

I feel like I'm intruding on what should've been a private conversation. Since I'm still in between the two, I press my back to the wall to try to disappear as much as possible.

"You think I don't know that? Fu…fudge," he growls, catching himself before the f-bomb even though Finley's at school. "None of this is what I wanted, but it's out of my control! I hate it as much as you do."

"When? When will you know?" Maya asks, folding her arms over her chest.

"Soon, hopefully," he tells her. "Tommy says I would be stupid not to accept an offer in case I screw up in a game and the team changes their minds."

"How…why…why can't you stay in D.C. with the Warhawks?" she asks.

"Because they don't want to keep me on the team. I don't get along great with my teammates or the coaches. They would rather pass and move on from me."

"Then they're a bunch of freaking jerks!"

"Yes, they are."

"We've only been here for three years. I thought…" She shakes her head and says, "I know things change often in the pros, but I thought we would stay a little longer."

"I know. I did too. I'm sorry."

"And I'm sorry for opening this can of worms," I whisper to them. "Should I go?"

"No," they both respond when they turn to toward me. Maya shakes her head and says, "It's not your fault my brother likes to keep secrets, to put all the burden on himself instead of letting others share it."

"She's right," Preston says, reaching for my hand and pressing a kiss to the top of it, as if letting me know we're okay. "It's for the best that Maya's all caught up with where things stand. Now we can figure it out together."

I'm not sure if I'm included in the together, and I don't ask.

As much as it sucks, waiting and seeing what happens between me and Preston after the finals are over is all I feel like I can do at the moment, too.

28

Preston

When Maya brings Finley home from preschool, he's a ball of energy like usual. Recognizing Elle from the few minutes she was at last night's game, he instantly grabbed her hand to pull her along to see all his cool toys in his room and then out to the backyard.

She seems most impressed with the treehouse.

"You built this? Seriously?" Elle asks again as the two of us huddle up inside the small fort that's five feet off the ground. There are three steps built into the tree as well as a rope in the middle of the floor that Finley can climb to get in or out.

"I'm not just an amazing hockey player," I tell her, placing a quick kiss on her cheek while Finley's gone to get us juice boxes and goldfish so we can have a picnic.

"What else are you good at?" she asks. "Well, besides the things that I have already experienced."

231

Rubbing my scruffy chin, I consider her question, trying not to think about the things she and I experienced last night and this morning. "I'm a decent cook."

"Yeah?"

"I'll show you tonight. We're having Tuscan ravioli with Arugula salad and chocolate filled cannoli."

Her blonde brow shoots up. "Wow. I'm already impressed."

"Okay, so the cannoli may be store bought this time since I've been busy, but I can make it."

"I can't wait to try it all."

"Uncle Pres!" Finley calls from below us when he returns with the goods. I reach down to grab the Warhawk lunch box from him, and it suddenly hits me just how devastated the little guy will be when I'm playing for a different team. He loves the Warhawks so damn much.

Clearing my throat, I reach my other arm down to pull him up through the hole in the floor where the rope hangs from. "Thanks for the snacks, buddy."

"Welcome," he replies proudly before he sits down near us and begins laying out a juice and snack pack for Elle, then me, then himself.

"This looks so delicious," Elle says as she jabs her tiny white straw into her box and sips it before popping a cheddar cracker into her mouth. "Wow, the apple juice and the goldfish taste great, Finley," Elle tells him before she takes her second and final sip from the juice. "Thank you so much. I was starving after Uncle Preston told me about his dinner plans."

"You're welcome, Ellie," he says triumphantly, flashing her a big grin. "I'm glad you came to visit us."

Elle completely freezes at his remark, as if he just told her the secret to curing cancer or some other miraculous shit.

I nudge her gently with my elbow to her side. "What's up?"

"Nothing," she whispers to me. "He just...he gave me a nickname."

"Yeah, he likes you," I tell her quietly. And it's true. Elle is great with the little guy, a natural, making me certain that she'll be a great mother someday.

God. I shouldn't be thinking shit like that, not when it's becoming more and more obvious that the two of us won't have a future together.

A move to the West Coast would mean juggling my time between traveling for games, practices, and seeing Maya and Finley as often as I can. That won't leave me much time for a relationship with Elle.

She won't marry me or have my kids. She'll be a mother to some other man's spawn while I'm alone and miserable in California.

I should tell her and Maya about the offer from the Grizzlies, but I haven't even laid eyes on the contract yet. It's still just one possibility. Maybe I'll get more offers if I have a great game tomorrow night or if the Warhawks win the championship trophy.

Elle

"Are you sure you don't need my help?" I ask Preston and Maya as they work on preparing dinner and Finley huddles down in his room to do his reading for the night.

"Heck no," Preston replies. "Just sit down and relax. You're our guest."

"We don't get many guests, so we have to try to impress you," Maya says, flashing me a grin over her shoulder.

"Trust me, I am already impressed. My dinners typically consist of takeout."

"That is a shame," Preston says with a shake of his head while making the ravioli.

Seeing Preston in the kitchen is almost as sexy as seeing him on the ice. He cooks while Maya makes the salad and sets the table, the two moving around the kitchen with an ease of people who have lived together for years. They've obviously made a lot of dinners together, just the two of them because their parents are apparently assholes.

And Christian may or may not know he's a father. Either way, he's not here to help out, to spend time with his adorable son who also calls me Ellie.

When dinner is ready and we sit down to eat, Finley talks a mile a minute between each of his bites, telling us about what he did at school, all the funny things his friend Joey said and did. The way he speaks and laughs with such an easy-going personality reminds me so much of his father that it's scary. The only difference is that Finley was shy at first, but the longer I'm here, the more he seems to relax.

I still can't believe that Christian wouldn't step up and be a father if he knew about him. He's a good man. Or at least I thought he was, despite his philandering ways.

But maybe I'm wrong. Maybe it's Preston who is the good man, and I was with Christian for all the wrong reasons.

All I know is that as soon as dinner is over, I'm going to block Christian's number in my phone once and for all.

Maya interrupts Finley's play-by-play of his day, currently describing the lineup order for the entire class, by asking him, "Would you like to have a sleepover tonight with Joey?"

The boy's brown eyes widen. "Tonight? But it's a school night, Mom."

"Yes, sweetie. I know it's a school night. And usually, we don't do sleepovers except on Fridays or Saturdays, but Joey's moms have made an exception. They even invited me to stay over too."

He frowns and says, "Oh man. It won't be as much fun if you're there!"

Maya rolls her eyes and then boops the tip of his nose with her finger. "Too bad, buddy. I'm coming too, and it's going to be awesome."

Later that night, I finally do what I should've done the day he dumped me—I block Christian's number, closing the book on him for good.

Even though I haven't known Preston for very long, everything already feels different with him. Like he wants more from me than sex. He's not rushing me, giving me as much time as I need to move on from the destruction of my heart and trust issues that Christian left behind.

After Finley and Maya leave, Preston and I are curled up on the sofa watching cooking shows.

I go up on my knees to kiss his cheek and then his lips when he turns his head to me.

"You know I don't expect anything tonight, right? Just because Maya and Finley aren't here..." Preston tells me.

"I know you don't expect anything. That's not why..." I trail off as I try to figure out how to explain it. "I'm ready, Preston. His number has been permanently blocked. I know that's not much proof, but in five months I never felt the way I feel for you after only seven days. And while I know you have rules about sex before a game..."

I don't get to finish my thought. Preston scoops me up and is then striding through the house toward his bedroom.

Winding my arms around his neck, I ask, "Is this a yes?"

"It's a hell yes, cupcake."

Finally!

But once he lays me down in the center of his giant, king-sized bed, Preston's face falls as if he's having second thoughts.

"What's wrong?" I ask him, sitting up on my elbows.

"I was just thinking that this is still so new with us, and the future is uncertain."

"I know that, Preston. And while I don't love the idea of the unknown, I just want to enjoy this time with you for however long I can." When he still doesn't look convinced, I cup the side of his fuzzy face and tell him, "Don't worry. You're not taking advantage of me. I won't think it's more than it is between us just because we have sex."

"I want it to be more, though," he says. And I hear everything he doesn't say as well. *But it's unlikely to become more, given that we live so far away from each other.* "And I want to see all of you this time."

"All of me?"

"Last night you kept on my jersey."

"Oh. Right." He's asking me to get completely naked. And while I'm nervous that seeing every little inch of my imperfect body will disappoint him, I still sit up to whip my shirt over my head because I don't want any barriers between us.

"God bless America," Preston says. Pausing the undoing of his pants, his eyes linger on my breasts for a long moment before he crawls up on the bed. When he's on his hands and knees above me, he runs one finger down the center of my cleavage. "I could spend the entire night with these beauties."

Lowering his head, his tongue follows the same path as his finger. The scruff on his cheeks grazing my breasts through the red lace bra makes all the insecurities disappear, along with the ability to hold myself up. I lie flat on the mattress again, and Preston's tongue follows. He groans as he flicks it back and forth between the mounds. Then his mouth is covering my entire nipple through the lace, warming it with his breath, lavishing the hard point with an open-mouthed kiss that ends with a gentle tug between his teeth.

A jolt of desire shoots straight to my core. Needing to feel his mouth on my bare flesh, I tug both cups down, tucking the fabric under the weight of my heavy breasts.

"Oh yeah. All night," Preston says again before he devours my boobs with the same zest as he licked another part of me.

His obsession with a certain part of my body, while flattering, quickly becomes problematic the longer it goes on. I'm wet and aching, without any relief in sight. My pants and panties are still on, and Preston is still fully dressed other than his shoes.

But I don't have to wait long for this amazing man to come

to the rescue. Without removing his mouth from my nipple, his hand lowers to the crotch of my jeans, cupping me possessively.

"*Yesss*," I moan when he applies pressure to that ache, causing my back to arch. His mouth frantically covers more of my breasts now thrust in his face as he rubs me through the denim.

"Give me a few more minutes up here," Preston says, flicking his tongue over my other nipple now. "And I'll spend as much time as you need down here. I want you soaking wet before I get another taste." His hand applies more pressure to my mound. Just thinking about how good it feels when he's "tasting me" down there has me trembling all over with pleasure.

I fly so high I get dizzy for several wonderful seconds. When I come back down, I open my eyes and find Preston moving down my body. His big hands tremble, trying to work the much smaller button and zipper on my jeans. When he gets them undone, he jerks the denim down my legs with a muttered curse, like they're the bane of his existence. Then I'm lying underneath him in just my panties, and a matching bra still tucked underneath my heaving breasts.

"These pretty red panties are drenched," he remarks, rubbing a thick finger over the damp crotch. I'm still so sensitive from my orgasm that I squirm at his touch. "But you're still not ready to take my cock yet."

"Please," I whisper, wanting him, needing him inside of me. Like a little tramp in heat, I shove my panties down my legs and kick them off my ankles. I'm way past having things like modesty.

The way Preston looks at me like I'm precious to him, like

I'm the most beautiful woman in the world, makes all my insecurities disappear.

He doesn't waste any time teasing me. No, he gets right to stroking me with his tongue while simultaneously sliding a finger inside of me, getting me ready for him.

Every moan he pulls out of my mouth has his eyes lifting to mine, watching the pleasure visible on my face. I run my fingers through his hair and whisper his name, a plea for more. I need more of him, all of him. His tongue becomes frantic. He adds another finger, sending me flying so high I never want to come down.

But when I do, I open my eyes and find his face hovering above mine.

"Should I get a condom?" he asks, his voice so deep and rumbly a shiver runs through my entire body.

"Only…only if you want to," I tell him. "I'm on the pill and I used one with…with everyone I've been with. Tested recently and was all clear. Very recently." I don't say Christian's name, but we both know that's who I was referring to.

"I haven't been with anyone in years, and I have never gone bareback."

"So, we could be each other's first?"

"God yes. Even if I won't last five seconds once I get inside of you."

"That's fine." Grinning up at him, I run my fingertips over his broad shoulders and say, "I bet you'll make up for it in the second period after a short intermission."

"Damn right," Preston agrees.

29

Elle

The morning after with Preston isn't the least bit awkward. Yesterday, he was in a hurry to leave for practice, but even then, I never felt like he was rushing off to be free of me, of the consequences of the night (and the morning).

There's no regret, no wondering if Preston is plotting some sort of escape plan on his side of the bed, silently facing me with a sleepy grin and bedhead.

Christian used to tell me he was starving for—just fill in the blank that constantly changed—and could only get said food from a shop or diner on the other side of town. He never once asked me if I was hungry or if I wanted to go with him. It was clear that he was just ready to get away, to flee my bed or his own.

That was usually the worst, having to do the walk of

shame out of his fancy penthouse apartment to make my way back to my little shitty one wearing last night's wrinkled clothes.

"We need food," Preston eventually says, as if he overheard my internal thoughts. But he's not abandoning me—he used the word "we." "What are you in the mood for?"

"I'm not picky," I assure him. "And I could use a shower before I think about leaving this bedroom."

"Same," he agrees, rolling to his back to stretch his thick arms over his head. "I had no idea bareback was so…"

"Messy?"

Chuckling, he turns his face to look at me. "Messy, but in a damn good way. Totally worth it if I'm so sticky down there that I may have to shave my pubes."

I can't help but giggle at his ridiculous TMI comment.

"What are you laughing at?" he asks. "I would be surprised if you can even spread your thighs apart today after the mess I made on them."

"You're not wrong."

Rolling to his side, his big palm smooths its way down my thigh and back up. "I could help you with that if you want."

"Help me spread my legs? Oh, I'm sure you could. My thigh muscles are aching from how long you kept them apart last night."

"My new favorite place in the world is being between your thighs with my face in your tits."

I can't help but voice the concern I had after every round. "You aren't worried about tonight, given how many times you came in the past twenty-four hours?"

"Nope. If anything, I'm much more relaxed, less likely to

get into any fights. Nothing could drag me down today, not even a little shithead whose name rhymes with Miley."

"Good," I say, smiling in relief, hoping Preston doesn't change his mind if the Warhawks lose. "In that case, would you like to join me in the shower?"

"Fuck yes. I'll even let you stand in the warm stream," he offers. Reaching around, he cups my ass cheek, giving it a squeeze. "God, I'm so glad that Maya and Finley had sleepovers last night. There's no way either of us could have been quiet unless we were gagged."

"Agreed. Although, I do feel bad about kicking your family out of their home."

"You didn't kick anyone out. They left voluntarily."

"Same thing."

"No, it's not."

"What about tonight?"

"What about it?" Preston asks, hiking my thigh up over his hip, spreading me open and lining a particular part of my body up with his hard one.

"Do you think we should get a hotel room for privacy?"

"Hmm. That depends."

"Depends on what?"

"If the Warhawks win, I'm going to throw a party."

"A party? You?" I scoff in disbelief.

"Yeah, here at the house. Since it's the weekend, Finley can stay and talk to all the guys for a while."

Mr. Grumpy Antisocial wants to throw a party?

Maybe that was some life-changing sex last night.

"And if the Warhawks lose?" I ask him with a wince.

Swatting gently at my bottom, he says, "That's not going to

happen, so we better get a shower and grab some breakfast because we've got a party to plan."

Preston

When I get to the stadium, I am in a damn fine mood thanks to the amazing night before and my surprise shower blowjob. Elle is enthusiastic about giving head. Or maybe it's just been a while since a woman went down on me. Either way, I could get used to her mouth sucking the life out of me on a daily basis.

I have zero concerns about playing shitty tonight because I blew my load before the game. Several times over.

I'm going to try to put that stupid superstition and the past behind me for good. I'll give it my best on the ice, and however the game ends tonight, I know one thing for certain—I'll be going back to my house, to my bed, with Elle.

I still haven't opened the email on my phone from Tommy with the contract offer from the Grizzlies. It feels like once I read it, it'll be real that I'm moving to the other side of the country. It may as well be the other side of the world for how far I'll be from Elle.

I could ask her to come with me, but that's unlikely since her family, her friends, and her salon are all in or near Greensboro.

Maybe I could suggest that she open up a second salon in

California, like a franchise. I could give her the startup money. It could be great.

Another thought suddenly occurs to me.

Tonight's game could be the last one I ever play in the Warhawks arena if we win it and game five in Greensboro. And isn't that a kick in the nuts?

The city may not be my original hometown, but it's been good to me the past three years. The fans pack the stadium, selling out every game to cheer on the team, even if I'm nobody's favorite player.

I'll miss this place, the familiar house I share every minute with my sister and nephew. I think that's subconsciously the real reason I wanted to celebrate tonight. It's the end of a chapter in my life.

In a few weeks, I'll have to start over somewhere else all over again. And I'll probably have to do it alone.

Whatever happens, I know I'll always cherish these last few days with Elle, playing in the championships, having all the family I need coming out to support me.

While the team is getting dressed in the locker room, I slam my hand against my locker to get everyone's attention. "Listen up!"

All conversations stop. The look on my teammates' faces reminds me of when Finley gets caught sneaking cookies before dinner. It's a mix of guilty and reluctant acceptance of the berating he knows his mom is going to give him.

Damn. Maybe I am a little harsher than I need to be with my critiques if that's automatically what all the guys expect whenever I open my mouth.

"Tonight, after we win, getting one game closer to the

trophy, there's going to be a party at my house. I'll have someone text the address to everyone."

It's so quiet I can hear the announcer testing the audio equipment all the way down the tunnel and out in the arena. *Testing. Testing 1-2-3.*

"That's all," I tell the men when they seem to be holding their breath, waiting for me to finish speaking.

"So…there's a party tonight at your place?" Bryan repeats slowly.

"Yes."

"And we're all invited?" Vincent asks, pointing a finger at his chest, then the rest of the locker room.

"Yes. Bring some friends or significant others if you want. There should be plenty of beer and pizza. Maybe even cake," I add with a grin. "We'll have earned a night of a little junk food, right?"

I left the food and beverages for Maya and Elle to handle. The three of us spent some time straightening up the place earlier. We don't have to worry about any breakable possessions since the house is always kid and giant-clumsy-uncle-proof.

Everyone continues to sit or stand so still and motionless that I feel like I'm in one of those creepy wax museums. "If there are no other questions, then get your asses on the ice for warmups."

Finally, a few shoulders slump, breathing resumes, gaping mouths close.

Still, I'm not even a little surprised when Saul says, "A party at your place sounds cool and all, Pres, but what if we –" That's all he gets out before the guys on either side of him slap both of their palms over his mouth.

"We're winning this game tonight," I assure my teammates. "How do I know? Because this is our fucking year to bring home the championship trophy. Forget the last game. Shit happens. Flush it and get off the pot. Tonight, just play like it's the last game of your life because it very well could be. And we're all a bunch of idiots if we take this opportunity for granted. We're the goddamn Northern Conference champs and we're only two games away from kissing the trophy that we've all dreamed about, the trophy every hockey player in the world dreams about from the moment they lace up their first pair of skates."

"Couldn't have said it better myself," Coach Ramsey agrees when he walks into the center of the locker room. "You heard the man—get your asses out on the ice for warmups, then clinch that W tonight."

He gives me a nod that I return before putting on my gloves and taking my own advice, heading out to the arena.

The first test of my new inner peace comes when the Bobcats skate out of the visitor's tunnel. I remind my temper, my jealousy, that nothing I can do to Christian Riley will change anything. He'll still be a prick until the day he dies, and I'll never forgive him for taking advantage of my little sister and then abandoning her when she needed him most.

After he sent the cash to Maya, I lost it, lost all respect for him for refusing to even talk to her about the pregnancy he caused.

I know it wasn't Elle leaving the arena that caused me to play awful in the last game. I was so damn worried that Riley would see Maya and Finley in the stands and finally start asking questions. Maya isn't on social media, and her and Finley didn't travel for the two away games I got ejected from when playing Riley. Seeing them at game three in D.C. would have been the first time Riley could possibly realize that Maya didn't terminate the pregnancy five years ago.

I waited for him to come up and ask all three periods. But I should've known that the idiot wouldn't even bat an eye because he's so self-centered.

His past with Elle is no different. He doesn't care about her, never did. If he had, he wouldn't have broken her heart. So, all the talk is nothing but him regretting letting her go and unintentionally sending her right into my arms.

If anything, I should be thanking the prick.

30

———

Elle

"Oh my god, I'm so freaking nervous," I tell Maya as the two teams face off for the puck drop.

"Even if the Warhawks lose this one, it's not over," she says cheerfully, giving my knee a comforting pat.

"No. I know. That's not what I mean." Rubbing my sweaty palms on my leggings, I tell her, "I'm worried that I may have jinxed Preston."

"Jinxed him?" she repeats, turning to face me with her brow furrowed. "How could you jinx him?"

"Uh, well, you probably don't want to know this, but Preston has a rule about not...*indulging* before a game."

"Yuck," she mutters, her nose scrunching up. "And let me guess, you think you were solely responsible for him *indulging* during your sleepover?"

"Yes."

"Come on, Elle. Look at him," she says as the Warhawks get possession of the puck, and charge toward the Bobcats' goal. "Preston has an extra pep in his skates. He's practically floating out there. I bet he'll play his best game ever tonight."

"I hope you're right," I tell her. Then, shaking my head to clear the thoughts about last night from it, I say, "Enough about me. We need to get you back out in the dating world."

"I don't know…"

"There must be some decent guys on the Warhawks. I bet Preston could introduce you tonight at the party."

"No. That's not a good idea, considering how the last time ended when he introduced me to a teammate."

"Oh. Right. Well, you're a grown woman. You can choose a man to date all on your own."

"Right," she agrees with a heavy sigh, her eyes locked on a player, not the puck. I don't have to even follow her line of sight to know who she's looking at. She's still not over Christian, even after all the trouble he caused her five years ago.

"Hey, Mom?" Finley asks, tugging on the sleeve of her black Preston Lawrence jersey.

"Yes, sweetie?"

"How does that guy skate so fast?"

Again, I don't have to look to know who the boy is talking about. The fastest man on the ice is always Christian if he's out there.

"Wh-which one?" Maya stammers as if she already knows too.

"The one who keeps stealing the puck from the Warhawks. Number nineteen."

"I don't know, sweetie. Maybe because he doesn't have a soul," Maya replies, then winces.

"Huh?" Finley asks, turning to her with a raised eyebrow.

"I meant, he probably has light soles, you know, in his skates that weigh less than everyone else's."

Finley nods as if that makes perfect sense before his attention returns to the game. "Uncle Preston must have soles like bricks in his skates. He's not very fast, and he barely touches the puck."

Maya and I both laugh at that keen observation.

"Uncle Preston's job isn't to be the fastest, but to be the biggest and toughest, so he can prevent the other team from scoring."

"Oh. Okay."

Leaning around Maya to speak to Finley, I say, "Are you excited about showing the team your house tonight?"

Maya hums and frowns at me. "They might be busy, not able to make it on such short notice."

"All of them?" I ask in confusion.

"Uncle Preston isn't the most…agreeable human to be around," she explains.

"But surely they'll all want to come celebrate a win, right?"

"We'll see," Maya replies. "It's the first period and nobody has scored yet. There's still a lot more game to be played."

"Preston seemed pretty confident the Warhawks would win, despite my own concerns."

"Yes, well, we know that Preston's optimism stems from over-indulging last night and probably this morning, so he may not be thinking clearly."

"True," I agree with a grin.

"This is the slowest game ever," I mutter during the third period, when the scoreboard still sits at a big fat zero for both teams. The goalies have both been hot tonight, stopping every single puck. Well, except for one of the Warhawk's goals that was reviewed and taken away because the player was offsides.

With less than two minutes to go, I dread having to sit on the edge of my seat in overtime for who knows how long before someone freaking scores!

"Mom, I'm sleepy," Finley says into the silence. The rest of the arena must be too, if I can hear him so easily.

"Me too, sweetie. Me too," she agrees around a yawn that causes me to yawn as well.

"When will the game end?"

"When someone finally scores a point that doesn't get taken away," Maya tells him.

"How much longer will that take?"

"I have no clue, sweetie. We could be here quite a while tonight."

"All night? We get to sleep in the arena?"

"No, sweetie. We won't sleep here. We'll stay for the first overtime and then…"

She trails off when there's suddenly a burst of movement on the ice. And it's…

"Preston?" we both say at the same time.

Like Finley pointed out, he rarely touches the puck, usually only doing so to pass it to one of the forwards. But he just stuck out his enormous skate to block a pass from a Bobcats player in the neutral zone to head in the other direction, toward the Warhawks goal.

He looks left and right for someone to pass it to, but his teammates are slow and tired, some even changing up, so he's on his own at the other end of the ice, facing off with the goalie. He picks up speed, dribbling the puck left to right before shooting it…

"Gooooallll!"

The buzzer goes off and the entire stadium erupts. Everyone is on their feet, jumping up and down, myself included. I swear the floor shakes from the excitement.

"He scored!" I exclaim as Maya and I stop jumping long enough to hug each other.

Preston's teammates surround him, hugging him as well.

With less than a minute to go in the third period, all the Warhawks have to do is keep the Bobcats from scoring.

Everyone starts chanting, "Warhawks! Warhawks!" for the entire sixty seconds after the puck drop until the final buzzer.

"Oh my god! Oh my god! They won! They freaking won!" I shout. "I didn't jinx him!"

"Told you!" Maya says with a smug grin. "You're Preston's lucky charm!"

"He is definitely getting lucky tonight!" I say before slapping my palm over my mouth. "I meant, with the game and party, he's so lucky tonight."

Maya leans over to whisper, "Nice save."

"Almost as good as your light soles, right?"

"Right," she laughs with a shake of her head. She throws her arm around my shoulders and Finley's in a group hug. "Well, kids, it looks like we've got a party to host!"

31

Preston

"Yo, Lawrence," Saul calls out from the group of our teammates huddled around the sofa. Finley's been taking them on, one by one, and beating them handily in the hockey pro video game while Maya supervises like a mama hen.

"What's up?" I ask when I join the group.

"Why didn't you tell us you had a little hockey genius nephew or a smoking hot sister?"

"Why do you think?" Vincent responds with a slap upside the back of Saul's head, saving me the effort. "He was right to hide them from the likes of you."

"How is he so good at this game?" Maya comes up and asks me. "He's only allowed to play half an hour on weekdays and an hour on weekends!"

Holding up my palms defensively, I tell her, "Don't look at me. I know better than to break any of your rules."

"Joey has this game, too," Finley informs us. "We played for four hours straight one day while he tried to beat me."

"That is…I'm going to have a talk with Joey's mothers tonight," Maya huffs. "Which reminds me, it's way past the little hockey genius's bedtime." She rolls her eyes at Saul, but there's still a smile on her face at his nickname.

I wonder what the guys would say if they knew his genius was possibly skills inherited by his hockey pro father they beat earlier tonight.

"Just one more game, Mom. Please?" Finley begs when he finishes whooping Darrell's ass. "This is the only time I'll ever be able to beat these guys."

"Yeah, Mom," Nick echoes. "One more game with the champ. I haven't had my turn."

"Fine," Maya huffs. "But this is the last game, so make it count." To me she says, "You've created a monster. He'll be bragging about tonight for years to come."

"Just wait another few days when he can brag about beating half the players who won the championship trophy."

"Damn, right," Saul agrees proudly with a smirk before he sees Maya glaring at him. "I mean, heck yeah. Warhawks! Warhawks!"

The whole room chants the word while I go in search of my girlfriend. Now that I have proof that indulging before a game makes me play better, not worse, I intend to indulge the hell out of Elle multiple times tonight.

Tonight was the first score I've ever had in a playoff or championship game, and it feels fucking fantastic.

My good mood quickly deflates, however, when I find Elle

just outside the front door, talking to three pricks who sure as shit weren't invited to our little shindig.

"What are you doing here? How did you get this address?" I hear Elle hiss at Riley.

"Oh, I saw some pics of players celebrating. Did a little digging. It wasn't that hard to figure out."

His eyes lift from her to over her shoulder on my approach. "What do you want? Elle is done with you."

"I came to hear it straight from her mouth," he replies. "Damn, I miss that mouth of yours, babe," he says to my girlfriend. Then to me, "She's got an amazing one, doesn't she? Unless…maybe you don't know."

"I'm about to hit you so hard your mouth will have to be wired shut for months," I warn him, my fists clenching at my sides, ready to haul back and knock his ass out. The only thing standing in my way is Elle.

"Ah. So, maybe you haven't gotten the full salon experience yet. Too bad. Guess Ellie doesn't get all cute and horny whenever she sees you like she did for me."

That would have been his last words if I didn't have my sister and nephew to support thanks to his sorry ass.

Before I can ram my fist into his face, Elle reaches back and covers my clenching right hand with her much smaller one. She intertwines our fingers to hold mine hostage from doing something that will land me in hot water not only with the Warhawks but with the local cops.

"Why did you block me, Ellie? I know we're not finished. Did this asshole make you do it?" Riley asks, nodding his chin toward me. "He loves convincing women to stop talking to me."

Ah, so he's pissed at Elle and still not over her. At least

Elle seems to have moved on. I hope she has. Blocking his number and sleeping with me made me assume so. But then again, he's her actual ex and not a man she pretended to want to be with. They were together for months, while I've only known her a few days. Those details make me hate him even more.

"Shouldn't you be weeping about tonight's loss between some puck bunny's boobs?" Elle asks the asshole. Yeah, I think she's definitely over him. And I'll have to fist bump her later for that killer insult.

"Can't seem to find a rack that's better than yours to weep into, Ellie," the asshole replies with a wink. "Tired of pretending with the yeti yet?"

"Not sure if you noticed, but I gave Preston the full yeti makeover. Left just enough scruff on his face to tickle me in the best way." She turns to face me, between me and Riley. Turning her back to him, she reaches up to run her fingers over both sides of my face, around to my chin. When I capture her thumb between my teeth, she laughs and shivers. Without looking at the jerk behind her, she says quietly, "Just so you know, Christian, women like when men get on their knees too."

Damn. That was one hell of a burn, hitting the asshole where it hurts the most.

The fucker opens his mouth as if to make a snide remark, most likely about me not knowing my way around a woman's body, when Elle turns around and says, "You'll also be glad to know that all my STD tests came back negative. It was a stressful few days waiting to hear back after you admitted to dicking around all over the country."

"You need us to escort these guys out of here, Pres?"

Vincent asks when him and Spencer come up on either side of me and Elle outside on the porch.

"Nah, the playboy and his friends were just leaving before he has to watch the rest of the finals from his hospital room."

Riley scoffs, lifting his middle finger to flip me off before he turns around and walks off, knowing better than to push me. I don't miss his glance back toward the windows of the full living room as he goes, like he's looking for someone else. Thank god Maya was distracted with Finley's game play and didn't see him.

Even after he's gone, I can't relax. Riley isn't going to just give up on Elle and go away, either because the prick actually cares about her or just wants to hurt me.

And once the championship games are over, I won't be in Greensboro as often, while he lives there so close to Elle.

What kind of future can Elle and I even have with her living in North Carolina and me living in California? How could long-distance work for us when she won't ever trust me because of the dick that admitted to cheating on her during all of his away games?

Elle

"Let's take a moment to recover from the unwanted visitor," I suggest to Preston when I take his hand and lead him down the hallway to his bedroom.

Once we're inside the dimly lit room, I shut and lock the

door. When I turn around, he's looming over me, so close I have to tip my head all the way back to see his face. His large hands grab my hips to push my back against the door. This new aggressive side of Preston is one I like a lot.

"I hate that he called you babe," he confesses. "And Ellie."

Finding words when he's so close I can't breathe without our chests rubbing isn't easy, but I manage. "I-I just think it's cute that Finley calls me Ellie, too."

"What's not cute was the fucker talking about how much you apparently enjoyed going down on him in the salon chair."

"I'm sorry," I tell him when I hook my fingers into the waistband of his jeans to tug his big body against mine, so there's not the least bit of space between us. "But in my defense, my enjoyment of that particular activity is not exclusive to him. In fact, the bigger the stick, the more I love doing it. And it doesn't get any bigger than yours, Pres." Done with teasing him, I palm the front of his pants, humming with approval at the hard bulge rapidly forming. I give it a squeeze and stroke it through the denim.

"You're just…trying to distract me from my anger…at that son of a bitch," he says through pants.

"Would you rather keep talking about Christian Riley or let me do something more fun with my mouth? I'm already wet just thinking about it."

It takes less than a second for Preston to undo the button on his pants, then lower the zipper.

I drop to my knees and reach up to take over lowering his jeans down his thighs, then his boxer briefs. His long, thick erection pops up, nearly slapping me in the face.

The man obviously isn't in the mood for teasing, so I open

wide to cover him with my mouth. I get in five good strokes of my mouth up and down his shaft before Preston grabs me underneath my arms to lift me not only to my feet, but off the floor, taking me to his bed.

Tossing me down on the mattress, he quickly works to remove his shoes and clothes while I do the same. We're both naked within seconds.

Preston crawls up over me, taking a second to run his fingers between my legs, then groaning at the proof of my claim when two fingers easily slide inside of me. "Jesus, Elle."

My palms press on his shoulders, then slide down his back to his ass, needing more of him. "I told you I...enjoy it."

Those are the last words I get to say. Preston's mouth claims mine at the same time he enters me with one deep thrust.

Unlike the night before, he doesn't make love to me. This time isn't slow or sweet. It's hard and rough. Fast and furious. His need for me is so overwhelming that it's all that matters as he pumps in and out. Our tongues push and pull desperately. My fingernails dig into his backside with my enthusiastic encouragement. And when Preston's thrusts speed up, chasing his release, he doesn't forget about me. His fingers slide between our bodies, rubbing me in that perfect spot that sets me off. My mouth opens on a cry of pleasure against Preston's. He swallows it down, then roars through his own release.

"Sorry that was...so...fast." He apologizes with his face pressed against my neck, lips pressing open-mouthed kisses to my sweaty skin.

I run my palms up and down his damp back, wanting him to stay right where he is, buried inside of me, weight on top of me. "I didn't mind. Sometimes fast is good. Really, really good."

Groaning, I feel the twitch of his shaft inside of me as one of his palms cup my breast, weighing it, squeezing it. His mouth lowers to kiss it with swipes of his tongue.

"Good. Because I'm going to put you on your hands and knees, and it'll probably be even faster."

"You can have me anyway you want," I assure him. "Fast, slow, soft, rough, just don't stop."

Preston lifts his head from my breast to cover my lips briefly. "What about the party?"

"Oh, fine," I huff. "One more round, then we'll go back out?"

"Deal," he agrees. "But I want you riding me as soon as everyone leaves."

"I don't know," I whisper. "There will be a lot of jiggling."

"Hell yeah," Preston replies. Sitting up, he pats the undersides of both my breasts. "The jiggling is my favorite part."

He knows I'm referring to other parts of my body, but when he stares down at me like I'm the most beautiful woman in the world, it's easy to momentarily forget those other parts.

32

Preston

Sunday afternoon comes way too fast.

Having to say goodbye to Elle after spending an entire day and night in bed with her feels impossible.

While driving her to the airport, I thought about telling her that our future is fucked and beg her to come with me to California. Despite scoring a goal in game four, no other offers have come in.

Now, we're standing on the sidewalk outside the front doors of the airport and Elle looks so beautiful in her short, red floral dress. Her blonde hair glows like it's blessed by the sun. Her cheeks are still rosy from our detour to the crowded parking lot. I pulled her onto my lap and, without removing her panties, she just tugged them to the side and rode me. We mauled each other and fucked like the world was ending around us.

While I'm still having flashbacks, the beautiful woman looks up at me and says, "See you tomorrow in Greensboro?"

"You bet. As soon as the plane lands," I assure her. That's less than twenty-four hours from now but feels like a lifetime.

"Okay, good. I had a great time with you this week."

"Me too, cupcake." I press a kiss to her lips, then her cheek and neck. "Although, 'great' seems like a massive under-statement."

"True," Elle agrees, her body shivering when I kiss her collarbone.

I just need one more day where everything is so perfect between us before I tell her about California. I know that once I do, Elle will probably start pulling away, unable to imagine us having a relationship from two sides of the country.

Maybe by the time I see her tomorrow, I will have come up with some way to convince her. Opening another salon is the best I've thought of so far, but it doesn't solve the problem of Elle leaving behind her best friend and family.

"I...I'll miss you," I say instead of the other three words trying to burst free from my mouth, my heart.

"I'll miss you too," Elle replies, giving me a smile. Standing on her toes, she kisses my cheek.

And before I can blink, she's slipping away, rolling her luggage through the sliding doors.

When I get home, Maya is straightening the living room from the night before.

"Hey," she says in greeting as she tosses the throw pillows

back on the sofa. "I'm not even going to complain about the mess this morning because Finley had so much fun last night."

"Good," I say, since I'm not in the mood to hear her griping.

"I like Elle. She's so sweet. She's perfect for you, isn't she?"

"She is, but…" I rub the back of my neck, thinking of the next conversation I'm going to have to have with her.

"But what?"

"I don't know how this will work with her in North Carolina and I could end up anywhere." I intentionally don't mention California to my sister until it's a done deal with signatures on the page.

"If it's meant to be, then you two will figure it out."

"I hope you're right."

"Speaking of the future," Maya starts. She flops down onto the sofa cushion and pats the seat next to her for me to sit, which I take. "I think…I think I may want to stay here with Finley if you have to move."

Nodding, I tell her, "I understand. Even if it sucks." If Maya doesn't want to relocate, then that gives me one less thing to worry about, I guess.

"We'll miss you like crazy, but there's no telling if you'll have to up and change teams again in a year or two. I don't want to keep relocating Finley once he starts kindergarten in the fall."

"I know. I get it. I wouldn't want to upset him with so many changes."

"That still doesn't solve one of the biggest changes—not having you around."

"I'll visit as often as I can," I promise her. "And you two can come to the weekend games, right?"

"Right. We'll figure it out, just like you and Elle will."

I know Maya's words are meant as encouragement. It has the opposite effect.

Between hockey and finding time to see Maya and Finley, that won't leave much time for Elle, and I fucking hate it.

33

Elle

"Hey, I'm almost ready!" I call out to Preston from the back when I hear the jingle of the front door opening. Then I step into the salon and find the last person I expected to see.

"Christian?" As always, he looks like the good ole golden boy next door, not a blond hair out of place, his jeans and tee just a little snug to show off his lean, muscular frame. "What are you doing here?" I ask him.

"I fucked up," he says with a shrug, his hands sliding into his front pockets.

"Ah, what?"

The hot shot stands there in my empty salon, portraying the picture-perfect definition of humble. I didn't even know he was familiar with the word.

"I'm sorry about showing up at Preston's the other night."

I cross my arms over my chest when I remember him strolling up to the porch like he owned it with his two teammates, trying to start shit to get Preston arrested. "You shouldn't have done that. If you all had got into a fight…"

"I know. It could've landed us all in jail and out of the championships. I went too far."

"Yes, you did."

"I just wanted to see you and talk to you since you blocked my damn calls and messages."

"Blocking your texts should've made it clear that I don't want to see or talk to you, just like my previous texts before that specifically told you that, which you ignored."

Christian takes two steps closer to me, and says, "Ellie, please. I didn't know what I had with you until I lost you. Now I want you back. I'll do whatever it takes."

"Oh, I find that very hard to believe, Christian. You only think you want me now because I'm with Preston."

He flashes me his panty-dropping smile. "Come on, babe. I know you two aren't actually together. You were just trying to screw with my head because I messed up and dumped you right before the finals. I get it. I deserved it, from you and from Preston."

When I don't answer either way, he says, "Tell me that you don't miss me."

Okay, so a teeny, tiny part of me misses the prick, but with each day I'm with Preston, it diminishes. I don't want him back, that I'm certain of, but I can't lie. "I…I don't know what to say, honestly."

"How about you start with the truth? I never lied to you, Ellie. Not once."

"You didn't tell me you were screwing women in every city you played in, did you?"

"That wasn't a lie. You never asked if we were exclusive. I thought you knew we were just having fun. I've only ever tried to be with just one woman before and that went to hell. But since you've been gone, I've missed you so damn much."

Oh, wow. He is laying it on thicker than a brick wall. Still, I can't help but ask, "Who was the one woman you tried to be with?"

"It doesn't matter now."

"No, seriously. Tell me, Christian." When he doesn't answer me, I go with my hunch. "Was it maybe Preston's sister Maya?"

His eyes widen, and the man goes as still as a frozen ice sculpture. "How did you…how did you know about her? That son of a bitch told you?"

"Preston told me that you got her pregnant during her freshman year of college."

With a scoff, he scrubs both hands down his face. "Well, now you know why he wants to kill me."

I have to choose my next words very carefully because I will not be the one who tells him about Finley if he hasn't figured it out for himself. "Preston doesn't want to kill you. You two were good friends, right? He just blames himself for introducing you to his little sister, for wrongly *trusting* you."

Christian's arms fall to his sides. "I know he trusted me, and I fucked up everything! One mistake cost me my best friend and the girl I…" He stops speaking so abruptly that I have no doubt what he was about to say.

"The girl you what?" I want him to say it. If he does, then, I don't know, maybe not all hope is lost and there's a chance for the three of them to be a real family. I like Maya and know she's not over Christian yet. While she said she blames being a single mother on her lack of dating, Christian is the only man she's ever been with, as if no other man could compete with the memory of him.

"Loved, okay. I thought I loved Maya and that she felt the same about me. But after I knocked her up, Preston wouldn't let me anywhere near her again!"

"He kept you from her?"

"Hell yes. I couldn't even say her name to ask about her without him kicking my ass all over the ice. He literally threw me and all my shit out of the apartment we shared."

"Can you really blame him, Christian? He's protective of Maya and he trusted you to be safe with her. She was just out of high school!"

"I know all of that, Elle." I'm a little surprised when he uses my actual name and not the nickname he and his son use. "And I've apologized. I offered to go with Maya to the doctor and shit until she made her decision. I even sent her money in case she needed it for whichever way she went. Preston told me she didn't want anything to do with me anymore and to stay away from her."

Could there be more to the story? More than Preston shared, that makes Christian look a little bit less like an asshole?

"I want to believe you. I do. But I find it hard to trust anything you say, Christian."

"Funny, since there's only one of us here who is a proven liar," he replies with his jaw clenched tight. "Tell me the truth. Tell me you haven't been pretending with him," he says through gritted teeth.

Taking a deep breath, I give him what he wants. "Fine. Preston and I weren't really together."

"I fucking knew it!" he exclaims in triumph.

"At first," I quickly add. "When that photo of us kissing was taken, we weren't actually a couple yet. But then we got to know each other better and became closer. It is real now. It has been since the first night I went to D.C."

"And you actually believe he feels the same way? He's just using you to get back at me, Ellie! Can't you see that?"

"I thought so at first, but it's more than that for both of us now."

"I find that very hard to believe. He's turning you against me, just like he did with Maya."

"That's still your version of what happened, not either of theirs."

"Then ask Maya! She knows I tried."

"Does she?"

"Yes!" he shouts. "When my calls and texts stopped getting through to her, I wrote her actual fucking letters."

"Letters? You wrote letters?"

He nods. "Every day for weeks until I got called up to the majors."

"You wrote her every day, huh?"

"Handwritten letters every single day. And she never responded to any of them. I haven't spoken to her since the day she told me…since the day she told me she was pregnant."

I hate to admit that he actually sounds believable, like he may have really cared about her, especially if he wrote her love letters.

Jesus. The only time I've ever seen him with an actual

writing utensil in his hand is when he's using one to sign autographs.

Still treading very carefully, like I'm walking on a frozen lake in spring, I ask, "Did you happen to see Maya at the D.C. games?"

"Of course I saw her. It was the first time I had seen her since that day. I don't know how many years it's been, five or six maybe. She wasn't at Preston's away games where we fought. At least I don't think she was…" He says this as if he looked for her in the stands those games. Was he unable to resist asking about her? If so, is that what set Preston off both times?

"You didn't notice anything different about her?"

Christian's golden brow furrows. "What do you mean? Maya looked exactly the same as she did the day we met."

"Forget it," I say before the subject of Finley comes up. "We got way off topic. You and I are done, so you should leave. Preston will be here any minute."

"He will, huh? Maybe I'll wait around to say hello."

"Christian, please go." I walk past him to the door, holding it open, hoping he'll take the hint.

"Fine. But I'm not giving up on you. I won't let him screw things up for me again. Just tell me what it will take, Ellie."

"Just so you know, I hate the name Ellie. It makes me feel like a cow," I inform him, even if it's adorable when Finley says it. "And there's nothing you can do."

"Do you want a ring? Is that what it will take? Because I'll do it. I'll buy a diamond and ask you to marry me if that's what it will take to prove I'm serious about giving up other women."

"Don't be ridiculous," I tell him with a roll of my eyes. "You are nowhere close to being ready to marry any woman."

"Oh yeah? Well, I stopped fucking around. I haven't been with anyone since the night we broke up."

"You mean you ended things with me that morning and slept with someone else hours later?" I ask.

Christian winces. "Yes. But that was the only time. After I was with her, I realized how much I missed you. That was before I heard anything about you and Preston. I was going to come see you after the first game, and you were waiting for him at the gate. Now I know that you actually cared about me. You didn't want me just because I'm a millionaire athlete. You knew me better than anyone. I could just be myself with you."

"Stop stalling and go. It's too late. There's absolutely nothing you can say or do to change my mind. Goodbye, Christian."

"This isn't over," he says as he thankfully walks away.

I wish I knew if he meant even half of what he said to me.

Not that it matters. I'm with Preston now and I...I think I'm falling in love with him. Even if I still cared about Christian more than a tiny teaspoon amount that he occupies in my heart, he wouldn't deserve a second chance.

34

Preston

By the time I find a parking spot downtown near Elle's salon, I'm running late for our lunch date. Or maybe I just wasn't in a huge hurry to have to break the news to Elle about California. As much as I want to see my girl, I'm dreading her reaction.

Distracted, I round the corner of her building and run smack dab into someone else.

"Shit. Sorry," I say before I see the face of who I just bulldozed—a blond man a few inches shorter than me, and smug as shit. "You!"

"Hi, Pres," the asshole says while grinning at me. "Crazy running into you here of all places."

I lift my eyes to the front of Elle's salon, trying to figure out why he was coming out of it. It's lunchtime. She doesn't have customers right now. Even if she was cutting Christian's hair she would've told me, wouldn't she? Yes. Of course, she would have.

"Why the hell are you here bothering her?" I ask him.

"How do you know I was bothering her?"

"Because she can't stand your ass after you hurt her."

"Are you sure about that?" he replies. "Ellie seemed pretty happy to see me. We both know that she's still not over me."

"Bullshit."

"We were together for five fucking months. How long have you two been pretending? Less than two weeks?"

"I'm not wasting my time on you, and I sure as hell won't throw a punch in broad daylight that will land my ass in jail."

With a chuckle, the prick walks around me, giving me a wide berth on the sidewalk. "Whatever you say, Pres."

The roaring in my head is back like before by the time I stomp into Elle's salon. She's standing next to the row of chair with her purse on her shoulder, a distant look on her face.

"What was that asshole doing here?"

She blinks at me and there's suddenly a storm brewing in her eyes. "Hello to you too, Preston."

"Cut the shit, Elle. Just tell me what he wanted."

She shrugs her shoulders as if the prick coming by isn't a big deal before she replies. "He said he wants another chance, that he would stop messing around and buy me a ring if that's what it would take to prove to me that I could trust him."

Jesus Christ. He offered to propose to her? He's so full of shit.

"And? What did you say?"

"What do you think I told him?" she asks, but I don't even try to guess. "I told him I was with you now, and that there wasn't a single thing he could do or say to change my mind."

"You told him that?"

"Yes!"

"Good."

"He also told me a few things about you and Maya."

"What the fuck did he say?" I growl. "You didn't tell him…"

She shakes her head. "No, of course I didn't tell him about Finley. Do you think I would blurt out something as important as the fact that he has a four-year-old son?"

"No. Shit. I'm sorry for making the accusation."

"You convinced Maya not to tell him she was keeping the baby, that he's Finley's father, didn't you?"

"What are you talking about?" I ask, caught off-guard by the sudden change of topic. One second, we were talking about her and Riley and now she brings in my sister and the asshole?

"Did you convince her to keep Christian away?" Elle repeats.

"Maya didn't want anything to do with the prick after he gave her some money to make it all go away."

"He said he tried to call her, text her, wanted to see her and go with her to the doctor, but you wouldn't let him near her. He claimed he wrote her handwritten love letters."

"That's bullshit. There were no fucking love letters. He probably can't even spell his own name."

"Why would he lie?"

"Look, Elle, no offense, but this all happened years ago, and you weren't there. Maya was a freshman in college. She had just turned nineteen, for fuck's sake. She was devastated to be pregnant, to have our parents and Riley abandon her. I did everything I could to stop her from completely falling apart."

"And you don't think letting Christian be there during the pregnancy and after would've maybe helped her more than his absence hurt her?"

"Hell no! Riley is a selfish asshole. He only cares about himself. You know that better than anyone! That son of a bitch didn't waste time signing a contract and leaving town, either. He didn't give a shit about Maya."

"I know that you feel guilty, that you blame yourself for introducing Christian and Maya, for trusting him to be careful with her."

"I regret that every single day."

"Do you think Maya regrets it, though?"

"Of course she does! He ruined her life. Dropping out of school was nothing compared to what she dealt with at home."

"I know. You told me it was bad with your parents. And I'm so sorry. I can't imagine how hard that must have been for her and for you."

Choosing between my judgmental parents and my sister who needed me, was easy. I don't regret it, even if it means shouldering the burden to make sure Maya and Finley have whatever they need.

"Like I said, between Riley bailing and our parents disowning her, Maya was a distraught mess, panicking to try to figure out how to be a single mother. She had to give up everything, all her hopes and dreams. I did what I had to do to take care of her. I'm just lucky that I went to the pros before she had Finley."

"You're an amazing brother, Preston. They're lucky to have you looking out for them."

"I'm the only one who has ever looked out for them, so I

sure as shit wasn't going to let Riley hurt them. He was my best friend. I knew him better than anyone else. He wasn't ready to settle down then and probably never will be. All he talked about was going pro, the money and women it would mean."

"You're right," Elle says with a sigh. "I'm sorry I brought it up. Can we please just try to calm down and go to lunch?"

"Yeah, cupcake. Let's go eat something," I agree, even though my blood pressure is still sky high.

And after what felt like a heated argument with Elle, I scrap my plan to tell her about California.

I'll tell her tonight, after the Warhawks win the championship.

Or tomorrow, since I don't want to ruin the celebration.

Definitely tomorrow.

~

Elle

I can't even begin to understand the situation Preston and Maya were in when she got pregnant so young. Even if Preston had to work two or three jobs, he would've done it for her and his nephew.

So, while I want to give Christian the benefit of the doubt, I let it go.

It's none of my business. I'm not the one who kept a roof over their head and made sure they were fed after their parents kicked her out.

"I hate that you both went through all that with Christian," I tell Preston on the walk back to the salon from our mostly silent lunch. "But you don't have anything to worry about when it comes to me and him. You believe me, don't you?"

When he hesitates with his reply, I know I'm not going to like it. "I'm still not convinced that you're completely over him. I think you're getting there…"

Taking his hand in mine, I tell him, "Christian and I had a few fun months together. That's it. I'm not still pining for him. If I was, don't you think I would've said yes the first time he texted me, asking to come over?"

"Yeah, I guess so. And you know his offer of proposing is bullshit, right?"

"Absolutely," I answer without needing to think about it. "You're right about him. He's selfish, arrogant, and only thinks about himself. You two may be the same age, but he still has a lot of growing up to do. And I want…"

"What do you want?" Preston asks, stopping to face me on the sidewalk when I pause.

Looking up at his handsome face, I tell him, "I want to be with someone who makes me feel safe and happy, day and night, not just occasionally when it's late and he's lonely."

"And I make you feel that way?"

"Yes."

"Good."

"I still worry that you'll end up hurting me."

"I won't."

"Only time will tell, right?" I say with a forced smile.

The one thing I've learned about Preston that never waivers is just how important his family, the family he works so hard to provide for, is to him. Nothing is more important.

Especially not me. I understand, even if it makes me a little sad. After all, the two of us just met and started out in a fake relationship.

I'm still expendable to him, even if he won't admit it to himself.

So, if he ever had to choose between me or his sister and nephew, I know who he'll pick every time.

It certainly won't be me.

That's something I have to understand and respect as part of our real relationship.

35

Preston

The Warhawks are one game away from winning the championship trophy. Unfortunately, that game has to be played in the Bobcats' home arena and not our own.

We won the first two games in Greensboro, so I know we can do it again.

For some reason though, this game day feels different. It's not just because I'm still reeling from the confrontation with Riley, followed by the argument with Elle, either.

There's so much riding on tonight that you can practically see the nerves on every single player's face. It's in the way shots go just a little too wide during warm-ups, when they would've sailed into the goal yesterday.

The pressure is getting to us all to pull off the win today and clinch the championship.

If we don't, we'll be back on the road and in D.C. for game six the day after tomorrow.

I'm trying my best to get focused during warm-ups, to forget about everything but playing my best when Riley starts circling me like a vulture.

"Hey, Pres. How's my girl doing? She *coming* tonight?"

I ignore the asshole, pretend like he doesn't exist, just like I did in the last game.

"She can't resist me," he calls out. "You both know it. It's only a matter of time before she's back in my bed, begging me to take her harder, faster. You know how she gets. Oh, no. I guess not since she's faking it all with you and you've never had her."

Fuck.

The roaring in my head drowns out everything in the arena, as well as weakening my restraint to not take his bait.

"She admitted that you two are just pretending," Christian shouts loud enough for all our teammates to hear. "That photo of you kissing? You did it just to stir shit up before the first game. It's all a lie to try to hurt me, to turn her against me, just like you did with Maya!"

That's it. I throw my stick down and skate toward him. "Keep my sister's name out of your goddamn mouth!"

Before I can plow into the asshole, Vincent gets between us, keeping me back. "Don't lose your head now, Lawrence. He's trying to get you to screw up," the goalie tells me.

"I hate that son of a bitch!" I yell as he pushes me back to the other side of the ice while Christian cackles behind him.

"Then smash his ass into the boards when the game starts. But remember what's on the line."

"Yeah, I remember. I can never forget," I tell him. Maya

and Finley are depending on me to keep my cool, to win the championship, or at least finish it without fucking up and losing the offer from the Grizzlies.

Nothing is more important to me than they are.

And Elle.

The longer I wait to tell her about California, the more it feels like a festering open wound in my chest, spreading every second and getting infected.

It's impossible to stop thinking about it, that this trip to Greensboro could be the last time I see Elle if she refuses to give long-distance a chance.

If Riley keeps pursuing her, she may even cave eventually. After all, he lives right here in her town and won't be going anywhere for several years.

Hell, if anyone could make that prick settle down, it would be her.

The two of them could live happily ever after while I live alone and miserable on the opposite coast.

It just gives me one more reason to hate that asshole.

Elle

The score is two to one, the Bobcats in the lead during the second period. There's been a lot of shoving and hard hits by both sides the whole game. It's like the Bobcats are giving it their all and the Warhawks are just...angry.

Or maybe that's just Preston.

Preston who comes onto the ice and goes charging straight toward Christian.

"Oh no. Oh no, oh no, oh no," I chant over and over as I watch. The two get in each other's faces, pushing and running their mouths. Somehow, I just know this is it, Preston has snapped. All that cool and calm he felt in the first four games is completely gone.

"Why does Preston look so pissed?" Audrey asks from beside me. Preston was somehow able to get us great seats yet again.

"I don't know. Christian's probably been running his mouth."

"Does he know he came by the salon yesterday?"

"Yes. They ran into each other when Preston was coming in and Christian was leaving."

"Uh-oh."

"My thoughts exactly. Preston was…I've never seen him so angry this afternoon."

"Until now, you mean?"

"What?"

"Your man just threw his gloves off and took a swing at Christian."

I look back at the ice and see she's right. Standing up, I cup my hands to my mouth as I shout, "Don't do it, Preston! He's not worth it!" as if he could actually hear me over the packed crowd that's cheering, rooting for a brawl between the known rivals.

"This isn't going to end well for either of them," Audrey remarks as helmets are thrown down too.

Fists fly and then Christian goes down on the ice. Preston is right there on top of him, punching him repeatedly in the face. The refs even give the two a chance to get a few hits in before they try to pull Preston off Christian. But Preston isn't about to let up. His elbow rams into the face of the ref behind him and then there's more blood spraying.

"Crap. He's going to get thrown out for that!" I remark as I cover my face with both hands, unable to keep watching.

"Oh, what a mess," Audrey mutters.

As the ref blows the whistle and calls for Preston to be ejected to the cheers of the Bobcats crowd, I can't help but feel like it's somehow all my fault.

I was supposed to help Preston keep his cool around Riley. Instead, I may be the reason he just lost it and hurt a referee.

I've become a distraction he didn't need. After all, it's the whole reason why he doesn't date.

And I think he may be right to blame me for this as well.

"I need to go talk to him."

"Now?" Audrey asks. "Are you crazy? What if he throws a swing at you?"

"He won't hurt me," I tell her confidently. *At least not physically.* I keep that part to myself. Even if the truth hurts, I want to hear it now before his team leaves after the game.

Downstairs in the tunnel leading to the locker room, I manage to throw Steve's name around to some security guards, who go retrieve the man.

"What do you want, troublemaker?" he asks when he finally walks up.

"I need you to get me in the locker room to see Preston."

"Are you nuts? I can't let you back there. Not without a press pass. This is the Bobcat's arena. I don't have that kind of pull here."

"Please, Steve. Let me check on him, make sure he's okay."

"You're not worried about your Bobcat boy? Looks like he took most of the damage."

"Is Christian still able to play?"

"Maybe. The docs are checking him out."

"He'll probably be fine, right? Do you know what he said to Preston?"

"No clue. And trust me Elle, even if I could get you back, you don't want to be around him right now. He's destroying the locker room."

"Destroying?" I croak out.

"Lawrence has lost his shit. He's going to be fined out his ass for the hit on the ref and the property damage."

"Then let me talk to him. Maybe it'll calm him down and prevent any more destruction."

"You seriously believe you have that much power over him? You think awfully highly of yourself, don't you?"

"No, I just I want to try to help him."

"Fine. Give me a minute and I'll see what I can do," he huffs.

"Thank you."

He steps away, talking into his intercom for several minutes before he goes up to the Bobcats security guys and tells them, "Riley needs an escort to the hospital. Go! Get over to the Bobcats locker room."

Once they take off, he comes back over to me just as the crowd and the arena roars in triumph of something good happening for the Bobcats, possibly a score during the five-minute power play Preston caused.

"Is Christian really going to the hospital?" I ask in concern.

"Nah. But they don't know that, do they?" he asks with a grin. "Come on. Hurry it up. You've got less than five minutes before intermission when the rest of the team comes in and you'll need to get the hell out of there."

"Okay," I agree, hoping five minutes is enough time.

Inside the quiet row of players cubbies, doors hang off hinges, clothes are scattered around, and Preston is still dressed in his uniform, stomping around on his skates with his back to me.

"Preston," I say softly. A second before he picks up his helmet or someone else's and slams it into the wall, startling me, making me second-guess coming down here. Maybe Steve was right.

When he turns around, his eyes are glazed with fury as he glares at me, looking nothing like the sweet man I know he is inside. "How could you tell him, Elle?"

"Wh-what?" I ask in confusion. "I never told him about Finley."

"You told him about us, that it was all fake!"

"I…that's not even close to what I said. Not exactly."

Before I can even say another word, Preston drops to the bench. His head is hanging in his hands between his legs as he shakes it. "I just lost my entire bonus for the postseason."

"I'm so sorry," I whisper, knowing how infuriating that must be to lose after one mistake.

"I can't do this anymore with you," he says. "We were down two to one before my penalty. I heard the crowd. They scored again during the power play, didn't they?"

"Y-yes, I think so."

"Fuck!" he shouts. Getting up and turning around, he punches his bare fist straight through the wall.

"Preston…"

"We're done, Elle!"

Done.

We're done.

I knew it.

I knew it would come to this and still I stupidly fell for him. Preston all but warned me that he didn't date, wouldn't date if it jeopardized his hockey career, if it meant hurting his family.

And now it has.

The Warhawks are probably going to lose game five.

Preston lost his playoff bonus and won't be getting a contract extension he was so desperate for.

Now, if another team wants him, he'll have to up and move with or without Maya and Finley.

I know Preston is furious at himself for lashing out, but it's me who gets all the blame right now.

Without another word, I slip off his jersey, glad I'm wearing a black lace cami underneath, and toss it on the closest bench. He can keep it. I don't want a single reminder of him. It'll just make getting over him even harder.

36

Preston

The roar of fury in my head subsides as soon as I turn around and Elle is no longer standing in the locker room.

She's gone.

She's not just gone. She left my jersey behind, tossing it down like its trash. Like I'm trash and she doesn't want anything else to do with me.

My stomach clenches, feeling empty and nauseous at the same time when I realize what I've done.

I blamed my temper, my fuck up, on her and pushed her away when I needed her the most.

Walking over on my skates, I pick up the sweater and hold it up to my nose. It smells like her, like the fancy shampoos she uses in the salon.

Hell, I know this is all my fault, and my fault alone.

My fault for letting Christian get to me.

He knew Elle was my weakness, that I still believe she hasn't got over him and may never be able to forget him.

But it's really just my own insecurities. I don't think I can compete with the blonde jackass, that I'll never be the man Elle needs. Especially not from the other side of the country.

When my teammates fill the locker room, none of them will even meet my eyes. They're pissed that I lost it, and my penalty meant putting pressure on our goalie and the four men who had to play against five Bobcats for five minutes to try to prevent them from scoring, a nearly impossible task.

"This is why you're a free agent, Lawrence," Coach Ramsey comes up and says to me. "You're a damn good player, but that temper of yours hurts the whole team."

My temper.

It's not Riley or Elle or anyone else's fault but my own.

And it's time for me to take responsibility for my actions.

"I'm sorry I lost it," I tell Coach and the entire room that's solemn now that we're losing three to one.

The trophy seems out of reach, at least for tonight, no matter how hard the guys fight to try to make a comeback.

But the loss from pushing Elle away feels a million times worse.

Elle

I text Audrey to grab our things and meet me at the main exit, needing to escape the arena as soon as possible.

As soon as she sees me in the empty lobby, her face falls.

"Oh no, Elle."

"I don't want to talk about it," I tell her as I push open the exit door.

"Sure thing. I'm here whenever you're ready –"

"I'm never dating another hockey player again," I tell her between sniffles as soon as the cool night air hits me.

"Damn all those stick-wielding pricks."

"No more athletes, period. They just want to play stupid head games, and I don't want any part of it!"

"Absolutely not."

"They're all a bunch of selfish assholes!" I rant.

"Damn right they are."

"It was stupid to think Christian or Preston would ever really want someone like me…"

"Whoa!" Audrey says, jumping in front of me on the dark sidewalk and pressing a hand to my chest. "It wasn't stupid. You are a beautiful, sweet, kind woman, Elle. And if anyone isn't worthy, it's those brawling idiots who are too stupid to realize you're the best woman they'll ever know."

"Thanks, Audrey," I say with a shaky smile as tears roll down my cheeks. "I thought…I thought I loved Christian, but I knew…I loved Preston."

"I know, honey. Come here," she says, pulling me into her arms where I cry on her shoulder.

37

Preston

As soon as I walk into the house, I smell the warm, delicious brownies. Loser brownies, she calls them. My sister's made them after every loss since we lived together in Raleigh.

From the living room sofa, Maya whispers, "Sorry about the loss."

"It was bound to end anyway," I grumble as I flop down in the closest chair, letting my duffle slide onto the floor. "I don't know why I let it go on as long as it did."

"Uh, what are you talking about?" she asks.

"Elle."

"Oh. I was talking about the game, and you getting ejected. What happened with Elle?"

"I told her I was done. We were done."

"What? Why in the world would you do that?"

"Why do you think? It was a mistake. She's a distraction I didn't need. Riley used her to get to me tonight. And it worked. My penalty cost us the game, and my fucking post-season bonus."

"But wait a second. I thought Elle was helping you with your temper. That being with her and rubbing it in Christian's face kept you from fighting him."

"Yeah, well, she was the cause of our fight today."

Going up on her knees to lean in closer to me, she says, "What did he say?"

"He talked shit."

"What did he say exactly?" Maya asks with an impatient huff.

"He's convinced she'll eventually want him back and said she told him that she was faking it all with me." Faking it in bed with me is what I know he meant. Was she? Fuck if I know. I thought we were good together, amazing in bed, but what do I know? I haven't been with a woman in years, and she was just in a relationship with a man who should be a pro at sex after all the women he's been with.

"Faking it?"

"Riley went to see Elle at the salon yesterday. She told him it was all fake."

"Did you ask Elle what exactly she may have said to him?"

"It doesn't matter." She told me he wanted another chance, would buy her a ring. She didn't mention telling him anything about us was fake.

"Yes, it does matter, Preston! Christian was probably lying!"

"He knew about the kiss the day we met being staged."

"So? That could've been a lucky guess. Come on, Pres.

Don't let that jerk make you lose something great. You should never believe him over her."

"The truth doesn't matter as much as the consequences. Those are all still the same. I lost my temper because of him talking about her, and we lost the game because of that power play from my ejection. Now I've lost money since I broke the clause in my contract."

"You lost the game because the entire team was playing like a bunch of nervous little shits tonight. And you have no one but yourself to blame for losing money, breaking whatever rule of your contract."

"We're so close to the championship trophy. One game away. I'm not going to let Elle get in my head and make me lose focus again."

"So, you'll just decide to stop thinking about her and that will be it?"

I nod. That sounds like a great plan. "Yes."

"I hate to break it to you, Pres, but love doesn't work like that. It's not something you can turn on or off whenever you want."

"I don't…" I start to say that I don't love Elle, but that would be a lie. "How the hell would you know?" I ask my sister instead of lying or confessing how I feel about Elle.

"You've never loved anyone before."

"Yes, I have."

"What? When?"

"I was young and naïve to think he felt the same about me, but that doesn't change the fact that I loved him."

"Hold on. Are you talking about *Riley*?"

"Who else would it be? You're not the only one who hasn't had a date in five years!"

Jesus. She *loved* that fucker? "I didn't know you felt that way about him."

At the time everything happened, Maya cried a bunch. Like every day and night. I thought it was the pregnancy hormones, not that she was missing the man she thought she loved. Or she did love him, but I was too blind to see it.

"Would it have mattered?" she asks.

"Maybe." Thinking about what Elle said yesterday, I ask her, "Do you regret, you know, ever being with him?"

"No, of course not," she says faster than I was expecting. "It wasn't easy to give up on my college degree, to know Mom and Dad couldn't accept me 'living in sin', but I don't regret one second of having Finley in my life. You gave me the strength and stability I needed to get through those first few months when I had a screaming newborn and no clue how to be a mother."

"You were a great mother to him even before he was born."

"I loved him before he was born, but that doesn't mean I knew what I was doing once he came into the world. I felt so…lost. Alone. If you hadn't been there to help, I'm not sure what I would've done." I'm still wrapping my head around everything she's just confessed when Maya says, "Enough about me. What are you going to do to fix things with Elle?"

"We may as well be planning a trip to the moon, since neither of those things are possible."

"Sure, it is. Well, the Elle part. It could be a few years before we can get to the moon."

Shaking my head, I tell her the truth. "Elle doesn't want to be with me. If she felt something, she wouldn't have told Christian that it wasn't real and that we hadn't slept together…"

Oh shit. How could he say it was all fake if he thought we hadn't even had sex?

"You didn't sleep with Elle? I find that *very* hard to believe. I was here during your disappearing act on the night of the party."

"No, we did. I mean, Christian thought we hadn't. He made it sound like Elle told him we hadn't been together."

"So, in other words, he was lying, or at best taking a shot in the dark?"

"I think so."

"Then you screwed up big time with her, didn't you, big brother?"

"It still doesn't really matter. Whether or not we slept together doesn't prove anything. She was using me to get back at Christian. Hell, maybe to get him back."

"I don't believe that for a second, Preston. You shouldn't either. Elle loves you. So, what if it started out with her wanting to hurt Christian? That lasted like a day before you made her forget all about him. Don't you remember how hurt she was when she came to D.C. and found out about Finley? She thought you were only with her to pay him back for getting me pregnant."

"She was…I had never seen her so sad," I say, hating even thinking about the look on her face when she opened her hotel door that night.

"Because she loves you, you big dummy! You have to fix this before it's too late! Being with Elle doesn't make you lose or win games or lose money for breaking your contract. That's all on your team and you personally for having a temper and not being able to let shit go!"

I consider my sister's perspective for several long minutes.

Our team did play awful. The guys put too much pressure on themselves tonight, me included. We fucking choked. The stakes were the highest they could get, so we played like we were scared of losing instead of playing to win the trophy.

And, well, I got angry and lost it on Riley twice before I even knew Elle because I was angry at him for getting Maya pregnant. Yes, working with her to make him jealous kept me level-headed for the first four games, but it was never Elle's responsibility to control my temper.

That shit is on me. Nobody else. I'm the only one to blame.

Just like how deep down I still blame myself for thinking that Maya and Riley dating was a good idea. My best friend and little sister together seemed like a great idea at the time. I thought if anyone could get the playboy to settle down, it was my sister. The way he looked at her, there was no doubt in my mind at the time that he adored her. Which made me think he would treat her like a queen. And I was dead wrong about that.

Me.

I had lived with him and played with Riley for years, watching him go from one woman to the next. It was stupid to think Maya would be any different.

I'm the one responsible for putting my sister in the position that got her pregnant. That's why I've done nothing but help support her with raising Finley since she decided to have him.

And I'm also the one responsible for hurting Elle tonight because I was angry at myself for losing my temper. She came down to the locker room to check on me, to try to calm me down because she cared, and I was an asshole who lashed out at her.

I ended things with Elle because I was upset and scared to tell her I was moving, hurting her before she could hurt me back by calling it quits rather than have a long-distance relationship with me. That's why I put off telling her. I didn't want to leave her, didn't want what we have to ever end because I love her so damn much. So why the hell did I tell her we were over?

"Oh god. I've made a huge fucking mistake," I mutter aloud.

"Yes, yes, you have. So go fix it!"

"I can't go to Greensboro now. We have a game here in D.C. in two days."

"The chance Elle will forgive you dwindles every second since the one where you broke her heart, Preston. The sooner you show up at her door begging her to take you back, the better your chance of getting her to forgive you."

She says that like she's experienced something similar. No. No way. Still, I have to ask. "Is that…are you still waiting for Riley to show up on your doorstep and beg for another chance?"

Maya shakes her head. "No. I gave up on Christian four years ago."

"After Finley was born?"

She nods. "Then later, I thought he would find out I had a baby, that he was a father, and he would come running…"

She waited for him. Even after Finley was born. She wanted him to figure out he was a father, to have him beg her to take him back. All because she loved him.

I don't think Riley felt the same or would've stepped up if he knew he was a dad, but what if I'm wrong?

What if I've been so angry at him, at myself, that I've been wrong for five years?

"Shit, Maya. I think I may have made a huge mistake with you too," I admit to her with a wince.

"What do you mean?"

"I sort of kept Christian away."

"What?"

"He asked about you. Several times. And instead of telling him you were going to keep the baby, I would just get into fights with him."

"When? When did he ask about me?"

"Pretty much every day of practice after you found out until he left for Greensboro. He still asked, even though he knew I would kick his ass for saying your name."

"Wow. So, for months you kept us apart?"

"I didn't think you wanted anything to do with him after he ruined your life!"

"He didn't ruin my life, Preston! Christian and I got pregnant *together*. It was on both of us for not being smart. The pullout method is not a real method."

"I'm sorry," I tell her, and to keep her from giving me any more details. "You have no idea how sorry I am for introducing the two of you and for interfering afterward. I shouldn't have trusted him alone with you."

"You've always been there for me and Finley, Preston. I can never repay you for that. So, if you thought we were better off without him, then I trusted you. I trust you more than I would ever trust him."

She trusts me. She trusted me when I said she should go out on a date with my best friend and look where that got her. But this time, keeping Christian away, it may be a bigger screw up than letting him get her pregnant as a teenager.

"There's, ah, something else I need to tell you."

"What now?"

"I got an offer from the Grizzlies, the team in San Diego. Well, that is, if they don't withdraw it after my ejection..."

"Okay. So, if the offer is still on the table, you're going to up and move all the way to California?"

"I told you it's the best offer I got. The other...I can't afford a pay cut to stay closer..."

"I could get a job to help out. You don't have to keep supporting me and Finley."

"Yes, I do. Who else will do it? Christian?"

"I never asked you to take us in. Yes, it was my only option when I was a depressed, pregnant, teenager. But now that he's getting ready to start school full-time in the fall, I could get a job. I can take care of myself now, you know?"

"Earning a living to support you and him isn't as easy as you think it is."

"Well, I'm not asking you to move to California for us. I never asked you to take out vengeance on Christian, either. That...what happened should've been between me and him. You shouldn't have had to give up your life for us."

"And you think he would have?"

"I doubt it, but I'll never know now, will I?" For the first time in as long as I can remember, there's anger in my sister's voice.

"If you want to tell the son of a bitch, then tell him! You could have done that at any point, but you didn't, did you? If you think he won't abandon you both, then you're still the naïve nineteen-year-old you were when he knocked you up."

"Love makes you want to think the best about someone. It has nothing to do with how young I was at the time."

"Love is nothing but a pain in the ass."

"Forget about me and Finley, and what happened in the past. What about Elle? You're just going to up and leave her?"

"I don't know what you want me to do, Maya. I have to go."

"You don't have to do anything, Preston. There's another team who wants you, isn't there?"

"Yes. But like I said…"

"It's less money. You would have to take a cut in pay. So what? Some things are more important than money. And one of them is in Greensboro. You would be crazy to choose anything over Elle. Trust me, if you give up on her without trying to fix things with her, you'll regret it for the rest of your life."

38

Elle

I'm folding towels in the laundry room when I hear the door chime, quickly followed by Audrey exclamation of, "What the hell are you doing here?"

Based on her angry tone, my first thought is that it must be Christian popping in again, maybe even asking for a haircut before he leaves for game six in D.C. tomorrow.

The urge to shave his eyebrows off has lessened, thankfully. I'm too sad about Preston to even be malicious toward the jackass.

Despite how much Preston hurt me, unlike Christian, I don't want to do him harm or try to get payback. Mostly because I don't blame him for pushing me away before he hurt his career even more.

"Ah, Elle?" Audrey asks from the doorway of our tiny laundry room.

"Yeah? Christian here for a cut? I don't mind fitting him in."

"Christian?" she repeats. "No, he's not the walk-in."

Turning around to face her, brow furrowed in confusion, I ask, "Then who were you yelling at?"

"Preston."

"That's…no," I say, shaking my head in disbelief. "He's in D.C. The team left last night."

"I don't know about all the travel logistics, but Preston Lawrence is here right now. He wants to talk to you."

"Oh. Wow."

I was not expecting this—for him to show up here when there's no game in town. He should be at home, getting ready to try to win the series with his team tomorrow night, not wasting time on me.

"Do you want to run out the back or…" Audrey trails off, leaving the decision to me.

"Is your client still here?"

"Mrs. Bailey is sitting under the dryer."

"Then I guess you should probably send him back here."

"Are you sure?"

Am I sure? Taking a deep breath, I let it out slowly, searching for that answer. "Yes."

"Okay then. I'll be out front, so if you need backup just yell for me."

"Thank you," I tell her.

I finish up the last towel, then turn off the light and shut the laundry room door. When I step into our little waiting area, he's standing there taking up all the space. His eyes roam up and down me as if he hasn't seen me in months when it's been less than twenty-four hours since he gave me the boot.

"Hey," he speaks first.

"Hey," I reply softly. I shouldn't be happy to see him or hear his rumbly voice, not after how badly he hurt me the last time I saw him when he was throwing shit and angry, telling me he was done with me. "What do you want? Your hair doesn't need a cut yet."

"You think I came all the way here from D.C. for a haircut?"

I shrug, since I have no clue why he's in town.

"I miss you," he says. "I missed you within seconds of you leaving the locker room. And I owe you an apology."

"Oh?"

"I need to apologize for blaming you for my temper. It wasn't your fault I blew up and went after Christian. I did that way before you and I ever met."

"I became a distraction and not a fun way to torment your enemy. There's nothing to apologize for, Preston, especially not in person when you should be getting ready for game six. You could've put all that in a text."

"That's not...yes, it was fun tormenting Christian. But my anger at him was more about me. I blame myself for letting him near my sister, getting her pregnant, and then taking away his chance to redeem himself with her and as a father."

Wow. That is definitely a change in his tune.

"I'm glad you've finally realized that. Is Maya going to tell him about Finley?"

"No. I am."

"You are?" I ask in surprise, my eyes widening in disbelief. "Before game six of the championships? That's messed up, Preston."

"No, I'm not going to tell him to throw him off his game. I

swear. I just can't keep it from him any longer out of spite. I would want to know if…He'll probably slice *my* throat with a skate when he finds out I kept Finley from him."

"He could've figured it out if he really wanted to. It's not like Maya was hiding him."

"I'm gonna ask if he wants to meet him tomorrow. The real reason I kept Maya and Finley out of Greensboro was to keep them away from Christian. It wasn't my place, though. By trying to protect my sister, I overstepped. Now I know that I can still be a supportive brother and uncle to Finley, even if Christian is in his life."

I think this is the first time I've ever heard him call his nemesis by his first name, like he's an old friend.

"Your heart was in the right place. At least I think it was," I tell him.

"It was. I didn't want Maya to have to deal with any more heartache after all she went through with our parents abandoning her and their own grandchild, and then Christian up and leaving town."

"Well, I'm glad you are going to try to make amends with Christian."

Holding up his big palms toward me, he says, "Whoa, I didn't say anything about making amends."

"Telling him he's the father to your nephew is going to require some amends, Preston. Whether you like it or not, you'll have to get used to him being around without hitting him in front of Finley."

His big hand scrubs over his beard as he considers that. "Wow. I guess you're right."

"It's a good thing to let go of your anger, at him and at

yourself. And you have the best reason to do it now—for Finley's sake. He deserves to grow up with a father."

"How can you be so sure that arrogant prick will want to be a dad?"

Giving him a small smile, I tell him the truth. "I just know. He's arrogant and can be a prick, yes. But Christian has his moments of decency."

"Like when he asked you to take him back?"

"He was just jealous or wanted to hurt you back. Actually, I think he's still in love with your sister."

"Seriously?"

"Yes."

"Huh. She loved him, too. It's possible she still does."

"Maybe you could try to let them figure that out without interfering this time?"

"I will. And, um, I may not even be around them as much if I accept the offer from San Diego."

"Oh. You got an offer to play for the Grizzlies?" I say in understanding.

"I did."

"That's great, Preston."

"At least I don't think they've revoked it yet. My agent wanted me to sign it like last week, in case I screwed up and got thrown out of a game. I should've listened but..."

"You've known since last week? And you didn't tell me?"

"I wanted to, Elle. I did. But I was scared of how you would react to me moving to the West Coast when this was so new between us."

Preston's moving to California.

My stomach sinks and I'm not even sure why. Because I

thought he was here to ask me to take him back and instead he came to make amends before moving across the country?

"I don't think Maya is going to up and move Finley out of his school and home in D.C., though."

"Right. That-that makes sense," I say.

"So, it'll just be me this time, living on my own."

"Well, um, good luck. Not just in tomorrow night's game, but with the move and all."

"Elle, I know it may be a long shot, but is there any way we could try to give this, us, another chance?"

Ah, there it is.

It should make me happier that he even bothered to ask. He can't actually think that would work though, does he?

"I don't know, Preston. Even if everything was good between us, California is so far away."

"I'll have time off during the summer before I have to go."

I'm already shaking my head no. "I can't. I don't think it would be a good idea for us to spend more time together before you up and leave. It's too much. And I don't want to be a distraction. I know how important hockey is to you, for you to keep supporting Maya and Finley. If I messed that up again…"

"Elle, what happened in that game, it wasn't your fault. I'm sorry I put the blame on you."

"Well, you did, and you were right. So how about we just end on good terms as friends?"

"Friends?"

"That's all I can offer you, Preston."

His wide shoulders rise, then fall heavily. "Then, I'll take it. I wish you would come to D.C. tomorrow for game six. It could be the last."

"I know, but I can't up and leave Audrey again with the salon. Thanks, though. And I do wish you luck. Lasting the entire game would even be a win in my book."

"Thanks, Elle. It was…it was really good to see you."

"It was good to see you too," I tell him, giving him a small, sad, close-lipped smile.

For a moment, he just stands there, hesitating, like he wants to say something else. But he doesn't. He turns around and walks out the door, out of my life for good.

I make it a good three seconds before the first sob escapes past my pursed lips.

39

Preston

It wasn't all that hard to find Riley's address. Of course he's living it up in one of the most expensive penthouses in the center of the city, close to all the clubs and bars, within walking distance to the arena, and Elle's salon.

The doorman, unfortunately for Riley, is just a little too trusting. He let me up when I told him I was a friend. Guess he doesn't follow hockey headlines. All he told Riley on the intercom was that he was sending up a friend.

A friend.

It seems like forever ago when Riley was my best friend and roommate. For more than three years, he was the person I did everything with, spent nearly every second either just hanging in our apartment or on the ice. We had a stupid plan to go pro together, promising that we would both hold out until the same team agreed to draft us both.

And then everything went to hell when Maya came to the city as a freshman at NC State, wanting to be near her big brother for whatever reason. Maybe for the sense of safety and protection when all I did was mess up her life.

I take the elevator up, using the code to the penthouse that the too trusting doorman gave me.

When I step out onto the penthouse floor, Riley's standing in his open doorway. He looks like shit thanks to the bruised cheek, busted lip and ear so swollen it sticks out from his thick head. All the injuries I inflicted on him last night and I still believe he deserved.

"So much for being a 'friend' coming up to visit," Christian grumbles. "What the hell do you want? Why are you even still in town? Did you come here to murder me without any witnesses? You should know there are cameras in the elevator and hallways." He points up to one in the upper corner of the hall.

"No murdering planned today. We need to talk."

"Talk? You mean you'll tell me I'm a piece of shit while beating the hell out of me some more until I can't play tomorrow?"

"No. I just mean talk. I swear I won't lay a finger on you." I hold up both of my hands in surrender. For this conversation, I'll keep that promise. It won't be easy to resist throttling the asshole, but I won't today. And if he hits me for keeping this from him, I won't even hit him back. At least not for the first punch.

"Whatever," he says, walking away from the door to leave the decision to come in or not up to me. I follow him inside, shutting the door behind me. His back and shoulders tense at the sound, as if he's regretting letting me in so easily.

"So, what do you want to talk about?" he asks as he slumps down in the middle of his leather sofa. His finger absently rubs along the cut in his bottom lip.

There are two other chairs, but I don't sit. I just go stand in front of the television and get right down to the purpose of this visit.

"You have a son."

"Huh?" he stares up at me, unblinking.

"His name is Finley. He's four and, of course, he loves hockey."

Christian is instantly on his feet, only a marble coffee table between us. "What the hell are you talking about, Preston? I think I would know if I had a son." It takes the blond moron a full minute before his eyes bulge with understanding. "Did you say…he's *four*? Like years? Like four years, the time since I've seen Maya plus about eight or nine months?"

"Yes."

He shakes his head, jaw clenched tight, pointing his index finger at me. "This isn't fucking funny, man. I'm tired of you fucking with my head, and now you're making more shit up!"

I ignore the roundabout mention of Elle.

"I'm not making this up. My sister gave up everything to become a mother while you skated off into the night, going pro and then screwing every woman you met."

Christian keeps shaking his head. "No. You're lying! This is some trick to fuck with my head, so I'll lose the biggest game of my life tomorrow!"

If the Warhawks win, we get to kiss the trophy, and the Bobcats go home empty-handed. If the Bobcats win, it all comes down to game seven here in Greensboro.

"It's not your game to win or lose, jackass. It's the whole team."

Running his fingers through the front of his hair, he starts to pace across the room, along the wall of windows that showcases the city down below. "I saw…I saw Maya at game three with a little boy. I figured he was hers, that she had met someone else and they…you know…" he trails off as if uncomfortable talking about my sister sleeping with someone else.

"You didn't notice he looked four?"

"How was I supposed to know how old he was? I don't know shit about kids. I…I figured she ended the pregnancy in college as soon as possible, met someone, got married, and started a family with someone else! I didn't want any details."

"Right. You didn't *want* to know the truth."

"I would've wanted to know that I have a son!" he bellows, going from denial to anger in the blink of an eye. "Are you fucking with me? Please, don't joke about this. Are you sure, like a thousand percent certain that he's mine?"

Now I'm getting angry too. "Are you accusing my sister of sleeping around?" I don't know for sure, but I'm almost certain Christian was her first and last.

"No. No, I'm not…that's not what I mean. I just, I find it hard to believe now, out of the blue…"

"I'm not joking. I swear on my sister and nephew's lives. He's yours. There was nobody else. There hasn't been anyone else for Maya."

"But you both hated me. Why would she…how could she still have my kid and raise him on her own without telling me?"

"She wasn't alone. They both still live with me in a suburb

near D.C.," I admit to him. "And Finley will be at the game tomorrow if you want to meet him."

"Tomorrow?"

"Yes."

I expect him to accuse me of messing with his head again, but then he says, "What if I...what if we lose? I can't... I don't want my...son to see me for the first time as a fucking loser."

"That's too damn bad! You don't get to pick and choose when to be a father. It's either always or never. I'm giving you a choice, so neither you nor Maya can blame me for standing in your way anymore after today!"

I head for the door, figuring I've said everything I needed to say. It doesn't feel like enough to fix everything. I know it's not. Maya is probably going to be even more pissed at me for opening this can of worms with Christian now, right before I leave for California. Then there's Elle, who wouldn't even consider the idea of moving across the country with me or even keep seeing me long-distance. Not that I blame her after the shit I put her through.

"Preston, wait," Christian calls out when I have my hand on the doorknob. "I want to meet him. You said...his name is Finley?"

Wow. It looks like Elle was right yet again.

"Yeah, Finley."

"Could I...would it be possible to see him before the game, though? Don't make me face something this big after... It won't be fair to him if I'm in a shit mood."

"You that certain your team is gonna lose?" I turn around to ask him.

"I don't know and neither do you. Please, Pres. Just do this one thing for me. You owe me that much after keeping my son from me for the past four fucking years!"

He's not wrong. But, it's not exactly up to me.

"I'll talk to Maya and see what she says. The truth is, she doesn't even know I was going to tell you today."

Fingers raking through his hair, he tugs on the strands, his face twisted as if in pain. "Jesus. She didn't want me to ever find out, did she?"

"It was more me than her. I should've asked her what she wanted but I didn't. I thought I knew better. I will ask her for this, though. I have to."

"Okay. Let me know?"

"Yeah. I'll let you know."

"What are you really doing in town?" he asks. "Trying to make up with Elle?"

"Why do you think I need to make up with her?"

"Because I've been in her shoes. Your knee-jerk reaction to any problem is cutting people out of your life. It's easier that way, right? Then you don't actually have to admit when you're wrong or try to fix shit."

"You're right. I ended things with her after the last game," I admit to him for some stupid reason. "And now I'm moving to San Diego, so there's no reason for her to forgive me."

"San Diego? The Grizzlies?"

Shit. I really shouldn't have said that. Contracts are supposed to be kept confidential, especially when they're still in the negotiation phase. Now they may have another reason to yank it out from under me if he runs his mouth.

"It's not a done deal yet, but it's the best offer Tommy thinks I'll get."

"That's a fucking lie."

"What?"

"I know the Bobcats want you."

"How?"

"Management asked me about you, before the series started. They wanted my blessing."

"So that's why they haven't sent anything in writing."

"If they haven't made an official offer, then I honestly don't know why," he says, crossing his arms over his chest. "I told them I don't give a shit."

"You don't give a shit?"

"Maybe it was stupid, but I thought that if we finally got to play on the same team again, we could work things out. I'm not the one who always starts the fights."

"You run your mouth just to get me to lose it and hit you."

"True. You did break my arm and give me a concussion. You're the reason we didn't make it to the playoff those two years."

"Because you couldn't play? You think awfully highly of yourself, don't you?"

"It's the truth. The team can't score shit without me."

"You haven't scored much shit lately, have you?"

"And whose fault is that?"

"You really regret ending things with Elle?" I ask, changing the subject.

"Hell yes. Don't you?"

"Yes."

I don't ask if he agreed to me playing for the Bobcats because it might mean seeing more of Maya.

It doesn't matter, and it's not going to happen. No official offer from the Bobcats means it's Cali or bust for me. Tommy said they weren't nearly offering as much as the Grizzlies, anyway.

"Your phone number still the same?" I ask Christian as I pull out my cell phone from my jean pocket.

"Yeah."

"Then give me time to talk to my sister in person. Could be later tonight before I have an answer."

"Whenever is fine," he replies. "Do you have any pictures, you know, of him?"

Opening the photo app, I scroll through to the photos of Finley's most recent birthday party, which has some of him on the ice too.

"Here. You can scroll."

"Thanks," Christian says as he takes the device and stares down at the first image. His blue eyes shimmer as if he's about to bawl like a baby. Then he laughs and presses his fist between his teeth. "Holy shit. He already plays hockey?"

"Of course he does, on the ice a little and video game as much as Maya lets him. He wants to grow up and go pro like his uncle. He'll be thrilled when he finds out his dad's a pro, too."

"You think so?"

"Yeah, I do. And if you hurt him in any way, especially if it's by walking away after meeting him, I really will murder you by slicing my skate across your throat."

"Shit," he says as he continues to occasionally swipe images. "Always or never a father, huh?"

"You better be damn sure before you decide," I warn him. "There's no going back after you meet him. Not unless…"

"Unless what?"

"Unless you want to meet him as a friend of mine and not as his father."

"You mean…don't tell him who I am?"

"At least not at first."

"I don't know if I could do that."

"It would give Maya a chance to make sure you're gonna stick around. That could work best for everyone."

"Everyone except for me! What happens when he finds out I'm a fucking liar?"

I jerk my phone from his hand and tell him, "You were the one worried about how he would feel about you being a loser, remember?"

"Just talk to Maya and let me think about it."

"Fine."

"Fine," he says, and I show myself out, hoping I haven't just made a huge mistake for everyone.

40

Elle

I'm sweeping up hair between clients, replaying my last conversation with Preston, when a blond man bursts through the front door like he's being chased by the hounds of hell.

Ah, guess the team's plane is about to leave and he thinks he's so important I'll make customers wait to cut his hair.

"Christian," I say in surprise while I continue my sweeping. "What are you doing here? I don't have time to fit you in today."

"Do you know too?" he asks.

I look up to find his eyes glistening, his posture like that of a man who has been run over by a Mack truck. His face is bruised and battered, distracting me. It's the first time I've seen it since the fight with Preston on the ice. Too busy cata-

323

loguing his injuries, it takes me longer than it should to grasp the meaning of his question until he repeats it.

"Just tell me the truth. Do you know about him, Elle?" This time, the question is asked through gritted teeth.

Him. Oh crap.

"I…I…we should talk somewhere else," I quickly suggest. There are two clients in the waiting room, so we can't go back there. The little old ladies are the worst gossipers around town. "I'll be right back, Mr. Richards," I yell to my client before I head outside and around the side of the building with Christian right behind me.

"Christian, I'm sorry, but I couldn't tell you. I promised Preston and Maya," I tell him softly. "I'm so sorry."

He doesn't say anything else; he just throws his arms around me and doesn't let go. I can barely breath he's gripping me so tight. I'm about to push him away when his shoulders begin to shake.

The man may be a prick, but I let him cry on me and even return his hug, patting him on his back to try to console him.

Eventually, he asks without releasing me, "What the fuck am I going to do?"

"Try to be a good father?"

I feel his head shake from side to side. "What if I can't…if they never tell him…"

"What do you mean?"

Releasing me, Christian paces away, his back to me as he lifts the bottom front of his tee up to wipe his face. Without facing me, he says, "Preston suggested I meet him tomorrow, as Preston's friend…"

"Oh," I say in understanding. Playing it cautious rather than throwing the truth at a sweet four-year-old boy in case

Christian flakes, stops coming around or whatever else he could do to screw up his chance to be a father. "Maybe that's best for everyone."

"It's not best for me!" he huffs.

"Sure, it is. There will be less pressure on you to be… anything except for a cool new hockey player friend when you meet him."

A scoff with his back still to me says Christian disagrees.

"I heard Finley ask Maya about you during game four."

Now he spins around to face me, the red around his eyes the only proof he's been crying. "He asked about me?"

"Yes."

"Why? What did he say?"

"Oh, well, he asked how you were so much faster than all the other players."

"Yeah?" a smile spreads across his face, as if proud that his son was impressed with his skills.

"He beat half the Warhawks on a hockey video game the night of Preston's party."

"Really?" he says in surprise. Then, "He was…he was there when I was there?"

"Yes."

"What else?"

"He calls me Ellie too, just like out of nowhere."

"No shit?" he says with a chuckle. Swiping a hand under his nose, he looks at the pavement and says, "I bet Maya's a really good mother."

"She is. The best," I tell him.

"And does Maya…is she married? Seeing anyone? She's not on social media so…" he trails off after admitting to trying to stalk her.

"No. She's not married or seeing anyone." His hunched shoulders lower a few inches. Since he looks like a man who needs some good news, I add, "In fact, Maya doesn't date anyone, like ever. I don't think she's been with anyone since you."

He snorts and says, "That's impossible. She's gorgeous."

"She's a single mother. Her entire world revolves around Finley."

Christian nods, but turns his back to me again to dry off his face.

"I know this is a lot to absorb right now, especially with the pressure of finishing the championships. You don't have to become a father overnight, Christian. Meet your son. Just focus on being his friend to give Finley and yourself time to get used to the idea of you being a permanent part of his life."

"Always or never a father. That's what Preston said I have to decide."

"We both know which one you'll choose."

"I never thought…I had no idea she had him. I was sure she would end it."

"Why did you think that?" I ask him.

"Because Maya was so young and scared. She actually broke up with me, you know, before she found out. Preston thinks I ended it, but it was all Maya."

"Why did she end things?"

"Well, we only sort of slept together once, and it was…bad. I was bad at it. It happened so fast and I knew it was her first time. Then I just panicked and left her."

It's hard to imagine Christian Riley being bad in bed, which means he was probably overthinking everything because he knew Maya was different from all the other girls.

"You can't panic and leave this time," I warn him. "No matter what."

"I know. I won't."

"Good," I say, and I believe him.

"I'm just…I'm so nervous about meeting him, my son. His name is Finley, right?"

"Right. He's adorable, so smart for his age, and kind-hearted."

"Would you…I know I have no right to ask you for anything, but could you maybe come with me? To meet Finley and see the game? I'll get you tickets. Audrey too, if she wants."

"I don't know, Christian."

"Please, Ellie. I don't have anyone else, and you're the only one who knows the truth."

I nod, caving, even though it feels like this favor will make everything more complicated.

Preston

"So? How did it go?" Maya pounces on me as soon as I open the front door back in D.C. as if she was pacing in front of it. "Did you apologize to Elle?"

"Yeah, I did."

"And? Are you two back together?"

"No, we're not."

"What? Why not?"

"I told her about California. She doesn't want to do long distance, which means she's not going to consider moving for me. I couldn't even talk her into spending time together during the off-season, so…"

"Aww. Well, if you care about her, then don't give up so easily just yet."

"I don't know what else I can do, Maya."

"You need to come up with more than an apology. It'll take a grand gesture to prove to her you're serious about making this work and that you won't push her away again when things get tough."

"Like what?"

She gives me a light punch to my shoulder. "That's for you to figure out, big brother."

"Yeah, I don't know if there's any figuring this out. I don't want to walk away from her. Being in D.C. without Elle doesn't even feel right."

And that's when an idea hits me.

It's a really, really stupid idea. If the Warhawks win the trophy tomorrow, I'll beg Elle to take me back on national television the first time someone shoves a microphone in my face.

But that won't fix anything for Maya.

Which reminds me…

I scrape my fingers through my beard then tell my sister, "There was something else I had to do in Greensboro, someone else to apologize to."

"Oh yeah? Who?"

"Do you think you and Finley could come to the game a little earlier tomorrow? There's something I was wondering if you would do before the puck drop."

"Sure. Is there a pre-game party or something?"

"No. I was hoping, well, let's sit down and I'll start at the beginning."

"Oh-kay," she drawls.

We both go over to the living room and take a seat on the sofa. "I told Riley about Finley."

Maya blinks at me, her face stunned. "You did what now?"

"I told him he's Finley's father. And he wants to meet him."

"Preston!" Getting to her feet, she explodes with her arms flailing all over the place. "What…why…you should've asked me first! How could you do this, after all this time, without talking to me first?"

"I know I should've asked what you wanted five years ago, and I didn't. I'm sorry. I just wanted to make things right as soon as possible."

Curses I've never heard before come spewing out of my sister's mouth as she storms around the living room, her fingers tugging on her ponytail.

Standing up, I grab her shoulders to stop her pacing. "Look, Maya, I know it's last minute, and I'm an asshole for springing this on you, but you don't have to tell Finley who Riley is. He can just be a friend of mine if you want to take things slow."

She shakes her head, shakes my hands off her by taking a step back. "I don't know. Lying to Finley about this feels wrong."

"I get it," I tell her. "So, you're going to tell Finley the truth and then let them meet?"

"I don't know. I just…I need time to think this through!"

"Okay. If Riley meets him and bails, I'll kill him for you."

"Ugh! I'm so pissed at you for putting me on the spot like this."

"I know. I really am sorry about everything."

Poking me in the chest hard, she says, "It's a good thing I love you. That's the only reason I'm forgiving you."

Her words make me wonder if the same could be true for her forgiving Christian too.

41

Elle

Being in D.C., walking around the Warhawks arena with Christian feels all wrong.

Even though it's nearly two hours before the game starts, the place is still packed with fans who are excited that this could be it—the final game that wins the Warhawks the championship trophy.

When we give a security guard our names, he takes us down to the hallway near the locker rooms. There's a huge open lounge for friends and family of the players, usually ones with small children. A jumbo flat screen hangs on the wall, no doubt for showing the games. Comfy chairs for nursing mothers are scattered around, along with several travel baby cribs, and a changing table. The rest of the room has toys scattered for older kids, including a picnic table full of Lego blocks, which is where Finley is playing across from Maya while Preston hovers behind them. All three are wearing matching black Lawrence jerseys, and Preston already has his full pads and skates on, ready for warmups. Christian had to ask his coach if he could be a few minutes late, and he thankfully agreed, even though he doesn't know why.

"Holy shit," Christian whispers from the doorway.

"Don't cuss," I remind him just as Preston looks up and sees us.

"Elle?" His brow furrows in surprise until he looks between me and Christian and I know he's assuming the worst.

Giving Christian a little tug on his arm, I lead the way over to the picnic table.

"I'm just another friend who wanted to come say hi and good luck," I tell them. "Hey, Maya. Finley." I give them a forced smile that Finley returns, but Maya looks frazzled, her knee bouncing uncontrollably as she eyes Christian.

"Hi, Ellie!" Finley says, then he throws his leg over the picnic bench to come over to us, arms open. I bend down and give him a hug as Preston comes over, Maya too, even though she stays half-hidden behind her brother.

"It's good to see you again, Finley. Are you excited for the game?"

"Yep! Preston said when the Warhawks win, they'll get to carry a big trophy."

"That's right," I agree.

The boy's eyes finally slide over to Christian. I look to Preston, who is staring at me, then at Maya, who is watching Christian through unblinking eyes. I'm waiting for one of them to make introductions, but when they both stand there silently, I decide to do it myself.

"Finley, do you remember the other day when you asked how that one Bobcats player was so fast? Number nineteen?"

He looks back at me and nods after he considers my question.

"Well, now you can ask him yourself. This is Christian Riley. He plays for the Bobcats. Number nineteen."

Christian is frozen in place, studying Finley's every move like he's going to be quizzed about him later and his life depends on acing it. I elbow him in the side, causing him to finally snap out of his daze.

"Hey, um, hi, Finley."

The boy looks up at him and asks, "You're the player that's really fast and steals the puck from the Warhawks?"

Christian's gaze goes from his son to Maya and quickly back again. Clearing his throat, he nods. "Um, yeah. Sometimes I guess I'm fast."

Finley's head cocks. "So? How are you faster than everyone else?"

"Ah, well, I practice a lot."

"Uncle Preston practices a lot too, and he's slow."

Preston growls quietly while Christian huffs out a laugh. "Preston could practice day and night and he would still be slow."

"Are you playing in today's game?" Finley asks.

"Yes. Yeah, of course."

"You aren't in your uniform."

"Oh right," Christian says, his hands that have been clutching his blue and yellow jersey relax as he untwists it. "I, um, I brought you one of my jerseys. If you want it, I mean."

"Cool. I don't have a Bobcats' jersey," Finley replies as he swipes it from Christian's hands. He holds it up in front of him, inspecting the front and then the back of the youth large he'll be able to grow into and wear for years.

I really hope Christian sticks around that long.

"Bobcats! *Rawr*! Will you sign it for me?" Finley asks, practically jumping up and down.

"Ah, yeah. Absolutely." Christian pats down the sides of his slacks for a writing utensil, even though he never carries one. "I don't have a pen or anything on me."

"I have one," Maya says, whipping one out from her clear cross-body bag. She offers it to Finley who snatches it up and holds the marker and jersey up to Christian. He takes both and looks at them as if he can't remember how to write his own name.

"You could use that Lego table over there," I suggest.

"Right. Yeah. Thanks," Christian says before he goes over and lays the fabric on the table with Finley hot on his heels. He points at the top white corner above the numbers on the front to indicate where he wants his father to sign.

"I'll just…I better get to my seat. Will you be okay, Christian?"

He nods without even glancing in my direction.

"Good luck," I tell him and glance over at Preston, who looks like a sad grizzly bear. "You too."

Preston

Elle's here.

Or she was here.

I was so shocked to see her with Christian that I couldn't even speak a word. And now she's gone, and I can't exactly chase her through the arena in my skates.

I'm not sure why I'm surprised she came with Christian.

The photo of them…embracing outside her salon was all over sports news and social media. I wanted to punch something or someone the first time I saw it, along with the assumptions that they were back together, and I had been kicked to the curb.

By the tenth time I had to look at the image, I had come to terms with the fact that I had lost her fair and square, and it was nobody's fault but my own. Winning the trophy and begging her on national television would be pointless now.

Maya looks about like I feel as she supervises Christian and Finley's first meeting. The two are making a spaceship out of Legos, that looks like a giant dick, complete with balls. I'm not sure if Maya's going to yell, cry, or laugh when this meeting is over.

And it will have to be over soon. Not just because I'm a little hurt that Finley put on Riley's Bobcats jersey over mine, but because we've both got a game to play.

What was with Elle's shirt? It had both Bobcats and Warhawk logos on it, as if she doesn't have a preferred team. I want her to root for my team, wear my jersey. But I fucked that all up.

"We need to get going, Riley," I remind him, a little harsher than I intended because of the reminder of how badly I screwed up with Elle.

"Oh. Yeah. Right," Christian agrees as he stands from the tiny chair and runs his fingers through the front of his blond hair. "I…thanks," he says to Maya. Then to my nephew, he reaches a hand toward him, turning it into a fist for him to hit. "It was nice to meet you, Finley. I heard you like video games."

"Uh-huh."

"Maybe…maybe we could play some time?"

"Could we, Mom?" he turns to ask Maya, who says to Christian, "We'll see."

Nodding in understanding, he backs toward the door with a wave, nearly tripping over a baby stroller before he makes it out the door.

"This way," I tell him, pointing down the tunnel. "Try not to fall and break your neck. Everyone will blame me for it."

"*Fuucck*," he whispers, scrubbing both hands over his face. "How badly did I screw that up?"

"I don't know," I tell him honestly. It didn't seem that bad to me, but I'm not sure what Maya thought. "It was…nice of you to bring him a jersey."

"I thought he might laugh or throw it in the trash."

"That's basically what Elle did to mine," I mutter. "So… how is she?" I cave and ask him.

"Who?"

"Elle."

His shoulders shrug as we walk. "How the fuck would I know?"

I honestly expected him to gloat, to say they were back together now that I'm out of the picture. After all, she came to D.C. with the prick.

"You're really going to play stupid? I know you came to the arena together. You don't want to try to piss me off before the game?" I ask in disbelief.

"I'm not playing stupid. I'm not back with Ellie. She came with me today just as a friend."

"I saw the photo of you outside her salon."

"Man, that wasn't…I didn't know there was anyone watching us, I swear. I just went to her because I was upset after you broke the news to me that I'm a father. Ellie was the only one who knew, the only one I could talk to."

"So, you two didn't…you haven't…"

"No. Elle is definitely over me."

"Are you over her?"

Snorting, he turns to me and says, "I've got more important shit to worry about now, don't I?"

"Yeah, I guess so," I agree.

"Ellie…she's probably the only person in the world who thinks I could be a decent father."

"You don't think you'll be a decent father?"

"I don't know if Maya will give me the chance."

"It won't be easy to convince her," I tell him honestly. "And if you fuck up this chance, I'll kill you."

"Nope. You can't get in my head today, man." With a grin, he says, "*My son* is wearing my jersey, and he thinks I'm fast."

"He's four. He doesn't know what the hell he's talking about," I joke with him. "And it doesn't matter how fast you are tonight. Elle's here. Maya said I've got to make a grand gesture to win her back, which means I'm about to go win that trophy for her."

42

Elle

I was so worried that showing up unannounced with Christian would go so badly that Preston would have a shitty game. Or that Christian would be off during this game because he just met his son for the first time.

Thankfully, I was wrong on both accounts.

Preston is playing just as hard and aggressive as usual, but without getting any penalties. And Christian is faster than ever. The score is tied up two to two in the third period, and everyone in the entire arena is on their feet for the last three minutes. We could be going to overtime where the Warhawks win the championship with one more score, or the Bobcats could make a comeback, win today, and take this whole series to game seven back in Greensboro.

While Preston may be hitting Christian every chance he

gets, it doesn't seem as personal as before, like it's all part of the game, both men doing their jobs to try to help their team win.

Christian spins around a Warhawk player, then he's racing down the ice, one on one with the goalie. He goes left, then right, then shoots.

And the goalie throws up his mitt and catches it.

Wow, that was close.

And I'm not even sure who I'm rooting for anymore. I want both teams to win so badly. But knowing this is Preston's final game in D.C. no matter what happens, I guess I'm rooting for him a little bit more.

Just because it's over between us doesn't mean I don't still care. That I don't still love the grumpy man. We just can't be together because he's moving to California.

Since he didn't even ask me to come with him, I think he knows as well as I do that it will never work.

Not that I would up and leave Audrey, our salon, all our customers, and being a short drive away from my parents. Still, it would've been nice to be asked.

The game does go into overtime, which means up to twenty more grueling minutes of hockey, where both teams are worn out.

Nothing much happens during the first ten minutes. It's like neither side can get the puck out of the neutral zone.

But then one of the Bobcats gets a penalty for delay of game, throwing the puck up into the stands, which means the Warhawks will have an extra man on the ice.

You can tell they smell blood as they get into position. Three different players make a shot. A Bobcats forward tries to steal the puck, but Preston keeps it in play, passing it to the teammate across the ice from him. The player draws his stick back and lets it fly from the blue line to the goal where it's deflected by the goalie.

But another Warhawk player is waiting right in front of the goal. As soon as the airborne puck lands, he taps it with his stick and it's in!

The Warhawks score and win!

Fans around me jump up and down, some even hug me even though I'm not wearing Preston's Warhawk jersey. No, for today's game, I bought a black tee promoting the series, the mascots of both teams and a vs. in between them.

It was my way of being neutral. Or as neutral as I could be when the man I love just won the championship trophy.

Black and red confetti rains down on the ice as the Warhawks celebrate by hugging each other. I watch as Christian fist bumps a few players on the opposing team before reaching Preston. They say a few quick words to each other, bump fists, and don't throw any other punches. Their truce feels like its very own miracle. One I hope will last for Maya and Finley's sakes.

I'm so glad that Preston is making the effort to forgive the other man, if for no other reason than for his nephew, who he knows is watching.

I stick around long enough to see Preston get his turn to heft up the trophy and kiss it before I slip out of the arena, telling myself I'm just trying to avoid the rush when everyone else leaves.

The truth is, I know it's time to let him go, to say goodbye, no matter how hard it is.

Preston

We did it.

The Warhawks actually fucking did it.

And I played a small part in helping my teammates finally get their hands on the championship trophy, everything they've always dreamed of.

While I may have won it back in my first year in the league, I was too young then to fully appreciate the moment. It seemed so easy, as if it didn't take a shit ton of work and a little bit of luck for such a huge accomplishment.

The Bobcats and the coaching staff actually stay on the ice through the entire ceremony, which is surprising, but also decent of them. They fought a hell of a series, almost taking it to game seven if Vincent hadn't stopped Christian's goal in the third period and Nick hadn't made that rebound shot in overtime.

All the little plays from an entire series added up to this win.

And I'm so glad Elle was here, even if she wasn't here for me but as moral support for Christian.

"Congrats, Lawrence," Coach Bell from the Bobcats says when he approaches me with his hand out.

"Thanks, Coach."

"It's too bad you prefer California to the Carolinas. It would've been good to have you playing defense for us."

"Ah, yeah, well, I never got an official offer from the Bobcats."

"Because your agent told us not to waste our time, that you were headed to the West Coast."

"That's…I didn't think I would be able to live and play in Greensboro," I tell him honestly as I see number nineteen, skating to the locker rooms, shoulders hunched in defeat but head up, searching the stands. "You know…I haven't signed a contract yet."

"Is that right?" Bell asks with a smirk.

"Is the team still interested?"

"We'll send an offer over as soon as we emotionally recover from today's loss."

"You've got a tough team," I tell him.

"Here's hoping it'll be a little tougher next season."

Shoving his hands in his pockets, he walks off the ice with his head still held high, proud of his team's accomplishment, even if they didn't win it all.

He seems like a decent coach. The team is stacked with great players in every position except for maybe defense. Christian and I have no choice but to be on good terms now, which means the only thing keeping me from moving to the city and team to be with the woman I love is what? A few dollars?

Okay, so it's probably more like a million of them, but Elle's worth every single penny.

I search the stands for her again, having no idea where she would be sitting in the packed house or if she's still here.

But I bet I know which hotel she's staying at tonight.

Heading off the ice, I stop in the locker room long enough to untie my skates and kick them off along with my helmet and gloves before putting on the dress shoes I wore to the arena. Then I grab my phone and I'm set.

"Nice outfit, Lawrence," Spencer says with a chuckle as I head out of the locker room. "Where are you headed looking like that?"

"I've got to go find my girl."

"We've got a trophy to celebrate tonight at the owner's house!" he calls out.

"Yeah, save me a beer. I'll be there as soon as I can."

Jogging out of the arena as fast as I can in the slippery soled shoes. I call my sister first.

"Hey! Congrats on the big win!" Maya answers.

"Hey, thank you. Now I'm going to find Elle."

"Oh. Well, good for you."

"And I may be moving to Greensboro."

"Oh?"

"Yeah. Nothing is in writing yet, but maybe you will reconsider moving…"

"I-I don't know. He's only met him once!" she whispers into the phone.

"I know that, but I've got a good feeling about this."

"Well, you and your good feeling can do whatever you want. I have to figure out what's best for me and Finley."

"I know. I get it. I just wanted to give you the heads up, so you could think about it over the summer."

"Okay, well, you have more important things to think about tonight. Finley and I won't wait up for you."

"You're that confident that Elle will take me back?"

"I'm that confident that you won't give up yet, even if she does."

"True," I agree. "Let me know when you two are home safe."

"We will. Love you, big brother."

"Love you too," I tell her before ending the call and taking off down the sidewalk in front of the arena. I don't even bother trying to get a taxi or Uber since the street is packed with fans celebrating, some of which high five me as I run by them.

43

Elle

I'm exhausted by the time I walk back to the hotel. And then, wouldn't you know it, my stupid keycard wouldn't work, so I had to come all the way back down to the front desk to get them to reactivate it.

There's a long line at the reservation desk too, lots of traveling fans checking in after the game, when I just want to go to my room and fall into bed.

And maybe turn on the television to see the rest of the Warhawk's celebration.

Behind me, I hear gasps and squeals. Turning around to see what the commotion is all about, I glance over my shoulder and my jaw drops.

Preston jogs in heading straight for the front desk still wearing his uniform and…a pair of men's dress shoes? His hair and beard are still damp with sweat. A red line slashes across his forehead from where he recently removed his helmet.

When his eyes spot me, he stops abruptly. "Cupcake," he says with a heavy sigh of relief. "I knew…you were staying… here."

"Preston, what are you doing here?" I ask as all the eyes in the entire crowded lobby are drawn to us.

"I needed to talk to you."

"Oh. Um, well, congratulations on winning the championship."

"Thanks." Leaning over, he puts his palms on his knees to catch his breath, while everyone in the entire lobby stares at us.

"Shouldn't you be celebrating with the team?" I ask.

"Yes."

He's still recovering, and everyone around us seems to be holding their breath.

"So, um, how does it feel? As amazing as before?" I ask into the uncomfortable silence.

"Second trophy…in five years feels…pretty damn good, yeah."

"I'm happy for you, Preston. I really do wish you the best in California."

"About that," he says, holding up a finger. "Give me another second."

"Okay."

Straightening again, he says, "I'm going to turn down the offer to play for the Grizzlies."

I glance around again, noticing all the eyes and ears on us. Nodding my head to the alcove nearby, I reluctantly get out of the long line and lead him over. He towers over me, standing close with his palm braced on the wall above my head. At least no one can hear us. Looking up at him, I say, "I thought…why would you turn down the Grizzlies? You said they were the only team to make you an offer."

"Not exactly. They were the only team I would have considered a few weeks ago. There was one other team that was interested but never sent the offer because my agent told them there was no point. One I never thought I would want to accept."

"Who do you…oh," I mutter in understanding.

"That's right. The Bobcats."

"But you won't play for them because of Christian?"

"I couldn't imagine playing on the same team as that…as Christian. But you are more important to me than a grudge. More important than anything else. I'm going to play for the Bobcats because that's where you are, and I want to be near you."

"What? No, Preston. I can't let you do that. This is a huge decision! Years of your life, right? Don't do this for me."

"Why not?"

He moves closer so our bodies are nearly flush, making it harder for me to think. What were we talking about? Oh right, moving to Greensboro. "Because you shouldn't! Think about yourself, about Maya and Finley."

"I have thought about them. Maya doesn't want to move but, in Greensboro, Finley will have more time to spend with Christian."

"Oh." I deflate several inches. "So you're moving for them. It was stupid for me to think…"

"No, Elle. I don't know what decision Maya will make. I'm

leaving it up to her. It's time I step back and let my sister make her own decisions. But I'm going to sign this contract as soon as I get it, even if Maya stays in D.C., just to be near you. I love you, and I know you may not be ready to forgive me yet, but I'm not going to give up."

He loves me? Those words cause warmth to spread through my chest, even if I know it won't last.

"But…" Struggling to figure out a way to prevent him from doing something he'll regret if we don't work out, I decide to go with activating his hair trigger temper. "I guess you haven't seen the photos of me and Christian yet. And you know I came with him to the game…"

"I have seen the pictures. And I talked to Christian about them and why you came with him to D.C. He told me the photos were taken right after he found out he was a father, and he needed a friend then and today. Just a friend, right?"

"Yes. That's…I thought you would assume the worst."

"I did. I did, but I'm not jealous of him anymore. What we have isn't something he can compete with, right cupcake?"

I nod, unable to say the words.

"I love you, Elle. And no matter what answer you give me today, I'm not giving up on you or us. Ever. You're the end game for me. I'll be here waiting for you, however long it takes."

With that pronouncement, Preston's lips brush lightly over mine just once. It's more than a kiss. It's a promise of more whenever I'm ready. Then, with a grin, he turns to leave.

I grab a handful of his jersey to pull him back.

His eyes widen in surprise, and I tell him, "I love you too."

When Preston just stands there looking stunned, I go up

on my toes to cup his cheek, pulling his mouth back to mine because I want to show him that I don't want to wait even a second longer to be with him.

351

EPILOGUE

Preston
Five months later...

"Hi, Preston. You are Preston Lawrence, right?" a woman calls out to me as soon as I exit my SUV with my duffle bag hefted over my shoulder. It's not just any woman, but a gorgeous blonde. "Could I pretty please have just one moment of your time?" she adds with a wink and a smile.

"Just one moment? That's all you want?" I ask as I approach the fence surrounding the player's parking lot.

"I know what you're thinking," she replies. "But I'm not a puck bunny."

"No? That's too bad."

Biting her lip to keep from laughing, she says, "Right well, I just wanted a selfie, or an ussie, since I would like for you to be in the photo with me."

"No."

"No? You won't take pity on a lonely woman?"

"Hmm. I don't know." I drop my eyes to her snug, blue and yellow striped tee. "You a Bobcats' fan?"

"Of course. I could show you my lucky Bobcats' panties to prove it." She hooks her thumb in her jeans to tug them down enough to show me the blue string.

"Hell yes. Let her through right now," I order the security guard manning the gatehouse.

I drop my duffle on the ground while he unlocks the gate to let her slip through, and then she's jumping into my arms. Our mouths meet, then our tongues as I back her into the fence to let her feel how hard I got just from seeing her lucky panties.

"Are you excited for your first home game in a new arena?" Elle asks against my lips when we both have to come up for air.

"More excited about using my teeth to pull off your little panties tonight when I get home."

She laughs and swats playfully at my chest, so I lower her feet to the ground again.

When I moved into my new apartment in Greensboro in late June, one in Christian's building, Elle refused to move in with me. But by the end of July, she was staying over every night, neither of us willing to sleep apart. By the end of August, Elle finally caved and made it official.

"You look very dashing in that new suit, Mr. Grumpy Hockey Player."

"Thanks," I say, while straightening the front of it. "My girlfriend helped me pick it out."

"Aww. You're taken. That's too bad."

"That's right, cupcake. All I can offer you is a picture before I have to get my ass inside." While Elle pulls out her phone from her jeans, I tell her, "I'll have someone bring you one of my jerseys before the puck drop. I can't believe it has taken this long to slap my name on one."

"Can't wait to wear it," she replies, holding up her phone to try to capture us both as I slip my arm around her waist, pulling her closer to my side.

"Do I need to stoop down a little?" I ask, since it's just my head showing up on the screen.

Giggling, she says, "Just a little bit." I hunch down and she says, "A little more."

"Let me try, since my arm is longer."

Taking the phone from her hand, I quickly swipe to the right to press the video option and hit the red button.

"A little lower," she says, not noticing that it's recording us now.

I drop to one knee and ask, "How's that?"

"Perfect! Smile…no, wait, it's on video mode."

"Then I really hope you say yes," I reply while retrieving the ring from inside my suit pocket. I had been planning to wait until after the game tonight, but I can't wait a second longer. Proposing in the exact spot where we first met is even better than doing it in a fancy Italian restaurant where we had our first official date or in the middle of a crowded arena with everyone watching.

"Yes?" Elle repeats, but it's a question, not an answer.

She finally glances away from the phone and at me, down on one knee, holding the black velvet jewelry box. I pry it open with my thumb to reveal the diamond ring inside while keeping the phone recording us. Who knows, maybe one day we can show this moment to our kids or grandkids.

Her palm slaps over her mouth as if she just figured out what's happening.

"Elle Townsend, the first time I saw you, I couldn't believe anyone would be foolish enough to ever let you go or to break your heart. But I'm glad he did. It gave me a chance to get to meet you right here in this very parking lot. And now that you're mine, I don't know how I lived in this world for so long without you by my side. So, will you try to overlook my grumpy ways, my past and future mistakes, and all my flaws, and believe that no matter how badly I screw things up, I'll always love you more than anything? Will you please be my wife?"

"Yes!" Elle exclaims as a tear races down her cheek. Ignoring the ring box, she throws her arms around my neck, sealing her answer with a branding kiss. I lower the phone and box gently to the ground to free up my hands, so I can finally pull her into my arms.

The kids and grandkids have seen enough.

The End

to show her that he's committed to being a father before letting him have a permanent place in their lives.

Proving to Maya that he can step up to be a father to Finley, and that his puckboy days are behind him, will be the toughest challenge Christian has ever faced.

Fate has finally given him a second chance to take a shot at love, so this time he better not puck around and miss.

Pucking Fate has a HEA and is perfect for fans of swoon-worthy athletes, sizzling chemistry, and second chances that come when you least expect them.

ABOUT THE AUTHOR

L.A. Hart is the alter ego of New York Times and USA Today bestselling author Lane Hart. Under this pen name she writes new adult and sports romance.

Most of Lane's steamy stories take place in her home state of North Carolina where she lives with her husband, fellow author D.B. West, and their two beautiful children.

Connect with Lane:

Newsletter Sign-up: https://8d74dec5662811e9930706b4694bee2a.eo.page/cg1j3

Instagram: https://www.instagram.com/authorlahart/

Facebook: https://www.facebook.com/SportsRomanceAuthorLAHart/

Bookbub: https://www.bookbub.com/authors/l-a-hart

Goodreads: https://www.goodreads.com/author/show/52249255.L_A_Hart

Website: https://authorlahart.com

Email: authorlahart@outlook.com